The Best Medicine

A BELL HARBOR NOVEL

D010664?

Other Titles by Tracy Brogan

Crazy Little Thing (A Bell Harbor Novel)
Highland Surrender
Hold on My Heart

The Best Medicine

A BELL HARBOR NOVEL

Tracy Brogan

Montlake
Romance

Published by Montlake Romance, Seattle

www.apub.com

ISBN-13: 9781477818350
ISBN-10: 1477818359

Cover design by Laura Klynstra

Library of Congress Control Number: 2013917677

Printed in the United States of America

To my real Gabby and my real Hillery,
my BFFs before BFFs were even invented.

Chapter 1

BIRTHDAY PARTIES ARE A LOT like pelvic exams—a little uncomfortable, a little awkward, a little too personal, but an unavoidable yearly nuisance—like a Pap smear, only with presents. So I should have known I couldn't tiptoe past this day with both my secret, and my *dignity*, intact.

There I was, just minding my own business, looking for a cup of coffee in the Bell Harbor Plastic Surgery Center staff lounge, when suddenly I was surrounded. They pounced, silently and with no warning. The air around me morphed into a shimmering tsunami of pink and purple metallic confetti, and throaty laughter filled my ears. Warm bodies surged forward, pressing me into the corner of the room. More sparkles flew, clinging to my face and hair like sparkly shrapnel.

They were on to me, and there was no escape.

I was a victim of the Birthday Ninja Glitter-Bomb Squad.

Because today was no ordinary day. It was, in fact, my birthday. A birthday I wasn't happy about. A birthday I wanted to ignore. A birthday that punted me from the eighteen-to-thirty-four bracket into the thirty-five-to-death category. Now I was trapped inside the birthday ninjas' rainbow-bright web. Resistance was futile.

"Surprise!"

"Happy birthday, Evelyn!"

"Happy birthday, Dr. Rhoades!"

Another cloud of confetti descended, and someone plunked a tarnished rhinestone tiara on my head, which assuredly clashed against my red hair. Quasi-benevolent good wishes blended with giggles and old-age jibes as the lounge filled with my six physician partners and members of our office staff, two dozen in all. Delle, our rotund, middle-aged receptionist, bustled forward importantly and placed a candle-laden cake on the table in the center of the room. She smiled wide, triumphant.

They all did. The whole herd of them beamed at me and shifted on their feet, expectation glowing in their shining eyes. They looked jubilant, the way people do when they want you to be overcome with delight . . . which I was not.

It wasn't that I didn't appreciate their efforts. I'm not a complete birthday Scrooge . . . except when it comes to my *own* birthday. I'm just not a big-celebration, look-at-me kind of woman. Having all that attention directed my way for something no more notable than aging seems silly. It's like getting the green participation ribbon for field day. I hadn't worked to earn this. I was being rewarded simply for showing up.

"Well, did we surprise you?" Delle demanded. She nudged thick glasses against the bridge of her nose with a pudgy thumb. She had different frames for each day of the week. These were teal. It must be Tuesday.

For a split second I hoped the open flames of all those candles might set off the smoke alarms, forcing us to vacate the building. But no such luck. Snagged in that moment, I had no choice but to take one for the team. I plastered on my fake happy birthday face.

"Gosh, you guys. Yes. Wow. You really did surprise me. I had no idea anyone even knew it was my birthday." My surprise *was* genuine, but I also did a pretty commendable job at sounding pleased. Score one for me.

"Dr. Pullman told us. You should thank her." Delle pointed at the tall brunette with the two-hundred-dollar haircut and ridiculously impractical high-heeled shoes.

I swung my gaze toward Hilary Pullman, the one person in town who knew unequivocally I didn't want a fuss made today. She was my professional colleague, my most trusted confidante, and until ten seconds ago, my closest friend. We'd met during our plastic surgery residency and bonded over the trials and tribulations of being a woman in medicine. Nothing quite cements a friendship like sharing a post-call toothbrush before morning rounds.

Hilary had grown up in Bell Harbor, and our friendship was half the reason I'd chosen to practice here. But friend or not, she knew I hated birthday parties in my honor. I squinted at her and tried to look fierce, but she was a foot taller than me in those damn heels. I was at a distinct disadvantage.

She returned a guileless smile and shrugged in her typical *sorry-but-not-really* fashion. She stepped away from the cluster of birthday revelers. The hem of her fitted black pencil skirt barely cleared the bottom of her white lab coat. Some might say that skirt was too short. And they'd be right. But in all honesty, if I had legs like hers, I'd wear skirts like that too. Unfortunately, I didn't, and so I couldn't. I was five two. Nothing was short on me except for me.

Hilary picked up a spatula from the table with her graceful fingers and handed it to me, handle first.

"Happy birthday, Evie. I know this isn't as sharp as what you're used to, but here you go. Don't stab me with it." She winked playfully.

I took the spatula and tried to glare at her without letting the others see, but she was entirely immune to my annoyance. It wasn't that she didn't notice. She just didn't care. Hilary thought her role in our friendship was to taunt me, and cajole me out of my comfort zone. Somewhere along the line, she'd decided it was her job to loosen me up. But I didn't need loosening up. I liked myself just the way I was. Most of the time.

Delle wheezed and clasped her hands in front of her massive double-Ds. "Well, make a wish, Dr. Rhoades. Blow out the candles."

I smiled at her and then the others, trying so valiantly to make it seem legit that it almost felt as if it were. Their intentions were good, after all. Maybe this birthday wouldn't be so bad. Thirty-five wasn't *that* old. At least there were no doomsday banners or balloons declaring me over the hill. No dead-flower bouquets or black decorations. Just confetti and a tiara. I could handle this.

I cleared my throat and took a breath. "Thank you, everyone. This is really very sweet. These past few months here in Bell Harbor have been wonderful, and you've all made me feel right at home. I can't think of anything else I need to wish for."

"How about a husband?" Delle called out, giggling again, and nodding at the others, perspiration gleaming against her dark forehead.

Oh, she was hilarious, wasn't she? Heckling me on my own birthday?

That was one disadvantage of moving to such a small, close-knit community—the complete lack of privacy. Being the newest doctor in town had made me as fascinating an object of curiosity to the good people of Bell Harbor as a meteorite striking the cross of the St. Aloysius Church of the Immaculate Conception. Everyone in town seemed to know I lived alone in a tiny apartment, wanted to buy a house on the lakeshore, and that I was perpetually single. That last fact weighed heavily on everyone's mind. Everyone's except mine, that is. I still had plenty of time to find a husband.

Assuming I even wanted one.

Which I didn't.

Most of the time.

I also didn't want this room full of people speculating about my love life, or current lack thereof. My private life was, well . . . private. If only they'd let me keep it that way.

I offered up a fake-sounding "heh heh heh" and turned toward the cake. I stared at the candles, pretending to ponder my upcoming wish with the proper amount of reverence. Having lived most of my life entrenched in a scientific, evidence-based philosophy, however, nothing about making a wish and blowing out a flame was any part of my reality. Birthday wishes did not come true, any more than wishes made on puffy dandelions blown into the breeze or pennies tossed into a fountain. Wishes were nothing more than unrealized goals.

Still, the image of me in a gauzy white dress floating down the aisle toward a faceless, tuxedo-clad groom burst into my imagination, like a rainbow brightening a dismal sky after the storm. There were bright pink roses and lavender chiffon–clad bridesmaids. Strains of Pachelbel's "Canon in D" hummed silently in my ears. My heart palpitated illogically, as if this vision were something to strive for. It wasn't, of course. Not for me. Not right now. I had my career. It was enough.

Most of the time.

I twitched, erasing my mental Etch A Sketch, and blew out the candles without making any wish at all. Everyone clapped and undulated forward en masse, synchronized like a school of tuna. Tuna who wanted cake. I was surrounded once again.

"Let me help you." Gabby, our office manager, stepped forward. She tucked a lock of blonde, pink-tipped hair behind her multipierced ear, her turquoise-and-orange skirt swishing around her ankles as she moved. She was twenty-eight but had the kind of youthful, flawless skin my patients paid thousands of dollars to recapture. She was also Hilary's little sister, which by association sort of made her like my little sister too.

"Here are the plates," she said, handing me a stack.

They were decorated with kittens wearing tiaras just like mine, as if I were turning five instead of thirty-five. Either these were left over from some child's birthday or someone was teasing me. I didn't want to know which.

"Who wants a corner piece with lots of frosting?" I called out instead, relieved to have something to do with my hands. *Let's get this party started—and finished—so I can get back to my charting and wrap up the day's paperwork. I have other places to be.*

I made short work of cutting the pieces. Being a plastic surgeon has some benefits. Gabby and Hilary passed out the plates then returned to my side to get pieces for themselves. I took a bite of my own, knowing I was obligated. Knowing it meant an extra forty-five minutes of cardio to work it off. Knowing the lard would clog up my arteries like old motor oil. But damn, it tasted good. Sticky and sweet and defiant.

Gabby stuffed a big red frosting rose into her mouth. *"Feliz aniversário,"* she said around it, her teeth coated in crimson. She looked like a vampire. "That's Portuguese for happy birthday."

"When did you start speaking Portuguese?" Hilary asked, taking a nibble of the minuscule piece she'd taken for herself.

Her sister shrugged, noncommittal. "A while. I've been teaching myself. Gorgeous language. Gorgeous men."

Hilary nodded. "Uh-huh. Speaking of gorgeous men, Evie, it wouldn't hurt you, you know." Her dark brown gaze turned back to me.

I looked up from my cake. "Learning to speak Portuguese?"

"No," she whispered. "Wishing for a husband. You know, and getting a little something-something on your birthday." She made a subtle bobbing motion with her hips as if her meaning wasn't clear.

Gabby giggled and I choked on my cake. I reached for my coffee cup, but it was empty. I swallowed as best as I could and whispered indignantly, "What makes you think I'm not?"

"Because you would have told me."

She's right. I would have.

"And because your mother called about dinner tonight," Gabby added. "I talked to her fifteen minutes ago."

"You talked to my mother?"

Gabby nodded, the pink tips of her hair sliding over her shoulders. "Yeah, and she said, '*Vamos ser tarde. Podemos encontrá-lo no restaurant.*'"

Curiosity spiked, along with my glucose levels. "My Portuguese is a little rusty, Gab. What does that actually mean?"

"It means your parents will meet you at the restaurant because they're running late." She scooped up another frosting rose.

"She also said she couldn't stand the thought of you spending another birthday alone," Hilary added, picking up a single crumb with her fork.

"She did not say that!" My voice scraped inside my throat, and I glanced around the room to see if anyone was listening. Fortunately, their cake held them spellbound. I lowered my voice to a conscientiously modulated whisper. "My mother would never say something like that. Not if someone held a scalpel to her jugular."

I didn't bother adding that my mother was even less sentimental than I was about stuff like this and knew I'd spent more than one birthday solidly, contentedly alone.

Hilary arched a cosmetically perfected brow. "All right. You caught me. She didn't say that. But, Evie, you've been here almost four months, and I haven't heard you mention going on even one date. It's time you got out and met some new people."

"Yes, men kind of people," Gabby said. "My boyfriend, Mike, knows lots of single guys you could go out with. Well . . . *lots* is a strong word. But he must know at least a couple. And a couple is all you need for a pretty fun party, right?"

The sisters shared a laugh, and I pondered her level of seriousness. "I don't think I want to know what kind of parties you have."

Hilary set down her plate. "Well, Steve and I have boring married-couple parties, but even those are better than spending your birthday alone. Honestly, Ev, you need to make more of an effort. Stop being so picky."

I stood tall. Well, as tall as I was able, and prepared to defend myself.

"I'm not too picky. I just haven't had time. I'm always working."

"You're always working because you don't have anything else to do." Her admonishment was gentle but familiar. I'd heard it before.

"It was all well and good to play the busy card during residency," Hilary added, "but you're an attending now. You have regular office hours. And no more excuses."

This conversation always made my skin itch. It was the one subject Hilary and I never agreed on—my dormant interest in finding a man. Just because she was happily married with two beautiful children, she couldn't understand why I was still putting off that phase of my life, why I was still focused on career instead of family. But I simply wasn't in a hurry. I'd seen the darker side of marriage. I knew the failure rate. I'd lived it with my own parents. My parents . . .

"Wait a minute!" I gasped as my subconscious pushed forward a thought. I clunked my plate down on the table and looked at Gabby. "Did you say *they* will meet me at the restaurant? They, as in *both* my parents?"

That couldn't be right. It must be just my mother. Just like we'd planned.

Gabby nodded slowly, wary at my change in demeanor.

"What did she say, precisely?" I asked, resisting the urge to grab her by the shoulders and rattle her around.

Gabby's brow furrowed. "She said, '*Diga a Evelyn estava tarde estávamos—*'"

"No! No, in English. Please." Seriously?

Gabby cast her blue eyes toward the ceiling as if I was the one being inconvenient.

"Oh, fine. Your mother said, 'Tell Evelyn we'll meet her at the restaurant because her father got delayed in surgery.' Why is that such a big deal?"

It *was* a big deal, but of course they wouldn't understand the magnitude of just how big a deal this was. It wasn't something I often talked about.

"My parents don't get along," I said. "Actually, that's an understatement. Cats and dogs don't get along. What my parents have is like mixing bleach with ammonia, then adding Coke and a Mentos. It's toxic and messy for anyone within a two-mile radius."

My parents were both cardiothoracic surgeons. Busy, important cardiothoracic surgeons, a point which I had been reminded of repeatedly throughout my youth as they shuffled me back and forth between the two of them. They'd been divorced for ages and the three of us hadn't shared a meal together since my matriculation into medical school. And *that* dinner had ended abruptly with my mother dumping gazpacho on my father's linen pants and stomping from the restaurant before the entrée was served. She'd left dents in the sidewalk.

"Didn't they tell you they were both coming?" Hilary asked. She'd heard a handful of stories about my parents' diabolically perverse competition with each other, but not all of them. But she knew I thought part of the reason they both practiced in Ann Arbor was to steal patients from one another.

"No, they didn't tell me." My mind flipped through a short list of possible reasons they'd be coming together. Maybe my father had been named surgeon general. Maybe my mother had invented another revolutionary new surgical technique. Or maybe one of them had been exposed to a virulent strain of monkey pox and had only days to live. We were meeting at a pretty nice restaurant, so I hoped it wasn't that. But something had prompted this surprise reunion. Not only were they both coming, but they were apparently riding together? Granted, Ann Arbor was a couple of hours' drive from Bell Harbor, but even so, one of them must be bound and gagged in the trunk by now.

This was all very curious.

"Dr. Rhoades." One of our nurses stuck her head in through the lounge doorway. "Dr. McKnight from the emergency department is on the phone. He says he's got a facial laceration consult. You're on call tonight, right?"

"You're on call tonight?" Hilary asked. "Why didn't you trade with someone since it's your birthday? I could've done it if you'd asked ahead of time." Her tone was a combination of surprise and condemnation. I'd obviously reinforced her belief I was deliberately keeping busy with work to avoid social obligations. But really, I just wanted the extra money. Every penny I made was being tucked away for my future house. I had my heart set on a place right on the shoreline, and those did not come cheap.

"I like taking call. And besides, everyone else has kids to go home to." I turned to the nurse. "Please tell him I'll be right there." I could deal with this patient and still make it to dinner on time. I just wouldn't be able to run home to my apartment and change first.

I raised my hand and waved to the remaining birthday crowd. It had thinned, and I realized my other partners had already returned to work.

"Thanks, everyone, for the wonderful birthday party. Sorry to carb-load and dash, but duty calls."

A few voices called out another round of birthday wishes as Hilary and Gabby followed me into the waiting room. I turned back toward them before leaving the office.

"And a big, fat thanks to you two for spilling the beans about my birthday." I shook my finger at them, but once again, Hilary was unimpressed by my impotent frustration, and I was secretly glad. I had to admit, I felt a little warm and fuzzy down deep inside, knowing the group had gone to this trouble on my behalf. Sure, maybe they just wanted cake, but they *had* all clapped when I blew out the candles.

"*Não há problema.*" Gabby smiled. "By the way—"

Hilary interrupted her sister. "I know you secretly wanted us to make a fuss."

I laughed out loud at her misplaced certainty. "No, I really didn't. But I appreciate the gesture."

"Someone needs to teach you how to have fun, Evie. Live a little." Her smile was oversized for the occasion.

Gabby reached over and squeezed my arm. "I could send my friend Axel over to your apartment later for a *foda pena*. He's lots of fun."

"What's a *foda pena*?"

"It's a pity fu—"

"Shh!" I hissed and made a chopping motion across my throat. Delle, the receptionist, had deftly and strategically positioned herself behind them to listen to our conversation. Honestly, the woman weighed more than a linebacker, but she could sneak up and eavesdrop like a professional assassin. She wasn't brigade leader of the birthday ninjas by accident.

—⋀— —⋀—

I made my way from the plastic surgery center office down two flights of stairs and several hallways before arriving at the emergency department. Everyone I encountered along the way greeted me with a broad smile and even a few chuckles. Either news of my birthday had spread or I still wasn't accustomed to how friendly the locals were.

The Bell Harbor ED was a busy place, but not nearly as chaotic as where I'd trained in Chicago. Emergencies around here tended to be of the beach resort variety, and the whole department had a polite atmosphere. Not that there weren't car accidents and heart attacks and dramatic things of that sort, but nobody around here ever got stabbed or shot. There weren't gang signs spray-painted on the side of the ambulance bay, and I hadn't seen a strung-out hooker in months.

I pushed open the metal doors. A nurse in green scrubs seemed to skip a step at my entrance, then she too smiled wide. Her dark, wavy hair was twisted up in a bun, and I was nearly certain her name was Lecia, but since I wasn't positive, I just smiled back. Nurses really hate it when you call them by the wrong name. I learned that the hard way in medical school.

"Hi, Dr. Rhoades. You're fancy today. Are you here for the face lac?"

"Fancy?"

She pointed at my head.

Oh!

No.

Really?

I reached up, and yep, there it was. The tiara. I yanked it from my head, ripping out hair along with it. How could I have forgotten the flippin' tiara? No wonder everyone kept grinning at me.

"Sorry. It's my birthday," I mumbled and tossed it into the nearby trash can. I brushed my hair back from my face, feeling heat steal over my cheeks. I bet I was turning splotchy too. Oh, the joys of being fair skinned. "And yes, I'm here for the face lac. What's the story?"

She led me toward a curtained area. "Twenty-seven-year-old Caucasian male versus a fifth of whiskey and a boat dock."

"What?"

"He ran into a boat dock while drunk driving a Jet Ski. Broke the fall with his face. But according to his story, he did not spill any of his drink."

Her brows lifted as she nodded, clearly impressed by the order of his priorities. She pulled his chart from the rack and handed it to me, adding, "But he's pretty, and he doesn't want a scar."

She shoved the curtain to the side while I looked over his stats.

Tyler Connelly. Twenty-seven. Good vital signs. No employer listed. I stepped closer to get a better look.

He was tall and broad. I could tell that much, even as he lay on the stretcher. His eyes were closed, and his hair was messy with the sort of blond highlights that came from spending hours in the sun. That explained the tan too, which covered all that I could see except for his face—which had a slightly ashen pallor and showed signs of bruising on one side. A white section of gauze was taped along his jawline, from under his chin halfway back toward his left ear.

I tucked the chart under my arm. "Mr. Connelly, I'm Dr. Rhoades."

A soft snore came from the bed.

I looked at the nurse, who was fussing with a blood pressure cuff.

"Well, you've obviously managed his pain well enough," I said drily.

She chuckled. "We haven't given him anything. Whiskey, remember? He was half-anesthetized when he got here."

"On a Tuesday afternoon?"

It wasn't unusual for emergency department clientele to be drunk, but this patient didn't look like your average derelict. He was muscular and well fed, and even with the pale hue and gauze stuck to his jaw, that was one aesthetically pleasing face. Rugged model material. Not that I was affected by that sort of thing. But damn, this was a good-looking man.

I moved right up next to the bed and raised my voice. "Mr. Connelly, wake up."

He twitched and opened his eyes. They were bloodshot and a little glassy, but even so, they were still the prettiest, lightest blue I'd ever seen in my life.

I glanced at his chart once more.

Twenty-seven.

Unemployed.

Intoxicated.

Damn.

And damn again.

He looked at me and blinked—slow—as if his brain was downloading the instructions on how to do that. Then a lazy smile lifted one corner of his mouth.

"Wow," he said on a sigh as he closed his eyes again. "Sexiest nurses in this place."

The real nurse chuckled again, then leaned in close to his ear and shouted, "Hey! Sleeping Beauty! Wake up. This is the doctor. And she's going to put stitches in your face, so you might want to show a little respect."

Oh, I liked her! Whatever her name was.

His eyes popped open at her words, and he blinked faster. I could see his gaze slowly coming into focus. He looked me over, as if taking in a mental inventory of all my various parts.

"You're the doctor?"

I got that reaction a lot. The price of being a short, curvy redhead in the land of tall, lab-coated men and their biggie-sized egos. But if my mother had taught me anything, it was how to never let anyone make me feel like less than I was. I wasn't about to be reduced by an unemployed twenty-seven-year-old who had nothing better to do on a Tuesday afternoon than get drunk and play with his man toys. I crossed my arms and lifted my chin, making me at least half an inch taller.

"Yes, Mr. Connelly. I'm Dr. Evelyn Rhoades, a board-certified plastic surgeon. I hear you had an accident today, so I'm going to take that bandage off your face and take a look. Got it?"

I set the chart down and moved over to the other side of the bed.

"Sure. Yeah. Of course." His small nod ended in a grimace, maybe due to pain caused by his injuries, or more than likely, the onset of his inevitable hangover. The aroma of alcohol permeated the air around him. Not the stale, sour stench that usually accompanied homeless alcoholics. This was more of a sweet, cloying smell, like bubbly pink champagne left out after a party. Mixed with cocoa butter. Apparently my booze-swizzling patient was not so irresponsible as to forgo sunscreen.

"Are you in any discomfort, Mr. Connelly?" I asked.

"I'm fine." His glance told me he had more to say but that whatever it was had nothing to do with his medical condition and everything to do with his impression of me. He seemed intrigued but a little suspicious.

"Dr. McKnight is treating his arm and shoulder," the nurse said. "We're waiting on some X-rays, but he doesn't appear to have any fractures or signs of concussion."

I pulled on purple latex gloves. "It sounds like you could have been hurt much worse, Mr. Connelly. Statistically speaking, you were lucky."

His ridiculously silver-blue eyes met mine. "Yeah, I'm a lucky guy." He started to chuckle but seemed to reconsider and coughed instead. His hands moved guardedly to his chest, indicating some level of pain. Even though he was covered by a blue-speckled hospital gown, I noticed all kinds of muscles flexing and squeezing as he did that.

His, and mine.

Damn you, Gabby and your foda pena*!*

I nudged a black rolling stool closer to the stretcher with my knee while a voice in my head reminded me he was twenty-seven. And unemployed. And drunk.

And a patient! There was that little matter as well.

"Mr. Connelly, I'm here to address your facial injury, so let's deal with that first."

I ignored the way his gown slipped off his shoulder as he readjusted on the bed. I ignored the edge of his deltoid tattoo peeking out from the shifting fabric too. It didn't allure me in any way. I was a professional. I would simply concentrate on his injury, not his physique. Just because Hilary and Gabby thought I needed some sexual gymnastics, and just because it had been ages since my last horizontal workout with a man, and just because it was my birthday, this man-boy from Neverland was certainly not what I needed. What I needed was to get to work.

The nurse started setting up a suture tray without being asked, while I gently peeled off the gauze.

My patient had a jagged laceration running along the edge of his jaw, ending at his chin. It was about three centimeters long, deep but not all the way to the bone. Still, a wound like this would require a multilayer closure, and he'd most definitely have a scar. I could keep it minimal, though. I'd leave him dashing rather than disfigured. I could do that. I had mad skills.

"You're going to need some stitches, Mr. Connelly. Have you ever had stitches before?" I pressed at the skin.

He chuckled again. "Plenty of times."

"Are you accident-prone?" I'm not sure why I asked him that. It wasn't medically relevant, but something tugged at me, an inconvenient curiosity about how this patient spent his time.

"No. I just don't like sitting still." His voice was deep, with a pleasant raspy quality. The kind of voice that might make a less professional woman think illicit thoughts. Fortunately for him, and for me, I wasn't that kind of woman. Most of the time.

"What types of injuries have you had in the past?" I asked, while continuing to *not* peek at that tattoo.

He sighed, as if pondering my question hurt his head, which, under the circumstances, it probably did.

"Dislocated shoulder, torn ACL. Wrist fracture. Split my forehead snowboarding once." He reached up and touched the corner of his right eyebrow, indicating a pale scar.

I might have noticed that scar had I not been avoiding eye contact. I leaned closer to examine it. He turned toward me just as I did, and I found myself thinking it was diabolically unfair that any man should have such thick, dark lashes while mine required copious amounts of mascara.

"Do you want to hear them all?" he asked. "I told the other doctor everything."

I straightened up again and glanced at the nurse. "Could you hand me the chart, please?" She did and I flipped through it, taking in the laundry list of his previous injuries thoroughly documented by Dr. McKnight. Broken bones, sprains, contusions. This guy was either clumsy as hell or a full-throttle adrenaline junkie. And he looked a little too muscular to be clumsy.

"Well, Mr. Connelly, aside from all the physical damage done to your person before today, would you say you're in generally good health?"

"Yes, ma'am."

Ma'am?

Oh. That one stung. I was a feminist through and through, but no woman under seventy-five wants to be called ma'am. He may as well have called me granny. Sharp, useless distress pierced my lungs. Maybe this birthday thing was bothering me more than I realized. I suddenly felt . . . dare I say . . . crotchety?

"Don't you think it's rather reckless to be on a Jet Ski while drinking whiskey?"

Oh, yes. That was most decidedly crotchety. I could feel my lips pinching around the word *whiskey* like a prohibition-era preacher's wife.

But my facially gifted young patient just laughed. "Yeah, the whiskey was a bad decision. But I gave up beer for Lent. Plus I didn't plan to be on the Jet Ski. That was sort of an accident."

I couldn't imagine how one accidentally ended up on a Jet Ski, but really, this was none of my business. It wasn't my job to pass judgment on this unleashed puppy. It was only my job to fix what he'd broken. Not to mention the fact that I was pretty sure Lent was somewhere around Easter, and since it was June, he was obviously not going to give me straight answers anyway. Time to mind my own business and get to work.

"Well, let's give you some stitches and get you out of here."

The nurse turned, and I finally caught sight of her ID badge. Her name was Susie. Where the hell had I gotten Lecia? This was precisely the reason why I needed to be careful addressing anyone by name. I could not be trusted to get it right. I could list all the muscles in the human body, but ask me to name the clerical staff in my own office, much less random nurses in the emergency department, and I'd be sunk.

"Thank you, Susie," I called out as she walked away to tend to another patient.

I got myself situated with my instruments and supplies at hand and set about suturing this laceration. This was what I excelled at. Not names. Not chatting. This was my groove. The buzz of voices and pings of medical machinery blended into a common hum around me. This was the background noise of a better portion of my life, and I typically found the commotion soothing.

Not so much today as I tried to focus on the wound in front of me. But it wasn't the noise or the chaos of the busy emergency department distracting me. It was Mr. Connelly's face. From a purely scientific standpoint, his appearance was mesmerizing. He had a nearly perfect symmetry to his features, right down to his matching dimples, and very few people have that sort of balance. It was fascinating. That's why I kept looking at him. For science.

As a scientist, I also couldn't help but appreciate the broad musculature of his wide shoulders or the sinews of his forearm, which moved when he folded his hands over his lean, flat abdomen. There was probably a six-pack under that gown too. Not to mention some other fine example of well-proportioned mass.

Wow. Was it warm in here? I think it was warm in here. Or maybe this birthday had triggered my first perimenopausal hot flash. Because I couldn't possibly be getting this hot and bothered just because Mr. Connelly was attractive. That kind of thing never affected me. I created beautiful faces for a living. And besides that, he was only twenty-seven years old, for goodness' sake. Eight years younger than me. And he'd called me ma'am!

This was Delle and Hilary and Gabby's fault, putting crazy, lusty thoughts into my head. That's what the problem was.

Now maybe if I was a twentysomething-year-old woman, this agitation would be logical, in spite of his apparent lack of common sense or gainful employment. Or then again . . . maybe it wouldn't. My twenties had been spent in medical school, and then residency, and then a fellowship after that. I'd studied while my peers had partied and slept around. They had gone on spring break, and I had taken that extra time to volunteer at a free clinic. My parents taught me work always came before play. And this guy was all play.

Still, there was a secret part of me who missed never having been frivolous and carefree and stupid. Not stupid enough to play chicken with a boat dock, but maybe stupid enough to be drunk in the middle of the week.

An unexpectedly remorseful sigh escaped before I could catch it.

"You getting bored?" My patient's eyes were closed again, but a little crook bent the corners of his mouth.

"I'm doing a procedure, Mr. Connelly. I'm never bored during a procedure," I answered.

"Tyler," he said.

"Excuse me?"

"Please call me Tyler. The only person who ever called me Mr. Connelly was my high school principal, and that never ended well."

"Why? Were you a troublemaker?" I could picture it. A boy too cute for his own good. Rousing the rabble. Fraternizing with the cheerleaders. Ignoring the bookish girls like me.

He opened his eyes and peered at me without turning his face. "I wasn't a troublemaker. I was angelic. I just have a habit of being in the wrong place at the wrong time with the wrong people."

The curtain surrounding the bed whooshed abruptly to the side. "You got that right, kid. What the hell happened on that boat today?"

A silver-haired man with a deep sunburn and at least two days' worth of whiskers stood across from me and glared down at my patient.

Aside from a short, shallow sigh, Mr. Conn—I mean, Tyler— didn't show much reaction. "How'd you know I was here, Carl?"

"Word travels." The man pulled a can of soda from the pocket of his—oh my God—was that a bathrobe he was wearing?

It was.

Light blue terry cloth.

He cracked open the can as if to make himself right at home. "But the details are a little sketchy. So, either you can tell me now what happened or I can listen to you explain it to the police, because they're in the lobby, and something tells me they're looking for you."

That seemed to get my patient's attention. He raised his hand to halt my work and tried to turn his face, but I caught him by the chin before he pulled out my most recent stitch.

"Did you say anything to them?" Tyler asked.

The other man scoffed as if that were the most absurd of questions. "Of course not."

"Have you talked to Scotty?" Tyler asked him.

"Your brother? No. Why? What does he have to do with this?" The bathrobe-wearing soda drinker took to frowning, his lips pursed in concern.

"Find him and take him home. Tell him not to talk to anybody, OK?"

Carl took a loud gulp from the can. I heard soda fizzing and watched his Adam's apple bob while I pondered who he was—and more importantly—what the hell was going on.

"Your mother's not going to like this," he said to Tyler, taking another swallow.

"Mom is the least of my concerns right now, Carl. Just find Scotty. Keep him off the phone if you can. And keep him away from Mom."

Carl squinted and crossed his robe-clad arms. He'd yet to acknowledge me in any way. I'm not even sure he realized I was there. He just gazed down silently at my patient, until at last he said, "Little man fucked up, didn't he?"

Tyler glanced at me as if measuring my trustworthiness, then looked back to Carl.

"No. Scotty is fine. I'll take care of it. Now get out of here before the police see you and arrest you for vagrancy. You look like a bum in that bathrobe."

Carl smoothed one hand over the lapel as if it were mink instead of threadbare terry cloth. "I love this bathrobe. Your mother gave it to me for Christmas. I think she shoplifted it, but she wanted to get me something nice."

"It's for inside the house, not out in public. We've told you that a thousand times." Tyler sighed, this time deep and slow. A tension that wasn't there before showed in the clench of his jaw. But Carl's shrug was the epitome of indifference. He clearly found no issue with his attire or how it came to be in his possession. Finally, he looked my way, his eyes widening a little as they got to my face. He tilted his soda can toward me in a random toast. "Sorry for the interruption, Red. Family business."

"She's a doctor, Carl. Show a little respect." Tyler mimicked the nurse's earlier words, and I might have chuckled if I wasn't so bewildered.

"Nice to meet you," Carl replied. He held up the can, pinky finger extended. "Why do you have glitter in your hair?"

"What?"

No! I ran a hand over my head and metallic confetti drifted downward, right onto my patient's face.

"Oh my gosh. I . . . oh!" I brushed at Tyler's cheek to flick the pink and purple flakes away. "I'm sorry. It's . . . it's my birthday."

Tyler looked up at me, the corner of his blue eyes crinkling in what I could only assume was amusement at my expense.

"It is? Happy birthday," he said.

Carl raised his soda can higher still. "Happy birthday, Doc. Take good care of my boy here, will you?"

I nodded. "Um, yes. Certainly. Of course." Glitter in my hair? I was going to kill those birthday ninjas! Something subtle and untraceable.

"Well, I'm off. I'll try to head those cops off at the pass," Carl said as he turned.

"No," Tyler answered. "Let me handle this, Carl. Promise." It wasn't a plea. It was a directive.

I watched the terry-clothed shoulders lift in another lackadaisical motion. "OK, kid. If you say so. But your mother isn't going to be happy."

He stepped away from the bed and flung the curtain back to its original position. The metal rings jingled like chains rattling and then fell silent.

"I'm sorry about that," Tyler said once the curtain had stopped swaying. His skin flushed, and although I could credit it to him feeling better, realistically I knew it was from embarrassment. But I was in no spot to judge. I didn't usually treat patients with glitter in my hair.

"That's OK," I said to him. "Let's get these stitches finished, though."

I readjusted on the stool and picked up another suture, but my curiosity bubbled like a chemical reaction inside a test tube. I wanted to ask where he'd been today and why the police would want to question him. But I'd learned a long time ago that every patient has some sad or exciting story to tell, and it was always better to leave those kinds of messy details to the social workers. Sometimes that was hard to do, but whatever had happened before my patient hit that boat dock was no business of mine. I knew better than to get tangled up in it.

A moment passed, and I continued closing the wound until Tyler let out another big sigh.

"Do you have brothers and sisters?" he asked. His voice sounded wistful, and I felt my policy of avoidance weakening.

"No."

Actually, I had a couple of stepsisters somewhere, but I didn't really count them since most of my father's marriages had been so brief I'd barely had time to sign the guest book before the wives and their dependents were gone. It was better not to get involved in the details of their messy lives either. It kept *my* life much simpler.

Tyler crossed his arms over his torso. The gown slipped off his shoulder a little farther, revealing more of that tattoo, but not enough so I could make it out. It was ridiculously tantalizing. This must be how men feel when they see cleavage.

"Well, I have a couple of each," he said. "And it's a lot of work keeping them out of trouble."

My hand paused, my mind processed. I shouldn't ask, but I did. "Why is it your job to keep them out of trouble?"

His chuckle sounded full of resignation rather than good humor. "It just finds us. And that guy in the bathrobe is our stepdad. You think he's going to keep an eye on them?"

I wanted to hear more. I did. I wanted to know how my patient ended up being drunk on a Jet Ski on a Tuesday afternoon, and running into a boat dock, and what his brother Scotty had to do with it, and why his siblings were his responsibility, but I looked up at the clock on the wall, and it read 6:40 p.m. I was going to be incredibly late meeting my parents, and if left alone, they'd probably take to puncturing each other with steak knives.

This conversation with Tyler Connelly wouldn't help me get his laceration sewn up, and that was my primary responsibility. Technically, it was my only responsibility. And besides, hearing more would only draw me in further, an emotional complication better left unexplored. I remained silent and continued suturing.

After a moment, he closed his eyes and sighed again. "How long have you been at this?"

I gave the stitch a little tug. "About forty minutes, but I'm almost finished."

Now his chuckle was amused. "I meant how long have you been a doctor?"

"Oh." I smiled, though he couldn't see me. "A while."

"It can't be much of a while. You look awfully young. Which birthday is this today?"

I had no intention of answering that. But it was nice to hear I at least *looked* young. "Mr. Connelly, I need you to stop talking and keep your jaw still, please. I'm nearly finished."

A voice penetrated through the general din of the department, deep and authoritative. A few seconds passed, the curtain slid aside, and an imposing mass of navy blue appeared in my field of vision. I looked up to see a behemoth of a police officer standing on the other side of the stretcher. Next to him stood a second burly cop, with thick forearms and mirrored sunglasses.

"Tyler Connelly?" The bigger policeman stared down at my symmetrically gifted patient.

Tyler opened his eyes again.

"Is there a problem, Officers?" I said. I had the most spontaneous compulsion to tell them Tyler Connelly had just run out the back door. But since he was lying on the stretcher between us, I didn't think they'd be fooled. Besides, if the police wanted to talk to my patient, they probably had just cause, while I had no explicable reason to feel protective.

"I'm Tyler Connelly," he answered without a hint of hesitation.

"Tyler Connelly, you're under arrest for grand larceny of a stolen Jet Ski and destruction of property. You have the right to remain silent. Anything you say can and will be used against you in a court of law. You have the right to an attorney. If you cannot afford an attorney, one will be provided for you. Do you understand the rights I've just told you?"

Grand larceny? I looked at my patient, ripples of surprise giving way to a shiver of unease as I waited for him to explain. Surely he hadn't stolen that Jet Ski. Surely there was some mistake. Surely he'd defend himself and the police would go away satisfied no crime had occurred.

But Tyler Connelly looked up at me. No stain of embarrassment colored his cheeks this time. He was as cool as a jewel thief on the French Riviera, his icy-blue eyes clear of any doubt.

I couldn't pull my gaze away.

Even as he said, "Yes, I understand. But before you cuff me, do you mind if the birthday girl here finishes with my stitches?"

Chapter 2

MY HEELS CLACKED A STACCATO rhythm on the cobble-stone sidewalk as I rushed to the restaurant. It had taken twenty more minutes to finish with my patient—the alleged felon. Although there didn't seem to be much *alleging* to it. He'd as much as confessed just by virtue of saying nothing.

What a sad, sad tale. Tyler Connelly had seemed like a charming, if somewhat careless, guy, but harmless enough. Obviously his good looks had deceived me. A criminal lurked beneath that nice tan and all those muscles. And now I'd never even know what happened to him. He'd be carted off to jail, and all that beautiful facial symmetry would be wasted on a cell mate named Dutch.

I glanced at my watch as I reached the door of Arno's. Seven fifteen. Good grief. I hoped my parents hadn't caused a ruckus by getting into an argument. Visions of my eleventh birthday popped up like an evil clown. My parents had still been married that year, though the fighting had escalated, and the long hospital shifts had grown more frequent. I remembered staring at that store-bought birthday cake and making my wish with every ounce of naive hope strumming through my veins. I wished for a family vacation. Someplace with a beach and lots of sunshine.

Someplace warm and relaxing. Someplace that would fix all the things that seemed broken in our lives. Then I'd blown out the candles and watched as my parents had a knock-down–drag-out over who would cut the cake.

Typical surgeons. All we care about is who gets to hold the knife.

Before the wisps of smoke had cleared the air, my mother had demanded a divorce and my father had left.

Birthdays soured for me after that. But I'd tucked away the memory and moved on. It's not as if my situation was unique. Nearly all my friends had seen their parents go full honey badger on each other at one point or another. I grew up assuming divorce was just the final phase of marriage. That's why I often contemplated skipping it altogether.

Now here we were, together again on my birthday, having dinner at the only elegant restaurant in Bell Harbor. I walked through the door and looked around for signs of their scuffle but found none. Gentle music played, blending with the soft murmur of relaxed diners. There were no broken glasses or overturned chairs. No hastily thrown knives dangling from the woodwork. Not even any raised voices.

Nothing out of the ordinary.

Except . . .

Except for the sight of my parents sitting together. Harmoniously. Like normal people. It was like catching Batman and Bruce Wayne at the same party. My mother and father were on two sides of a square table, laughing.

Laughing?

My mother's head tipped toward my father, her cheeks flushed as if she'd already polished off a glass or two of chardonnay. My father was telling some story and gesturing with his hands. I looked back at the door behind me. Maybe I'd tripped through a wormhole into an alternate universe.

"There she is. There's the birthday girl," my mother said when she spotted me. She reached up her arms and I leaned over to give her an awkward hug. Personal space was very clearly defined in my family, and you did not invade someone else's bubble, but she seemed to be inviting me.

My father stood up and hugged me too, for a second longer than essential. Oh my God. One of them *was* dying from monkey pox.

I stared at my dad's face. He looked fit, if a little older. It struck me then that he would do that—age while I wasn't paying attention. But he sure didn't look like he was dying.

He pulled out my chair, and I sat down with a thunk.

"Happy birthday, Evie," he said, settling back into his own chair.

I was named after his mother, so he always called me Evelyn. This breach of protocol was as unnerving to me as if he'd pointed in my direction and said, "Pull my finger." None of this was making me remotely comfortable.

"I'm sorry I'm late," I said, hooking my purse over the back of my chair. If they were going to pretend like everything was nicey-nice, I should play along. "I had to finish suturing a laceration so they could formally arrest my patient."

My mother laughed, a kind of titter that I hadn't heard in ages. "Arrested in Bell Harbor? What on earth did he do? Skateboard on the sidewalk?"

My mother had made a joke, and my alternate universe theory started feeling more plausible.

"Practically," I answered. "He stole a Jet Ski."

She laughed again and took a tiny sip of wine. Her expensive white suit gleamed against the bronzy glow of her skin. She looked tan, but since she never left the operating room for more than two hours at a time, someone must have installed a tanning bed in the doctors' lounge. She'd colored her hair too. A rich caramel color. When did she start doing that? Oh, no! Maybe it was her who was dying?

The waiter came and gave me a glass of water. I took a sip and wished it was vodka. I wasn't much of a drinker, plus I was on call, but certainly a good stiff martini was in order. It was my birthday, after all, and they were about to ruin it with news of someone's imminent demise. It was the only explanation for their aberrant behavior.

"Stole a Jet Ski?" my father said gruffly. "Hard to make an efficient getaway on that, I'd imagine."

My mother nodded and laughed again.

What the hell? She was not a laugher. She was hardly even a smiler.

The waiter came back and handed me a menu, which I accepted with trembling hands. Not a good sign in a surgeon, but these were unique circumstances.

"Have you dined with us at Arno's before?" he asked. He was short with a goatee and reminded me a little of an elf.

I smiled. At least I hoped it looked like a smile. It may have been more of a grimace, because my parents were freaking me out. "Yes, I have. Thank you. I'll just need a minute to look this over."

"Of course." He nodded politely. "I'll check back in just a few moments."

"Thanks." I looked at my dad. "Did you guys order?"

"No, of course not, sweetheart. We waited for you. After all, it's not every day we get to have dinner with our best birthday girl."

My father usually displayed a level of sentimentality one might expect from a prison warden, so this hint at nostalgia only added to my disequilibrium. Everything was out of balance. Come to think of it, he looked tan too. That was odd. My suspicions began multiplying like mutant cancer cells.

"So, tell me, Evie, how goes the house hunting? Any luck?" My mother wiped a fingerprint off the wineglass with her napkin.

I pulled a piece of bread from the basket on the table. That cake had turned to pure crack in my system, and I needed to counteract it with something besides water.

"It's going OK. I haven't had much time to look, but my real estate agent and I are going to see some houses next week. Unfortunately, the places on the water are either huge and expensive or run-down little shacks. And expensive. There doesn't seem to be much middle ground."

"Sounds as if you're planning to stay here long-term then." My father picked up his glass of Glenfiddich and swirled the ice around.

"Yes, I'm planning to stay. That's why I took the job." I straightened in my chair as if titanium had suddenly surged through my spine, Wolverine-style.

My parents had always encouraged me to make my own decisions and pursue my own dreams—as long as that meant becoming a doctor, like them, and working at a prestigious university hospital, like them. Not only had I let them down by refusing to become a cardiothoracic surgeon, but I'd chosen a practice not affiliated with any major medical school, where my vast potential would surely erode faster than the dunes sinking into the lake.

But I had fallen in love with this town the first time I'd come to visit with Hilary and her family. Something about the beach and the dunes and smell of the water. It was all so peaceful and serene. Bell Harbor had a tranquility to it so unlike my crazy, hectic day-to-day life as a resident. I'd thought living here would be like a vacation. Of course, I hadn't fully comprehended the impact of moving to such a small community. I was still getting used to the well-intentioned busybodies and their fascination with my personal life.

"The hospital is a level-one trauma center," I added tersely.

In spite of my steely resolve, and the fact that one of them must be dying, I felt the need to defend my choice, which irked me. I was thirty-five years old, after all. Just barely. But still, too old to have to explain my actions to my parents.

My father nodded. "Well, it's your choice, if that's what you want."

"Yes, it's what I want." And it was. I was happy here. Very happy. I'd prove that to them even if it killed me.

My mother cleared her throat. "And how are things with your practice? Is everyone pleasant?"

Pleasant? Pleasant was a word for a Sunday afternoon drive or a midwinter's nap, neither of which were things our family indulged in. It wasn't a word I associated with my mother in any way. Skilled. Determined. Competitive. Even brilliant. Those were words that suited her. But not *pleasant*.

"Yes, they're very pleasant."

"I'm glad to hear that, darling." She toyed with the edge of the paper napkin resting under her wineglass and wiped at another smudge. "Are all of your partners married?"

"Married?" Was my chair tippy? Because I felt a little dizzy all of a sudden. "Um, most of them are married. One has a partner."

At least I think Chloe had a partner. There wasn't a lot of time for chitchat while we were seeing patients in the office or spending time in the operating room. All I really knew of her was that she was a good surgeon, loved to travel, hated golf, and tolerated staff meetings by playing video poker on her iPhone.

"Are they men or women?" my mother asked.

I crossed my arms and wondered if Tyler Connelly was having a better time right now than I was. It seemed we were both up for interrogation.

"Three men and three women. Why?" This awkward banter was making me twitchy, like when you think sandwich meat has gone bad but you smell it just to make sure. The truth was, the Rhoades family was not prone to tiptoeing around an issue. And even though my parents probably loved me in their own restrained, dysfunctional ways, we were not a nurturing, chitchatty bunch. We didn't mind sticking our fists into someone's open gut, but exploring another person's emotional state was far too risky. And this line of questioning was bordering on personal.

My mother pressed her lips together for a moment, then finally blurted out, "Here's the thing, Evelyn. Your father and I are a little worried you might get . . . bored. Bell Harbor is so small, and you've always been so driven and competitive. Things around here might get monotonous for you."

That's what this was about? The lack of professional challenges available in this town? My spinal titanium swelled again. When would they start giving me some credit?

"I'll find plenty of variety here, Mom. Aside from having lots of patients to see, there are other aspects of the practice that are incredibly rewarding. In fact, we've just partnered with an organization that arranges clinics in third world countries, doing cleft palate surgery, and one of my partners invited me to help with his research on melanoma in the local geriatric community. I won't be bored. Far from it."

She nodded, but a crease had formed along her forehead. She plucked at the napkin some more. "That's good. Of course. That all sounds wonderful. But I wasn't just thinking of your work, necessarily. I was thinking of, you know . . . the social aspect."

My mother leaned closer, her gaze intense.

I leaned back. I imagine my gaze was equally intense. I had no idea where this conversation was going. "The social aspect?"

She glanced at my father.

He looked down at his menu.

Mother gave a little huff, as if frustrated I couldn't intuit her meaning.

"Yes, Evie. You're thirty-five now. There can't be many men for you to date in a town this size."

"Men?" She may as well have said hippopotamuses. Or ostriches. Or aliens.

It was bad enough talking about this kind of thing with Hilary, but my mother and I hadn't discussed men since I was fifteen and we'd had The Talk, which basically consisted of her warning me to avoid penises at all costs. Then she'd handed me a box of condoms, patted me on the shoulder, and said, "Good luck." It was as close to a bonding moment as we'd ever had.

For the most part, I had heeded her advice. I'd had a few boyfriends over the years. I'd enjoyed the benefits of a well-utilized penis now and again, and even the occasional *foda pena*. But I'd learned from her that love and professional achievement didn't blend well. That for the most part, men were self-absorbed, maturity challenged, and not worth the trouble. Like Tyler Connelly, most of them were just one Jim Beam and Coke away from stealing a Jet Ski.

"I'm not sure where you're going with this, Mom."

She looked at my father again, and for the first time in twenty years, I felt as if they were united, and I was the one on the outside. He cleared his throat and lifted his menu so I couldn't see his face. I found myself wishing I had a case of monkey pox.

My mother turned back to me. "Your father and I think we may have done you a disservice. That perhaps our animosity toward each other may have caused you to avoid forming a healthy relationship with someone special."

"Someone special?" Fly ball. Left field. Clunk in the cranium. I smoothed my napkin in my lap. "I haven't avoided relationships, Mom. I'm just very selective. And I haven't had time."

"Well, you should make time." My mother reached out to pat my hand, and a flash of lightning caught my eye.

No.

Hang on a second.

That wasn't lightning. It was the high-powered wattage of a giant diamond ring flashing from her finger. The glare was like the beam from a lighthouse.

"Wow!" A huff of surprised laughter escaped me, followed by the swirling sensation that life as I knew it was twirling off its axis. "That looks like an engagement ring, Mom."

She squeezed my wrist and leaned closer still. "It *is* an engagement ring."

Bungee jumping in the Grand Canyon could not have created a greater plummet in my gut.

"You're engaged?" When did my mother have time to date, much less fall in love? I glanced over at my father. He must be as shocked as I was.

But he wasn't. She must have told him on the drive. That's why they rode together. He set down the menu and took a sip of scotch, as cool as Clint Eastwood had been before Clint Eastwood got old and curmudgeonly.

"Engaged to whom?" I asked. Was it that nice widower who lived next door to her in Ann Arbor? He'd always had a thing for her. Or was it her colleague, Dr. Bettner? That thin-lipped guy with the bad comb-over? Ack, I hated that guy. I hoped it wasn't him. Or maybe it was someone brand-new? Someone I'd never even heard of.

My mother sat back, pulling her five-alarm rock with her. "This is where it gets a little unusual."

Unusual? Really? Because my day had turned unusual right about the time I got confetti chucked into my face and then had my patient arrested right before my very eyes. And now this momentous news? I couldn't imagine what she could say to make it *more* unusual.

"It's your father," she said.

Except for that.

The bungee cord snapped. "What?"

"Your father and I are getting remarried."

My parents were not practical jokers, and if they were trying to be funny right here, right now, they were doing a piss-poor job of it. This wasn't funny. And they weren't laughing. What the hell? My father reached his arm around and draped it along the back of my mother's chair.

"I'm sure this is a bit of a surprise, Evelyn, but it's something Debra and I have been discussing for a few weeks."

"A few weeks?" My voice squeaked as if I'd been sucking on helium. *Vodka, vodka, vodka. Where was the vodka?* "Dad, it took two years for you to pick out a new car, but this? This you decide in a matter of days?"

I pressed my palms down on the table, trying to steady a world gone out of control. Could this be some kind of midlife crisis for them gone horribly awry? Or a dual break with reality? Once again, that alternate universe theory of mine started picking up steam.

"Well, it's not as if we don't already know each other. Isn't that right, Garrett?" My mother's voice was mellow as she turned and gazed toward my father's lean face.

His hair was completely silver; not gray or white, but a crisp silver. And although my mother often commented on how she was aging so much better than him, the truth was, my father had only improved with time.

But all that was irrelevant at the moment, because I needed to fix this. I needed to set things back where they belonged. Sure, it had been a relentless horror listening to them bicker all these years, but at least in that scenario, I knew where I fit in. This was marshy, treacherous new territory.

"Yes, you know each other," I said as calmly as I was able, given the fact that I could neither breathe nor blink. "You know each other, and you hate each other."

"That's not true." My mother looked back at me and had the nerve to sound surprised. "I never hated your father. I just hated some of his terrible decisions."

I let that statement dangle out there, but no, no, I was pretty sure she'd hated him. For two decades she'd called him Ferret instead of Garrett. And she once commented that his subsequent wives were nothing more than talking blow-up dolls, only dumber.

But my father's nod was solemn. "Evelyn, I was careless, and short-sighted, and selfish, but the fact remains your mother is the only woman I've ever truly loved. All those countless others meant nothing."

A telltale muscle twitched at the corner of my mother's eye. I sank deeper into my chair as if someone had cranked up the gravity.

"Is one of you dying? Is that what this is really about?"

My mother chuckled. "Of course not. What would even make you ask that?"

"Because this is insanity. The last I heard, you two weren't even on speaking terms. What the hell happened?"

They looked at each other like hormone-addled teenagers. My mother fluttered her lashes, and for the first time in my life, I saw my father blush. A serious case of the queasies mushroomed in my stomach. Apparently there is no age limit at which a child ceases to be nauseated by the gross reality of her parents being intimate.

"We ran into each other at a conference in La Jolla a few weeks ago," my mother said. "And there was a little wine tasting, and, well, one thing just led to another, I guess."

One drunken night of booze-soaked sex and my mother set aside twenty-plus years of resentment? This didn't add up. "Fine, so you had a fling, but how did *that* get to *this*?" I pointed at the ring.

"It wasn't a fling, Evelyn." My father still had the stones to admonish me. "You know your mother is the only woman who has ever challenged me, personally or professionally. She's the only one who has ever been my intellectual equal, and I've finally grown to realize that. The fact that she's still stunning after all these years is just a bonus."

It was my mother's turn to blush.

I needed a Dramamine. This ride was spinning too fast.

"We're getting married on our original anniversary," my mother added, fully not appreciating how the roaring in my ears made it nearly impossible to hear her. "I'd like you to be my maid of honor, Evie."

She squeezed my hand again.

"Maid of honor?" I choked out.

"Yes. The wedding will be a modest but tasteful event in Bloomfield Hills."

"Bloomfield Hills?"

"Yes. There's a lovely little bed-and-breakfast place there that does weddings. Your father and I have been spending our weekends in that area. We may even buy a house."

"A house?" I couldn't seem to stop repeating her words, like a foreigner trying to master a new language. But I could not wrap my head around any of this. I'd spent most of my life mediating communications between my parents, trying to keep that boat from rocking too violently, and suddenly here we all were, on a honeymooners' sunset cruise. I put my head into my hands, resisting the urge to cover my ears.

Fortunately, they fell silent, letting me process these words like a meat grinder processed sausage. My emotions were getting all chopped up and mixed together until I couldn't recognize any of them. My parents, remarried?

Finally, I looked up.

They peered back.

I shook my head.

"I don't know what to say to you guys. Except . . . why do you always do this kind of shit on my birthday?"

Chapter 3

"SO, LET ME GET THIS straight," Gabby said as she poked her fork into a piece of spinach salad. "Your parents have been divorced for twenty-three years, and now they're getting back together?"

We were having lunch at a new place that had recently opened near the hospital. I didn't normally take a break during my office hours, but I needed to talk to someone about this absurd turn of events. I'd fretted over my parents' announcement all night, and today, with Hilary in surgery, Gabby was the only other trustworthy person I knew.

Well, actually, I wasn't sure I *could* trust her, but I needed to discuss this with an impartial third party since trying to talk sense into my parents had proven fruitless. All my father kept saying was "Trust us." And all my mother kept saying was "It's really time you found someone special."

Found someone special? After a lifetime of her drilling me about the importance of independence, *now* she wanted me to find someone special? I had whiplash from last night's dinner conversation. And I was beyond confused. I rested my spoon against the edge of my bowl. I should have ordered something less spicy than tortilla soup. Like a shot of Mylanta.

"Yes. They're getting remarried," I said. "At some little bed-and-breakfast they've been spending time at over in Bloomfield Hills."

"A bed-and-breakfast?" For a grown woman, Gabby's sigh was princess sweet. "That's so adorable. Mike says if we ever get married, he wants his reception at the bowling alley. It's the only reason I haven't dragged him down the aisle yet. But a bed-and-breakfast is so romantic."

"No. No. No. It isn't romantic. It's ridiculous. My mother has lost her mind." My palm thumped on the table, making all the silverware rattle.

A diner at the table next to us turned to stare in our direction. I smiled apologetically. Sometimes I get a little shrill. People notice.

"Why do you think it's ridiculous? I think it's sweet. Imagine rediscovering love after all those years." Gabby took another casual bite of salad, eating as if this were just some random, insignificant discussion about something random and insignificant.

"Ever since the day my parents split up, all I've heard from my mother is what an egotistical douche bag my father is. He's been married three other times, you know." I counted on my fingers. "One, two, three other times! So including my mother, this will be his fifth wedding. Fifth!" I pushed my splayed hand toward her face for emphasis.

Gabby dodged my hand, and a few more diners turned to gawk. Maybe we should have gone someplace with fewer people.

She shook her head again. "But didn't he say he'd finally realized she was his . . . what was it? His *alma gêmea*?"

"Really? Portuguese? Is that necessary?" Impatience stretched my vocal cords.

Gabby smiled, unfazed by my distress. "His soul mate," she answered.

I gave an unladylike snort. "He said she was his *intellectual equal.*" I finger quoted in midair . . . with my middle finger. "But that's bull. He's just getting too old to attract younger women, so he figures being with my mom is the easiest way to still get laid."

A woman from the booth next to ours glared at me, and I finally noticed her three little kids staring at me with big, round Cindy Lou Who eyes as if I were the foul-mouthed Grinch.

Shit.

I mean . . . phooey.

I lowered my voice to a whisper. "It's bad enough my mother's offering him a little Frito penis now and then, but does she have to marry him?"

Gabby smiled. *"Foda pena."*

"Whatever." I picked up my spoon. Then dropped it back into the bowl again. "I just don't understand how she's had this complete reversal of opinion. She couldn't tolerate him before, so why now? What's changed? It just makes me so worried for her."

"Your mom sounds like a pretty smart woman," Gabby said. "Maybe she's just decided he's what she wants. Warts and all."

I looked out the window into the glorious sunshine. People were strolling down the brick-paved sidewalk, enjoying their day. I wanted to be one of them. Carefree. Unburdened. But I knew better. I knew how relationships could turn sour, how following your emotions could lead to disaster.

"That's the part I really don't understand, Gabby. She's got love goggles on. It's like she's forgotten all the rotten things he did. She was no saint, either, of course, but all of a sudden she's full of forgiveness. Maybe it's a menopause thing. Like a hormonal imbalance."

Gabby laughed and tipped her head to the side, making her pink-tipped hair catch the sunlight. "Evie, my mother is in the clutches of menopause. The other day she threw a six-pound raw chicken at my father because he asked what was for dinner. So I'm thinking forgiveness is not a side effect of menopausal hormones."

I looked out the window again. I knew she was right about that. I also knew it was unlikely I could explain to anyone the concern I felt over my mother's journey back to the dark side of unholy matrimony with my father. Maybe she'd forgiven him, but the truth was, he'd left me too. Without so much as a backward glance. And started playing house with some other woman. And some other woman's kids. I'd always found it the height of hypocrisy that a man who fixed broken hearts for a living could be so incredibly careless with mine.

Gabby sipped her iced tea. "You know, the fact that he actually married those other women does say something nice about him."

"What? That he loves to pay alimony?" Other than my mother, who earned every bit as much as he did, his other wives had all been utterly dependent on his income for their daily expenditures. Being Mrs. Dr. Garrett Rhoades required a certain amount of upkeep.

"No," said Gabby. "I think it means deep down he's a romantic at heart. He believes in true love and happily ever after. And maybe so does your mother. Maybe all this time they've just been looking for their happily ever after and realized they can find it together."

She was giving both of them way too much credit. My parents were not that self-actualized. "They cannot possibly be each other's happily ever after. This isn't some TV movie of the week where enemies become lovers. You don't know what these two have done to each other."

"Like what?"

I rarely shared these details. No one knew the level of passive-aggressive behavior my parents had displayed over the years. I guess I'd gotten used to it, but it was still embarrassing to talk about.

"Stupid stuff. Childish stuff. Like every time my mom finds a magazine subscription card, she fills it out with his address. I got his mail once. He had fifty-seven magazines. Even the mail carrier started complaining."

Gabby giggled behind her hand. "That's actually kind of funny. It doesn't seem that mean. Except to the mailman."

"OK then, how about the fact that she'd pick up his dry cleaning and donate the clothes to Goodwill?"

Gabby laughed harder, and I began to wonder if the rest of the world would see this as more funny than cruel. "OK, so somewhere in Ann Arbor is a homeless man wearing an Armani tuxedo." I smiled and took my first spoonful of soup.

"What else?" Gabby prompted. She was enjoying this. "Did he retaliate?"

"Oh, absolutely." I actually chuckled. Maybe it *was* kind of funny. "He sent a gorilla-gram to her office to celebrate the ten-year anniversary of their divorce."

"A gorilla-gram?"

"Yeah, you know. A guy dressed up like a gorilla who shows up and sings to you. She was furious. She had his car towed from the hospital parking for that one. My mother does not like to be humiliated."

Gabby shook her head slowly. "No one does. But it seems to me that if they kept pulling these pranks on each other, they never really did let go. Love ends when you stop thinking about each other, not when you're still trying to get a rise from one another."

Hmm. Maybe there was a molecule of truth to that. Or half a molecule, but it seemed unlikely. "These are two very competitive people, Gabby. I think it's more about getting in the last word."

"Well, whatever the reason, they need each other. You may as well embrace it, because you can't do anything about it." She stuffed another bite of salad into her mouth.

Embrace it? This conversation had not gone as I intended. Gabby was supposed to nod, and agree, and validate my feelings of irritation. I guess I should have explained the rules. I mean, what good did it do me if her only advice was to *embrace it*?

I'd left my parents at Arno's last night right after we'd finished our entrées. I'd said no thanks to dessert, claiming to be too full. But the real truth was that two hours of watching them canoodle had given me a stomachache. Too much sugar.

"Call me tomorrow, darling," my mother had said as I got up to leave the table, but when I turned to wave good-bye, they were already locked in each other's gazes as if I wasn't even there. It was spooky.

"Oh," Gabby said, pulling me back to the moment, "there's Jasper."

A tall, slender man in chef's whites had been moving around the small dining room, stopping to chat with this patron and that patron, until he reached our table.

"Hey, Gabby. I thought that was you. Love the pink hair." He gave her shoulder a quick squeeze.

"Hi, Jasper. Congratulations on your new restaurant. This place is *adorável*." She gestured to the room in general.

"*Adora* what?" He cocked his head to the side.

Gabby nodded and spoke slowly. "*Adorável. Minha salada é deliciosa.* That's Portuguese for this place is adorable and my salad is delicious."

"Portuguese, huh? Interesting. I think my mom speaks a little of that." He turned my way and smiled, extending his long arm. "Hi, I'm Jasper."

I shook his hand.

"Jasper, meet Dr. Evelyn Rhoades," Gabby said. "We work together."

"It's nice to meet you, Jasper. This is your restaurant?"

The place was *adorável*, just as Gabby said. It was cozy and quaint, with big windows and dark wood accents. Every table had a different-colored cloth on it, and all the chairs were strategically mismatched. It felt like the kind of restaurant that had been there forever, a place where the locals spent every Saturday night.

"It's mine for now." Jasper nodded. "If business stays good, I might even get to keep it." His smile was as bright as the gold wedding ring gleaming from his finger. It was so shiny I guessed it was nearly as new as this restaurant.

"Business looks good." Gabby looked around at all the tables. Nearly each one was occupied.

Jasper nodded. "It's been really busy. I actually need to hire more waitresses soon."

"Is Beth working here? I haven't caught up with her in ages." Gabby turned to me. "I went to high school with Jasper's wife."

Crimson splashed across his cheeks, and he looked over his shoulder as if someone might be eavesdropping. "She's sort of helping, but the smell of food makes her queasy. She's kind of a liability in the kitchen right now."

Gabby's eyes went wide. "Is she pregnant?"

Jasper looked around again, but his smile proclaimed his answer loud and clear. "I can neither confirm nor deny those rumors for at least another week. I've been forbidden."

"Oh, I can't wait to see her." Gabby's own cheeks flushed. "Tell her to call me, will you?"

Jasper nodded. "I will. I have to get back to the kitchen. I just wanted to say hi."

He left us with a wave, and Gabby gave up a forlorn little sigh. "I want a baby. Right now. I want Mike to marry me first, but I really want the baby. I'm almost twenty-eight. My eggs are deteriorating exponentially, and Mike is dragging his feet."

My ovaries waved at my uterus as if to say *are you hearing this?* If *she* was getting too old, what the hell did that make me?

"Babies are a lot of work," I said, speaking as much to my reproductive organs as to Gabby.

She gazed back at me, her expression earnest. "Is that why you're never having any?"

My hand paused, holding the spoon over my soup bowl. Never having any? Wasn't I?

"Who said I was never having any?"

Her cheeks flushed cherry red and she began to stammer. "Um, well, no one. But you're not interested in dating. And you're thirty-five years old. I just kind of assumed . . . I mean, no offense. I guess lots of single women have kids now and that's great. I just . . . well . . . do you want to have any?"

That was a very thought-provoking question. One I'd never been asked, even by my own self. Did I want children?

Kind of.

Sort of.

Maybe. I sure liked Hilary's kids, but truthfully I was a little afraid of babies. They were so tiny and fragile. Other than my pediatrics rotation, I had never been responsible for one. Maybe subconsciously I'd made that decision by postponing marriage until it was too late. I knew the statistics. Getting pregnant after thirty-five put me into the high-risk category. And without a man anywhere on the horizon, I wasn't likely to be married and pregnant anytime soon.

The soup suddenly tasted bitter on my tongue, and I started wishing Gabby and I had skipped this lunch altogether. It was only making me feel worse.

"I'm not sure about kids," I said. "I do kind of want them, or at least one, but I'd probably be a terrible mother." It felt a little sickening to admit that, but it was true.

"Why would you say that?" Gabby's tone held genuine concern.

"Because I wouldn't have a clue in the world how to entertain a baby."

Abrupt laughter dashed away any hint of sadness from her face. "That's what you're worried about? That your baby would get bored?"

"Bored and hungry. I never have any food in my apartment. And I'm hardly ever home. When would I ever even see it? If I don't have time to date, I guess I don't have time for a baby." That felt oddly sickening to admit too. I'd never been one of those women who coochie-cooed every time I saw an infant, but the notion of never, ever having any of my own made me a little sad. I guess I should have thought about this sooner.

Gabby's tone was gentle again. "You're a doctor, Evie. You take care of all sorts of people. You can certainly learn to take care of a baby, if you wanted to."

"My parents are brilliant surgeons, Gab. But they sucked as parents. Trust me on that one. Being a good doctor doesn't equal good parenting."

"But you're not like them. And don't you think you'll get . . . lonely? I mean, eventually? That's the nice thing about kids. Men might leave, but your kids are yours forever."

Forever. That was a long time. And I had no response for her. I was still in knots over my parents reuniting. I couldn't heap my indecision about another life-altering topic onto the pile right now.

"Are you done eating? I should get back to the office."

Gabby's cheeks flushed again. "Sure. Of course. But Evie, I

think you're wrong. I think you'd be a good mother, if you ever decided to be one. Your patients love you, and so do Hilary's kids."

My eyes felt inexplicably moist, and I made a production out of finding something in my purse instead of looking at her. "Yeah, maybe."

The conversation veered to other topics as we paid our bill and left Jasper's restaurant. But as we strolled back to the office, past the quaint storefront windows and big flowerpots full of freshly planted pansies and geraniums, I couldn't help but notice we were surrounded by women with strollers. Had they all been out here before and I just hadn't noticed? Tall women. Short women. Pudgy ones in oversized T-shirts, and other ones in sports bras with bodies so buff you could see the muscle definition under their skin. But regardless of their shape or size, they seemed to have one thing in common.

They were all smiling.

At each other. At their babies. At me. I was moving among them, but set apart. Like the hero in some mind-bending science fiction movie who suddenly realizes everyone around him is a cleverly disguised alien. My steps faltered. Was I the only one in all of Bell Harbor without the primordial instinct to breed? My ovaries rattled again, angry monkeys in the cage of my nonmaternal body. They were being very noisy today after a lifetime of silence.

A toddler with fluffy blond curls and a blue striped shirt stepped into my path. He was cute, in a soft, dimply way, and walked with an unsteady gait, as if he had something sticky on the bottoms of his shoes. He stopped when he saw me, and regarded me with dark chocolate-brown eyes. He lifted one chubby fist to wave a cluster of dandelions in my direction. His plump cheeks doubled in size when he smiled, and a little sparkle of drool escaped past his tiny white teeth.

My stoic heart turned to pudding. He was the sweetest thing I'd ever seen.

His mother reached over and took a gentle hold of his wrist. "Stay with Mommy, honey," she said. She smiled at me apologetically. "Pardon us. He's such a flirt."

"He's *adorável*," Gabby said, a wistful note of longing in her voice.

They moved around us as we watched them walk down the sunny sidewalk. The mom wore a neon pink tank top and exercise pants. Her blonde hair bounced from a high ponytail as she expertly guided a gizmo-loaded stroller with one hand and held on to the little boy's with her other. A golden retriever trotted alongside them, his leash looped over the woman's elbow. Away they went, probably to some house with a picket fence and a minivan in the garage.

That was her life, and she seemed pretty happy about it, but it all looked foreign to me. A place full of miniature beings and unfamiliar scenes. Navigating the streets of Bell Harbor with a baby, a stroller, and a dog would be like me trying to do surgery in the middle of a monsoon with nothing but a stethoscope and a pair of pliers. I'd be clueless, helpless, and lost.

Still, something deep inside me, something at a microscopic level, split open and began to swell.

Chapter 4

"MY HUSBAND ALWAYS DID SAY I have an impressive rack."

In a long line of interesting patients I'd seen this week, Dody Baker was my most colorful. In the five minutes she'd been in my office, I'd learned more about her than I'd personally discussed with a priest, a bartender, a psychiatrist, or my own gynecologist. She was as unfiltered as river water but refreshing in a clumsy, unguarded way.

"Of course, they're not as buoyant as they used to be," she said, arching her back to lift her front. "But my nephew-in-law recommended you very highly. He says you're probably the best plastic surgeon in Bell Harbor. And he'd know because he's a doctor too. Dr. Desmond McKnight? You must know him."

I nodded. "Yes, of course, from the emergency department."

Everyone knew Des. The nurses practically swooned every time his name was mentioned. Not only was he attractive, smart, and nice, he was also madly in love with his wife. The ultimate Prince Charming. Now if I could find a man like him, this whole dating thing might be more appealing.

"Des says you can hoist my girls back up where they should be and even things out a bit. I had that lumperodectomy two years ago and I've been a little lopsided since then. See?"

She whipped open her hospital gown to expose her bare breasts, and I just barely contained my gasp of surprise. I wasn't prepared for that spontaneous visual, but damn, she was right. She did have an impressive rack, especially for a woman of nearly seventy years old and with part of one breast missing.

Still, I took the edges of her gown and tugged the sides back together. "Let's go through a little of your medical history before I do the exam, shall we?" I looked down at her chart to get my bearings on her case and began reading the notes from her primary care doctor. She had a history of ductal carcinoma but otherwise appeared to be in excellent health.

"They're expecting any day now, you know. With twins, no less. Although it's no wonder, the way they go at it."

"Excuse me?"

"Des and my niece, Sadie. They're like bunnies, those two. Although my husband, Walter, and I were the same way." She squeezed her hands together, setting her dozen colorful bracelets to jangling. "Do you have children, Dr. Rhoades?"

There was the children question again. This seemed to be a theme among the Bell Harborites. It must have something to do with the small-town mentality. As if there wasn't much else to do around here but find your mate, copulate, and procreate.

I shook my head but didn't look up from the paperwork in my lap. The trick to dealing with overly social patients was to avoid eye contact.

"No, no children," I said.

"Why? What's the matter with you?"

Now I looked up. Even for a forthright old lady, that was a ballsy, brazen question.

"What's the matter with me? There's nothing the matter with me."

"Are you married? A pretty thing like you must be married."

I didn't bother answering that. "Do you take any medications, Mrs. Baker?" I asked instead.

"A few. Here's a list." She fished around in her blue flowered purse before producing a laminated index card and handing it to me. "My niece made me that. She's a professional organizer. Very fussy. So, are you?"

"Excuse me?"

"Are you married?"

"No." I looked at the handy little card, which appeared to be color coded by frequency of dose. Nice. I wished all my patients had organized nieces. I jotted some notes on Mrs. Baker's chart.

She crossed her legs, nearly kicking me with her foot. She wore flip-flop sandals with big pink flowers on them. "Well, in that case, let me tell you, I've discovered the most wonderful website, don't you know? Bell Harbor singles dot com. Computerized matchmaking. Can you imagine? In my day we had to look for hanky-panky the old-fashioned way, at church socials. But now everything is arranged online. I met a simply delightful man on my computer. His name is Brock Lee, but he looks just like Wolf Blitzer. Do you suppose that's his real name? Wolf?" She paused to examine her fingernail. "Who would name a child Wolf?" she said a moment later. "Unless . . . oh my. You don't suppose he was raised by wolves, do you? Then it would make complete sense."

"Mrs. Baker." I tried to sound respectful but authoritative. "Could we focus on your medical history and talk about what I can do for you cosmetically?"

"What? Oh, yes. Of course. I was just thinking you might want to check that site out, if you're unattached. But a pretty little thing like you must not have any trouble finding men. Now, about my boobies . . ."

The appointment continued on about as I expected, with several more verbal detours and anecdotes about her children. It was nearly five o'clock by the time I was finished with her. I'd just sunk into my office chair to face the stack of paperwork before me when Delle tapped on my office door.

"You've got one more patient waiting, Dr. Rhoades, and you might want to put on some lipstick. As Gabby would say, he's *adorável.*"

Ever since my birthday party a week and a half ago, Portuguese had spread through this office like a sexually transmitted disease, but I ignored it, just as I ignored her comment about the patient. I was done, D—O—N—E, talking about men, and babies, and marriage, and dating. Done.

"Thanks, Delle. I'll be right there." I pushed aside the stack of papers and rose from my chair.

She looked me up and down. "You should take off your lab coat. You have lovely arms."

"What?"

"You have lovely arms. And if you don't mind me saying so, quite a shapely backside, but it's all covered up by that awful lab coat. Let the man see your tushy."

All right. This needed to stop. The biddies and the bachelorettes in this town were ganging up on me, and it was starting to piss me off. Even if I wanted to find a man, I wasn't going to do it on a computer website, and I sure as hell wasn't going to date one of my patients. Honestly, what was the matter with these people?

"Delle, those kinds of statements are completely inappropriate. I'm here to do my job, not attract some man. Now, please, no more remarks about my appearance, or finding me a husband, OK?" I was tired and cranky, and that made my tone far more harsh than I'd intended. But still, it needed to be said.

Delle's eyes widened behind her red-framed glasses. Her lips quivered.

Oh, dear heavens. She was puddling up.

Life would be hell for me in this office if I made our beloved Delle cry. I stepped closer and rested my hand on her shoulder as she blinked rapidly.

"I know you have the best of intentions, and I don't mean to hurt your feelings, but I would never date one of my patients."

She pulled a tissue from the sleeve of her white blouse and dabbed frantically at her nose.

"I'm sorry, Dr. Rhoades. I don't mean to get all up in your affairs. I mean, your lack of affairs. It's just that my Ronald and I are so happy together. We've been married nineteen years come this August, and every year it just gets better and better. There is nothing quite as wonderful as having the right man by your side. I just want you to experience that special bliss."

Ah. Yes.

That special bliss.

I'd overheard Delle telling Gabby this morning about her latest interlude with *special bliss*. It involved something called a Vagazzler.

I patted Delle's shoulder. "Thank you, Delle. You're sweet to worry about me, but really, I'm very happy with my life the way it is. Even without a man in it."

She peeked at me over the rims of her glasses, her eyes bright with moisture. She leaned close, her breath warm against my ear. "I understand. If you like the ladies, I'm OK with that too. I just want you to be fulfilled."

A gasp of laughter escaped before I could swallow it down. No matter how hard I tried to establish myself as an authority figure in this office, my staff continued to mother me like speckled hens. It made it very hard to tell where genuine concern ended and plain old nosiness began. But in this instance, I believed Delle just wanted me to be happy. And that was sweet.

"I'm not a lesbian, Delle. But once again, thanks for your concern." I turned her around with my hands on her shoulders and gave a gentle little push. "Now let me go see my patient."

"Put some lipstick on," she said without turning around.

I caught my reflection in the tiny magnetized mirror stuck to the side of my filing cabinet. Damn it. She was right. I needed lipstick. I put it on hastily and made my way to exam room number seven, plucking the thin manila folder from the rack outside the room.

I tapped a knuckle against the door in a quick knock, then stepped into the room.

There, sitting on the paper-covered exam table with his long legs dangling over the side, was my felon.

Well, he wasn't *my* felon. Just *a* felon.

Tyler Connelly wore faded jeans and an aquamarine T-shirt that made those eyes of his a neon glow-stick shade of blue.

I stopped short when I saw him, nearly tripping myself in the process. Not because of his symmetrical perfection, but just because I was surprised to see him. Regardless, my entrance was not smooth. "Oh, hello."

I thought his cheeks flushed a little, but he was so tan it was hard to tell. He stood up and offered half a smile, as if not certain how I'd receive him.

"Hi." His voice still had that gravelly purr, and he'd gotten his hair cut very short. It made him look older. Not older than me. Just older than he'd looked before.

I glanced down at his chart, which was nothing more than a few sheets of paper. The one from the emergency department had obviously not made its way here. But at least this one confirmed his name was definitely Tyler Connelly.

As if I'd forget.

I took a little breath and held out my hand to shake his. "Mr. Connelly, correct?"

He nodded. "Yes. Tyler."

His palm was warm against mine, and it seemed as if he held the clasp a little longer than necessary. Maybe he was noticing my fresh lipstick.

I pulled my hand away and looked back down at his paperwork. "Tyler. Yes. Of course. It says here you need some stitches removed. I'm assuming those are the ones I did in the emergency department?"

"Yes." His cheeks definitely flushed that time.

"Excellent. That shouldn't take long at all. Please sit down." I gestured to the exam table and heard the crinkle of the paper as he slid back into his spot. I turned to find the suture removal kit already waiting on the counter behind me. I peeled it open, then pulled out some latex gloves from the box attached to the wall. "I hope you haven't been waiting too long. My receptionist could have had the nurse practitioner remove those stitches."

"I know. She told me that. But I wanted to wait for you."

One rubber glove snapped against my wrist. "The nurse practitioner is entirely qualified."

"I'm sure she is, but I wanted to see you." I heard him stand back up.

I snapped the other glove against my wrist. A little self-administered aversion therapy to remind myself that attractive men, especially charming ones with criminal records, usually equated with some level of pain. Even in my limited experience,

I knew that. I turned around to face him and took note for the first time of how tall he really was. Six two, at least.

"You wanted to see me? Why?"

He leaned back against the edge of the exam table and hooked his thumbs along the edges of his pockets. His head dropped a little as he peered upward.

A friend of mine had a big sloppy dog that used to look at her in much the same way when he was trying to sneak onto the sofa. As if she wouldn't notice a 160-pound Labrador inching his way onto her lap.

"I wanted to explain about the other day," Tyler said.

And I wanted to hear his explanation purely for the sake of my own curious nature, but I couldn't let this patient get under my skin. For that reason, it was imperative I keep this appointment well within the bounds of professional propriety.

"You don't owe me any explanation. My job is to take care of my patients, regardless of what laws they may have broken."

He moved one hand from his pocket to rub the back of his neck. "Yes, I'm familiar with that policy, but can I trust you with a secret? Rely on doctor-patient confidentiality?" he asked.

I crossed my arms and stood a little taller to illustrate my personal strength and moral fortitude. "If it's pertaining to any kind of criminal activity, I'd feel obligated to report it."

"It's not . . . exactly." His shoulders lifted and fell with his fast sigh, then he stared at me boldly. "I didn't steal that Jet Ski."

I'm not sure what I was expecting him to say, but that still surprised me. And confused me too. "You might have mentioned that to the police before they arrested you, then."

"I know, but it's more complicated than that."

Of course it was. Jail was full of innocent men caught in complicated situations, but the less I knew about this, the less I knew about him, the better off I'd be. Regardless of how he felt, or what his motivations were for seeing me, I didn't know him. And no matter how incredibly fine he looked in those jeans, which was *very fine*, by the way, I wasn't gullible enough to be swept away by anything he might say.

"Mr. Connelly, I'm very glad to hear you didn't steal the Jet Ski, for your sake. Is that what you wanted to tell me?"

His nod was almost imperceptible.

"All right. You've told me. Now let's get those stitches out, shall we?" I flicked my gloved fingers at him, indicating he should get back up on the table and let me do my job.

He didn't, though. He crossed his arms instead and stared at me with those irritatingly luminescent eyes. "You don't believe me, do you?"

I didn't. And even if I'd wanted to, charm was Tyler Connelly's superpower. In any other circumstances, I bet he was pretty effective with it. But I was immune. It didn't matter that my nerves were doing a two-step throughout my body or that my blood fizzed in my veins when his eyes met mine. It didn't matter that he made me acutely aware of being a woman. A woman alone with a man.

No, none of that was relevant, because this man was my patient. He was eight years younger than me.

Oh, and a thief.

There was that too.

"It doesn't matter what I believe," I said. I crossed my own arms. A standoff.

"It does to me." His tone was impatient, as if my dismissal was personal. But it wasn't personal. It was self-defense.

"Why?"

He stared at me a moment, unsmiling. "Because you're really beautiful, and I don't want you thinking I steal things. I don't."

His voice had dropped, nearly to a whisper. It was rich and deep and warm and sent shivers up my spine and down my legs.

This was a problem. Men had flirted with me before, but few had the physical goods to back it up. This one did. And it rattled me to the core, but I couldn't let him know that. It wouldn't be professionally ethical. And it wasn't logical. There was no reason for me to feel so fidgety and fluttery just because some man called me beautiful.

"You bumped your head pretty hard when you hit that boat dock, Mr. Connelly. I think you may have knocked something loose. Now sit down on that table and let me take these stitches out." I used my bossy attending physician voice, and it seemed to do the trick.

I saw the trace of his smile as he braced his palms against the exam table and slid backward, that dangerous tattoo swaying along with the muscles of his arms.

I took the forceps and the surgical scissors from the suture removal kit and stepped closer. My hip bumped against his knee, but he didn't move it out of the way. He just looked at me. All smoldery-like.

What a tease. There must be a pile of devirginated, broken-hearted girls in his past. Thank goodness I was beyond all that. I ignored the distracting heat flickering south of my navel. But biology was a funny thing. Apparently my body didn't care that he was too young, too duplicitous, too unreliable. A broken heart in the making.

"Turn your head toward the side, please. This won't hurt."

"I know." He stared out the window, silent, while I captured the loop of the first suture and snipped it, pulling the end free. Then the next, and the next. He had faint residual bruising, but I'd seen much worse, and his laceration was definitely on the mend.

I did good work. His scar would barely be noticeable, especially considering it ran along the edge of his jaw. If he were any other patient, I might have mentioned that, but something told me he'd take it as some kind of invitation.

He started to say something and I shushed him. "You can't talk while I do this."

He folded his arms across his middle and slumped down a bit. He let out a sigh, and I could see the muscles in his jaw clench for a second before he relaxed again.

I had the home field advantage here. First of all, I was the one holding the very sharp scissors pointed at his face. And second, I had every reason to be staring at that face. And leaning toward him. It crossed my mind to oh-so-accidentally brush a breast across his bicep just to see what might happen next, but besides being coy, and foolish, and not at all my style, it would also be the most unprofessional thing imaginable. I could lose my license.

Still, the idea was silly enough to make me smile. I pressed my lips together to keep my amusement hidden.

"You're laughing at me," he said with no heat or embarrassment in his voice.

"No, I'm not."

"I think you are."

"Now who is disbelieving?" I snipped and pulled the last suture and stepped back. "There. All finished."

"That's it? You're done?"

"I'm fast."

"I wish."

He smiled at me, so bright I was nearly toppled by the brilliance of it.

Really, I'd like to do a graph of his face. There are quantifiable measurements of facial features that all human beings find universally pleasing. And Tyler Connelly's proportions were damn near perfection.

I found myself smiling in return.

"Have dinner with me," he said, leaning forward.

I took a step back, bumping against the counter behind me. "I don't think so."

"Why not?"

Why not? There were a dozen reasons. Right?

"Because I don't date my patients." That was harder to come up with than it should have been.

"Aren't you finished with my stitches?"

"Yes."

"Do you need to see me in this office again?"

"No."

"Good. Then I'm not your patient anymore. Problem solved." He moved off the exam table and stood again. He seemed taller than before. Maybe because his ego had inflated.

"Mr. Connelly, I—"

"Tyler."

I harrumphed. "Fine. Tyler. You're still my patient. And there are several other reasons I cannot have dinner with you, none of which I need to share." He didn't need to know that the lower half of my body was saying, "Yes, yes, yes." Thank God genitals can't talk—for oh, so many reasons.

He frowned down at me. "Coffee, then. Let me explain what happened with the police."

I felt my defenses weakening, but that just wouldn't do.

"Coffee isn't necessary. You said you didn't steal the Jet Ski, and I'll give you the benefit of the doubt." I set down the instruments behind me.

"Fine," he said. "But don't tell anyone I didn't steal it."

Maybe he needed a CT scan. He wasn't making any sense. "Why on earth would you *not* want people to know that you *didn't* steal it? That's ridiculous."

"I have my reasons. Have dinner with me and I'll explain." His smile was coy, seductive. Oh, he was clever. Dangerously, tantalizingly clever. I was the mouse and he was the trap. I *did* want to know this story, if for no other reason than to understand why he would keep his proclaimed innocence unproclaimed. But being alone with him, even at a restaurant or surrounded by other people, had *bad idea* embroidered all over it. My curiosity about his situation, not to mention my curiosity about how he looked without that shirt on, must go unsatisfied.

"Do you know what I think, Mr. Connelly?"

His brows pinched together at my refusal to call him Tyler, but I needed to return this discussion to more impersonal and professional grounds. I moved toward the door, pushing down on the handle. "I think we're finished here."

Chapter 5

"AS YOU CAN SEE, EVELYN, this house provides a stunning view of the lake, and the property offers seventy-five feet of lakefront access just steps from the door."

My real estate agent, Ruby, gestured toward the two-story wall of floor-to-ceiling windows with her expensively manicured fingertips. Her voice had a two-pack-a-day huskiness, and her hair was the same deep, store-bought burgundy as her nail polish.

This was the ninth house we'd looked at today, and I'd started to feel like Goldilocks. Some of the houses were way too big, and others were way too small. But this place? This might be Baby Bear's house, because it was feeling just right. Of course, we were still standing in the foyer. It might not meet my requirements after further inspection, but I was finally starting to feel optimistic.

After years of living in dorms and apartments, I was ready to buy a house. My own house. I'd worked long, hard hours to earn it, and I wanted to get this right. In fact, I'd made a list of everything I wanted, weighted by priority. That was a habit I'd developed early in life to help me make decisions. That way I could rely on logic instead of emotion. That's how I'd chosen which medical school to attend, which specialty to choose, and even which residencies to apply for. I'd made a list before coming to Bell Harbor too, but that one was a little lopsided by the fact that I wrote it after I already had my heart set on moving here.

And now I was buying a home here. With my weighted list in hand. First and foremost, it needed to be close to the hospital. Hopefully close enough so I could walk to work.

Check that one off. This place was just over a mile from my office.

I also wanted a place where I could hear the waves. It was a silly thing, really, but important to me. I had a memory, a vague, hazy memory, of being with my parents and sitting near a bamboo hut. I think we might have been in Hawaii, but what I remembered most was falling asleep with my head in my mother's lap and listening to the sound of waves. That may have been the last vacation we'd taken as a family.

"This lovely home is thirty-two hundred square feet and has three and a half baths. All the flooring is Brazilian cherry," Ruby said, reading from the colorful brochure in her hand. "Oh, it says there's a balcony off the master bedroom suite. Let's go see that."

She led the way up a wide staircase. The railing gleamed in the sunlight as I trailed my fingertips along the top. This was just the kind of place I'd dreamed of. Not too big but full of upgrades. I'd feel pretty fancy living in a house like this. Too bad I'd thrown away that birthday tiara.

"Besides the master, there are three other bedrooms, plus a den on the first floor that could easily be converted into an office or another bedroom," she added. "You'll have to get to work to fill those up with babies."

Of course she assumed I'd fill them up with babies. This was Bell Harbor, after all. Where everyone traveled two by two. If I didn't couple up soon and hop on the Ark, it'd be just me and the unicorns swimming for dear life.

We walked down a spacious hallway into the oversized master suite. It was white with lots of windows. It was beautiful, but a little sterile. It reminded me of an operating room with all that absence of color. But it could be painted. An easy fix. And I was pretty good with cosmetic upgrades.

"This bedroom is very elegant. Very romantic. Those babies will come along in no time," Ruby said, stepping over to a set of French doors. She opened them, and I followed her out onto the oversized balcony. The view was amazing, with the lake off to one side and a copse of trees on the other, offering some privacy. There were even two Adirondack chairs with a little table between them, just waiting for a mister and a missus to enjoy the sunset while sharing a glass of wine. My heart gave a little extra pulse. I might feel a little silly out here by myself, staring at that other empty chair. Maybe I could move it someplace else.

Ruby moved back inside, her silk suit rustling. It was bright orange. I'd never seen silk that color before, but somehow, on her, it seemed stylish. I could never get away with a look like that. Growing up with red hair, I'd learned to keep my clothing choices subdued. Every once in a while, I'd go crazy and wear emerald green.

"Oh, come see this." Her reverent voice echoed as she stared from the bedroom into the bathroom. I crossed the plush white carpet to see whatever it was that had made her so breathy, and offered up my own girly sigh of rapture. The master bathroom was painted in dove-gray hues accented with rustic wood. Bowl sinks rested above the his and hers vanities, and taking up one entire wall was a shower so big I could wash my car in there. Six showerheads of various sizes pointed in every direction. A built-in bench filled one corner.

Ruby waggled her eyebrows and jabbed me with her bony elbow. "That shower's not for getting clean. That's a shower for getting down and dirty, if you know what I mean."

Yes, I did know what she meant.

But the last time I'd had sex in a shower was in a dingy frat house, and I'd learned too late that everyone in the whole damn place could hear us. I vowed to never bathe tandem again after that incident, but this shower might change my mind—if I had the right somebody to try it with.

A gleaming, soaped-up Tyler Connelly burst into my imagination, and I gripped the bathroom counter for support. Visions of him had followed me around like an eager intern ever since I'd seen him in my office days ago. It was terribly annoying, and yet picturing him in that shower, smiling his *I'm-not-so-very-naughty* smile and offering me a sudsy loofah, nearly made me gasp out loud. I turned my back on the shower. And on him. I saw my flushed reflection in the mirror.

"Looks like it would use up a lot of water," I said breathlessly.

"Sure, but what fun," Ruby answered.

Yeah. Fun. Everyone seemed to think I could use some of that kind of fun. I was starting to believe it myself. Why else would that encounter with Tyler have left me so exhilarated and yet so frustrated?

Ruby and I looked through the rest of the house, at all the nooks and crannies, and I could actually imagine myself living here. Other than needing fresh paint in a few areas, it was damn close to perfect.

"The kitchen has all-new stainless steel appliances," Ruby said as we entered the final room. "And this oversized island is perfect for making gourmet meals. Do you enjoy cooking for your family, Evelyn?"

I'd hinted repeatedly that there was no family to speak of, but it hadn't sunk in. She must have thought I was teasing. I shook my head at her question while noticing the flecks of black and gold in the granite countertop. "I usually just eat at the hospital, but maybe if I had a kitchen like this, I might learn to cook."

I'd never really had spare time before, so the idea of nurturing a hobby was a novel one. Maybe I *would* learn to cook, or play the cello. Or finally finish a game of sudoku.

Or go on a date.

And there was Tyler again, standing in this gourmet kitchen, holding out a chilled glass of pinot grigio as I came home from work. He was wearing an apron because *he* was a good cook. And he'd made me dinner. Chicken Marsala.

Apparently, if I was going to fantasize in the middle of the day, I was going to make it count. So of course my imaginary boy toy could cook. He probably did laundry too.

The Tyler of my brain shook his head and evaporated.

At last, my subconscious was acknowledging the futility of that fantasy. Thinking of him in a domestic setting was ridiculous. *He* was ridiculous, asking me out as if I were some sorority girl who would giggle over his brush with the law. I wasn't, and I wouldn't. Going out with him was out of the question.

It was as crazy as my parents getting back together.

I tamped down a sigh.

Tyler Connelly wasn't my real problem. He was just a symptom of it. He'd stirred up sensations in me I'd buried deep during the busy days of residency and fellowship training, along with every notion of love and romance that I'd denounced after watching my parents' marriage implode.

But they were blissfully back together again.

And I had moved to Bell Harbor where every day was a frickin' Viagra commercial, followed by a Toys "R" Us ad. Everyone else in this town was married with children, or at least on their way to that. There was just no avoiding it. And they all wanted me to join their matrimonial sect. How long could I swim against this tide?

Maybe it was time to drink the Kool-Aid. Maybe it was time for me to find myself a man. A real man. A grown-up man. A man who would want to get married and even have some children. Someone with a fabulously important career, who I could talk to while we drank outrageously expensive wine on the balcony off our bedroom and not even worry about spilling it on that stark white carpet.

"Well, what do you think of this place, Evelyn?"

What did I think of this place?

I looked over Ruby's shoulder. There was Tyler again, standing near the pantry, nodding at me with encouragement. His eyes were bedroom dreamy, his dimples cavernously deep. He was wearing the apron again—but nothing else. He reached down . . . and lifted the hem.

"I'll buy it," I gasped, and my stomach dropped to the floor.

—⋀⋀— —⋀⋀—

"You bought a house?"

Hilary stood in my office doorway holding a twenty-ounce cup of coffee. I looked up from my computer screen in surprise. I hadn't even realized she was there. She looked tired today, and thin. She always looked thin, but she'd lost weight recently. Evil friend.

"How did you know I bought a house? I only made the offer last night. They haven't even accepted it yet."

Hilary sank into the chair across from my desk. "Yes, they have. My cousin, Judy, lives next door to their cleaning lady, and they told her they were going to say yes. How could you keep this a secret from me?"

"Apparently I can't," I teased, but she looked wounded rather than amused. "Hil, I'm kidding. I didn't tell you yet because I wanted it to be official before I started spreading the word." I had underestimated the level of nepotism and grapevinery in this town. I should have known the offer would be broadcast far and wide before the sun rose.

"Well, it's nearly official. Congratulations. I guess." She took a sip of coffee and stared out the window. I'd seen that look before.

"Really? You're pouting because your cousin Judy's neighbor has a big mouth and told you before I could? Not fair."

The corner of her mouth twitched. "No, I'm pouting because Judy told Gabby before she told me. Now everyone in town knows, and the only person I got to tell was you."

I would never understand this small-town mentality. Wait until they found out I was ready to start dating. That might require a special meeting of the city council.

"Well, thank you for telling me. Now I don't have to bother waiting for my Realtor to call. But I do have some other news." My pulse picked up a little speed. This was going to trump buying a house.

"Me too," she said, totally cutting me off. "I want you to give me a tummy tuck."

Oh. She won that round.

"A tummy tuck? Do you need a tummy tuck?" She was teeny tiny beneath that formfitting dress. I'm not sure I could find much to tuck.

"Yes," she said. "No matter how many crunches I do, those babies of mine left me with a marsupial pouch."

I laughed, but she didn't. She seemed quite serious. In fact, now that I thought about it, she'd been kind of serious for the last few days.

"Of course I'll do it if you want me to. But, Hil, is everything OK? You've seemed a little off your game."

She reached over and shut my office door, her face as tense as her Botox would allow. "Everything is fine. Except I think Steve might be considering an upgrade."

Steve Pullman had never been my favorite guy. I found him condescending and abrupt, but he was Hilary's husband, and she loved him, so when they got married, he became my reluctant friend-in-law. "What do you mean, upgrade? Like Hilary 2.0?"

She shrugged and took a big slug of coffee. "Or maybe a whole new model. Some hotshot lawyer just joined his firm, and he can't stop talking about her. Apparently she does amazing things with the tax code."

"That whore."

Hilary smiled. "She is a whore. A tax-coding whore and she's trying to steal my husband."

I knew she was being deliberately dramatic, and I smiled for that. Even Hilary gave a tiny chuckle. But her eyes were still a little sad, and it made my heart hurt.

"Do you really think this woman is an issue, or are you just feeling like a little body work will remind him of how awesome you are? Because you are, you know. Most women would die to have your figure."

She rubbed her fingertips across her forehead. "I don't know. I'm probably just being silly. He's working on some big case, and I've been busy helping Chloe set up that mission trip in Haiti. We're both so tired and the kids are so demanding. We never have time to just sit and talk."

They lived in the same house, so it seemed odd to me that they wouldn't have time for that. But then again, I was no expert on marriage. Or parenting. Or relationships in general.

"Maybe you should go away for a long weekend or something. Without the kids. Go to Vegas, or Chicago, or take one of those wine-tasting tours up north. Isn't that what couples do?"

She took another sip of coffee and stared at me over the rim. "That's not a bad idea. We haven't gone anyplace, just the two of us, in about a hundred years. Will you stay at my house and take care of my kids and my dogs, and the turtle and the fishes? And the gerbil?"

My skin itched just thinking about all that dander and poo. "No. That's too many pets. But I will cover your patient load on a Friday so you can take a long weekend."

Hilary smiled again, her face relaxing into the original version, the one I'd met back in residency.

"You would? That would be fabulous. Really fabulous. I think I'll go do some web browsing and find a romantic getaway. Do you know of any?"

She burst out laughing at her own joke, because obviously I wouldn't have a clue about romantic getaways, even though the whole idea had been mine.

I crossed my arms while she cracked herself up. "That's just hurtful," I finally said, but it wasn't, really. It was actually kind of funny, and I was glad to see her spirits lift. Before, she'd been drawn and exhausted, but now she looked like her usual vibrant self, and all because of something I'd suggested. Maybe I was better at this relationship stuff than I'd realized, and she was going to be extra happy to hear I was ready for one of my own.

But she glanced at her watch and pushed up from the chair. "Oh, shit. Is that the time? I'm supposed to be in surgery." She dropped the coffee cup into my wastebasket. "I'm still serious about the tummy tuck, though. Marsupial pouch has got to go. I'll schedule it and let you know."

She was gone with a flutter of white lab coat and long, toned legs.

"You're late for surgery, Dr. Pullman!" I heard Delle's voice call after her. Then I heard footsteps coming down the hall toward my office, and seconds later the receptionist filled my doorway.

"I heard you bought a house, Dr. Rhoades. Why didn't you tell me?"

Chapter 6

THE BELL HARBOR COMMUNITY PARK sat halfway between my apartment and the hospital. It was a mystical green space full of big, old oak trees and lots of winding paths, and the perfect place to take my early morning jog when the weather got too warm for beach running. Today I had just enough time to get in a few miles before heading off to work.

As I walked underneath the arbor entrance and adjusted my ear buds, a symphony of high-pitched yapping caught my attention. I pulled the buds from my ears and spotted a cluster of yippy little dogs tangled up around a man's muscular legs. One fluffy pooch bounced around like a furry Ping-Pong ball, another stretched as far as his lead would allow and bayed at a chattering squirrel, while a third mutt sprinted in a circle around them all, tightening the noose on the whole crew.

The imprisoned dog walker lifted a foot to disengage from the mess, but a black-and-white spotted puppy rose right along with his shin. "Come on, Taffy, you furry little rat."

My gaze traveled up his leg and locked on his face. That face. I flushed all over as Tyler Connelly looked up from the canine chaos and peered straight at me. What was he doing here? Why was he surrounded by a circus of little dogs? And most important, why hadn't I put on some makeup before leaving my apartment?

For an eighth of a second, I considered dashing behind an oak tree, but he'd obviously seen me. I was only twenty feet away. Nothing to do now but keep on walking. I approached, nonchalant, and offered him an awkward wave. The ear buds dangled uselessly around my neck.

"Good morning, Mr. Connelly," I said, as if seeing him here had been my plan all along.

He smiled in obvious but unflustered surprise and pushed his sunglasses up on top of his head, no doubt to mesmerize me with his laser-beam eyes. Cheeky bastard.

"Good morning, Dr. Rhoades." He said my name as if he were tasting it on his tongue. "Are you stalking me?" He sounded playfully hopeful.

"Not at all. Just here for a little exercise."

My hair was in two short ponytails down low behind my ears. It was a childish style, but at my hair's current shoulder length, this was about my only option for exercising. I wished, at that moment, I'd left it loose, even while acknowledging that what my hair looked like was completely irrelevant. My appearance didn't matter because I was in no way trying to attract him. In no way. Trying to attract him. No way.

A long, skinny rust-colored dog pulled on my shoelace.

Tyler tugged on its leash. "Hey, Doxie, knock that off."

"That's all right." I crouched down to scratch the dachshund mix behind his droopy ears. That was my first mistake. It brought me eye level with Tyler's goods. I hadn't had my face this close to a penis since my last relationship and the celebration of National Steak and Blow Job Day, which is apparently a big deal among the steak-eating, penis-endowed community.

I averted my gaze from Tyler's wiener to the wiener dog instead.

One was trying to ruin my shoe. The other could ruin my life.

"He's a menace," Tyler said.

I could only assume he meant the dog.

"But cute," I said. "I wouldn't have guessed you to be a little dog kind of guy."

Tyler tried to untwist one leash. "I'm not. These aren't my dogs."

I stood up again and looked at his face just in time to see those dimples deepen. That was my second mistake.

"They're not your dogs? Did you steal them?"

I was teasing, and he knew it.

"No. I didn't steal them, just like I didn't steal the Jet Ski." His voice lowered to a whisper when he said that last part, as if we shared a special secret, but one I still didn't understand.

"So you've said," I whispered back. "But if these aren't your dogs, then why are you walking them?"

A sly, lazy smile curved his lips into nearly a pucker.

My mouth watered irrationally.

"That's kind of a funny story, actually," he said. "Have dinner with me and I'll tell you all about it."

Fate was a persistent bitch. She seemed determined to toss us together. Various scenarios flashed through my mind. Some involved nudity. Actually they all involved nudity. Damn, maybe I should take him to bed just for the novelty of it. I hadn't had a meaningless fling in eons, and he was big and beautiful and couldn't be *that* bad a man if he was out walking all these cute little dogs. But he was twenty-seven and I was thirty-five. If I was going to get naked, it had to be with someone from my own bracket. And besides that, I was a surgeon and he was a . . . a dog walker. Of someone else's dogs.

The canine chaos continued to yip and yap and twine the various leashes around his legs.

"I can't have dinner with you, Mr. Connelly."

"Tyler."

"I can't have dinner with you, Tyler."

"Why?" He was asking as if we'd never been through this conversation before. It was amusing. And flirtatious. And it made me want to change my mind.

But I should end this, fast and sharp, like the first incision with a scalpel. I crossed my arms. "Why? Because I'm thirty-five years old."

His head tilted to the side. "And?"

It wasn't obvious? "And that means I'm too old for you."

He looked me over, slowly, from the laces of my shoes up to the stupidly tiny ponytails behind my ears. Then his gaze came back to mine. His eyes had a perceptible twinkle, and a rush of heat cascaded over me.

"We could go at four o'clock," he said coyly.

I nearly stomped my foot. His persistence was both flattering and frustrating. "I didn't say I was *old*. I said I was too old *for you*. And besides that, I watched you get arrested. Remember? Or maybe you don't remember that part because you were drunk."

All the smirk left him, like a guillotine falling. He looked down at the dogs and started to earnestly untangle them. "You're right. I made a great first impression, didn't I?"

Oh, well, shit. Now I felt mean. I hadn't meant to embarrass him, but I *had* seen him get arrested! Common sense warned me to avoid him, even if all my other senses wanted to taste him, and smell him, and squeeze him like a horny anaconda.

The dogs seemed to sense something tense was going on above their heads and quieted down. Tyler looked back at me, his expression void of any flirtation.

"Community service," he said.

"What?"

"My lawyer thinks it'll look good to the judge if I'm doing some kind of volunteer work, so I've started walking dogs for the animal shelter. Community service."

My chest, which had been tight since the first moment I saw him, deflated.

"So you did steal the Jet Ski?" The words were heavy on my tongue.

"No. I didn't. I was returning it for someone else. But I did knock out the dock by accident. I misjudged the angle. Might have been the whiskey."

Maybe I was gullible, but I believed him. If he was going to lie, he'd have come up with a better story. Something more clever than misjudging the angle. Because of whiskey.

"Who were you returning it for?"

Tyler shook his head. "It doesn't matter. As far as the police are concerned, it was all me. No good deed goes unpunished, right?" His smile was tight. There was obviously more to say, more to the story. It was present right there under the surface of what he *wasn't* saying, but Tyler's demeanor had changed from swagger to sincerity. It made him seem younger than ever. And made me feel even worse for having been so sharp.

"Anyway, I don't want to keep you from your exercise, Dr. Rhoades." He said my name with emphasis now, heightening the barrier between us. Which should make me glad. Only it didn't.

"Enjoy your walk," he added. "It looks like we're heading in different directions." He gave me a fast nod and moved on down the path, the little dogs scampering alongside him.

I watched him go and bit my lip. I wanted to stop him and tell him I believed him. Because I did. But what would be the point? He was right. We were heading in two very different directions.

—ᨆ— —ᨆ—

"The wedding plans are coming along nicely, Evelyn. Have you found a maid of honor dress yet?" My mother was calling between surgeries. I hadn't spoken to her much since my birthday, which wasn't unusual. Schedules being what they were, it was hard to find the time to chat. Or dress shop, for that matter.

"Nope, no dress yet. I thought maybe I could pick something out when I visit you in Ann Arbor in a few weeks. There aren't a lot of options here in Bell Harbor." I was walking down the hospital corridor, on my way to surgery as well.

"No, I suppose there wouldn't be many places to shop. Have you found a date yet?" Her voice was light, but the implication was heavy. I thought about just hanging up and pretending to have lost my signal, but she'd only call back.

"Nope, no date yet either."

There was a significant, meaningful pause. The nonverbal equivalent of *I'm disappointed in you.*

"Well, your father was going to ask Uncle Marv to be his best man, but he could ask Dan Hooper. You remember him, don't you? He's single these days."

A knot the size and shape of an armadillo lodged in my chest. Now my mother was trying to fix me up? With a thrice-married partner of my dad's? That was not only insulting, it was nauseating.

"I'll find my own date, Mother. I have someone in mind already." That was a lie. I didn't.

"Really?" She sounded uncharacteristically optimistic, and I couldn't stop the vision of me strolling into the Bloomfield Hills bed-and-breakfast with Tyler Connelly on my arm. That would go splendidly.

My father would say, "You're not a doctor? What do you do for a living, son?" and Tyler would say, "Well, in between incarcerations, I like to walk dogs."

Then my mother would say, "Oh, Evelyn, he's going to leave you for a younger woman. He's far better looking than you are. And he's not even a doctor."

And then Tyler would say, "No, I'm not a doctor. Do they serve whiskey at this place?"

Yeah, scratch that idea. Tyler was not going to be my date to my parents' wedding.

"Yes, I have some options," I said. That was a lie too. I didn't have any options. But that wedding was coming up fast, and I was going to have to figure something out equally fast. The only idea I had seemed far-fetched and risky. But I might just have to go for it.

Chapter 7

"GABBY, I NEED A FAVOR."

She was hunched over the keyboard at the front desk. Everyone else had gone home for the day, so it was just the two of us in the office.

"Sure. What's up?" she said, not looking away from her computer screen.

I wound up for a grand slam. "I need a man."

Gabby straightened up so fast her chair nearly tipped over. She clawed the reading glasses from her face, then stuck an index finger into her ear and wiggled it in an obnoxiously exaggerated manner.

"Wow, for a second there I thought you asked me to find you a man."

The onslaught of teasing was inevitable. I'd braced for it. I'd even prepared some canned responses.

"Yep. Go ahead. Make fun, but you, and your sister, and my parents, and the rest of this crazy little town have finally won. I'm ready for a man. But I'm going to go about this scientifically. Methodically."

Her eyes narrowed. "Scientifically? Like in a lab? Please don't tell me you're going to build a man using parts you've scraped off of other people."

I burst out laughing, and I was suddenly very glad I'd decided to ask for help. The truth was, I'd been thinking about this for days. And days. And days. Ever since seeing Tyler in the park. And in my office. And in the emergency department. My attraction to him was undeniable, but it was purely physical. He was not the man for me long-term. If I was going to find myself a significant other, I needed one who was mature and settled. And preferably with a clean criminal record.

"No, I'm not going to build one. I thought I'd try a dating service, though, to help me weed through all the inappropriate men and provide the most optimal choices." I'd practiced my little speech in the bathroom before coming out here to ask her. My palms were damp with nerves, and I sounded like I was reading from a cue card. I pulled a sheet of notebook paper from my lab coat pocket and handed it over. "I've made a list of my husband requirements, weighted by priority, just like I did for my house. That's how I always make big decisions."

She took the list gingerly between her fingers and unfolded it as if it were hardwired to explode. She put her glasses back on and scanned it quickly. "Evelyn's husband requirements," she read off the top, then glanced at me. "Are you kidding with this stuff? These are your requirements?"

"Yes. Those are very logical criteria. And they're prioritized. Remember, this is a guy for me, not you."

"Oh, you've got that right. Advanced degree in science, mathematics, or engineering? That's your number one demand?" Gabby leaned back in her chair and slid the glasses to the tip of her nose.

"I need someone I can have an intelligent conversation with." I crossed my arms.

She nodded. "Uh-huh. Have you talked to many engineers or mathematicians?"

"Not really. Why?"

She paused, then shook her head. "Never mind. I'll let you sail that voyage of self-discovery solo. But what's this second one here about economic equality?"

That point was easy to defend. "I think it's best to be with some who earns about the same amount as I do. That way I won't have to worry he's just after my money, and he won't think I'm after his. It keeps the balance of power equal."

"Right. So you'll trust him in your bed, just not in your bank account?"

She was being kind of argumentative in the face of my sound judgment. "That's not at all what that means. My mother taught me to take care of my own financial security. There is nothing wrong with that."

"No, there isn't. I'm just not sure choosing a man based on his income is going to score you the best dates. Rich guys can be big dicks. And they usually don't have them." She giggled at her own joke.

I tapped my foot. "So you're suggesting I should choose a man based on the size of his penis instead of his wallet?"

Her smile indicated that's precisely what she was suggesting. "Not exactly. A great big penis can be kind of uncomfortable too. I'm suggesting in all things, moderation. You know, not too big, not too small, not too soft, not too . . . well, forget that last one. The point is, I think you're missing some of the more important details. Like how about good old-fashioned chemistry?"

I should have guessed she'd have opinions about this. But her opinions wouldn't sway me.

"Sure, chemistry is a factor, but physical attraction shouldn't be the primary reason for being with someone. My parents got divorced because every time my father became infatuated with some other woman, he thought he was in love. And obviously he wasn't, because none of those marriages lasted either. Now he's back with my mother because he finally understands what's important in a relationship."

"Which is?"

"Intellectual equality. Common interests. Similar goals. Stuff that still matters once the honeymoon is over."

Gabby's eyelids drooped. "Oh my God. You're going to take all the fun out of this for me, aren't you?"

"Yes, that's my hidden agenda," I said drily. "Will you help me or not?"

She folded up the list and put it in her pocket. "Of course I will. I'll come over tonight and we can check out some dating sites. I'll bring Chinese takeout. Do you have wine?"

"I'm not going to set up my profile while drinking. That's a recipe for disaster." Actually wine sounded pretty good. And this plan had disaster written all over it anyway.

"Fine. I'll get drunk by myself. What else is new?" Gabby rolled the chair up to the desk and gave me a sincere smile. "Honestly, I love that you are doing this, Evie. And I'm honored to help you. What did Hilary have to say?"

I felt a little pang of unease. "I haven't told her yet. I tried the other day, but she had her own stuff going on and I never got a chance. Tonight she's busy with family time. But I can tell you that she'd fully support my criteria. So don't lose that!" I pointed at the pocket containing my list.

Gabby patted it. "Oh, I'll take good care of this. Trust me."

I didn't trust her. Not as far as I could chuck a Volkswagen. But Hilary was unavailable and Gabby was all I had. Of course, I could have done this alone too, but since always being alone was what had gotten me into this position, I felt like I needed a buddy for this adventure.

—⩗— —⩗—

Gabby sat on the floor of my apartment an hour later, polishing off her plate of moo goo gai pan and her second glass of wine. I'd caved to her peer pressure and was finishing my first merlot. My laptop was perched on the coffee table like some magic portal into my future. But I hadn't had the nerve to turn it on.

"All right. The night's half over, Evie. Time to boot this puppy up." Gabby reached over, her fingers flickering over the keyboard, and the screen brightened instantly. "Bell Harbor Singles, you said, right?" She continued typing.

I nodded. "That's the one Des McKnight's kooky aunt-in-law suggested. I guess if it's good enough for her, it's good enough for me. Although she is seventy. And quite possibly suffering from dementia."

On second thought, maybe this wasn't such a great idea. As soon as I put my information out there . . . well, then my information would be *out there*. Where literally every Tom, Dick, and Harry could see it. And every Bill and Brad and Brian, and scores of countless others. It's not as if I had any privacy in this town anyway, but this was taking things to a whole new level of transparency. Maybe I wasn't ready for this.

But before I could stop her, the site popped up and nearly blinded me. It was a cotton-candy pink with a photo of two hands clasped in front of a setting sun. Gabby read the text out loud.

"Bell Harbor—where the sand is warm and the romance scene is hot, hot, hot. Whether you're looking for just a little fun in the afternoon sun or a stroll down the aisle, your ideal match is waiting for you. Log on now. Your happily ever after is just one click away."

She smiled over at me. "Just a click away, Ev. Are you ready?"

I felt a little woozy all of a sudden. I hadn't been on a date in ages. In fact, I'd looked at my calendar just before Gabby arrived and realized I hadn't had sex in nearly two years. With my fellowship training and traveling for interviews, it just hadn't happened. So no wonder I was ogling a young stud like Tyler Connelly. I was suffering from a severe case of vaginal cobwebs. It must be like an old, abandoned subway tunnel down there.

Gabby moved the mouse around and clicked on a little bell that said "Create your profile."

"Don't forget my list," I said.

"I've already forgotten your list," she answered. "There's a questionnaire. Let's just go through that, and we'll get to all your requirements that way. Even the stupid ones."

"But I've listed them in order of importance."

Gabby shook her head. "I had no idea you were so compulsive. I'll be sure to mention that charming little personality gemstone in your profile."

"I'm not compulsive. I'm decisive. I don't want to waste time with someone who doesn't meet even my most basic of requirements."

Like Tyler Connelly.

Gabby clicked away on the keys, ignoring me.

"OK, speaking of basics, let's start with those. What's your preferred height range?" she asked. "It goes from three to eight feet."

"Seriously?" I tried to imagine either extreme. Then I tried to block those images away.

"That's pretty broad," Gabby agreed and took a chug of wine. "How tall are you?"

"Five two."

"OK, so no offense to the guys under five feet, but I think we can find you somebody taller without much effort. Let's say five five to six two. I dated a Goliath once who was six eight, and the sexual mechanics were a hassle. Plus he didn't fit in my car. Don't go that tall."

"Would that be the guy with the overly large penis?"

"That's the one."

"Duly noted."

The idea of working out sexual mechanics with anyone suddenly felt very overwhelming. Yes, I wanted to be scientific in my pursuit of a suitable mate, but certain things, sex in particular, shouldn't be dealt with in such a clinical fashion. It was very Masters and Johnson-y.

"How about fitness level?" Gabby asked. "Looks like the range here is from couch potato to the guys who can't get change from their own pockets because their biceps are too big."

I took a sip of wine and blocked more mental images. "Is there a spot that just says physically active? Like enjoys jogging or something?"

Gabby's fingers did more clicking. "Yep, I put your preferences right in the middle here."

We continued through the profile questionnaire, eliminating men who smoked, lived with their mothers, had an excessively high number of ex-wives, or had done hard time for murder or extortion.

"OK, here are some questions about you," Gabby said, her hands poised over the keyboard. "What do you do for fun?"

"Fun? Fun is on there?" I set my glass down and scratched my chin. "Um, well, I work, which is fun for me. I read a lot. I like to jog in the park when I have a chance."

Gabby made a snoring noise and let her head fall back against the sofa cushion. "That's it? That's all you've got? You don't need a man for that kind of crap, Evie. You need a basset hound."

"That's not a very nice thing to say. I'm not going to lie on my personality profile."

"Then you'll be the only one who doesn't. Look, I'm not suggesting you lie, but this is a marketing exercise. You have to come up with stuff a guy would actually want to participate in. Any man who gets excited by watching you read is a pervert. How about sports? Do you like any? Or better yet, do you play something, like tennis or volleyball or something? Or golf?"

"I used to be pretty good at badminton."

"Badminton? You mean with the little rackets and the rubber birdies?" Her tone was as dry as the beach in August. Maybe I should have done this alone after all.

"It's a sport," I said defensively. Maybe that explained all those participation ribbons for field day. The truth was, I'd never been very outdoorsy or sporty. I'd liked track well enough back in the day, and I still jogged regularly, but that was about it.

"How is it that you don't play golf? You're a doctor. I thought all doctors play golf," Gabby complained.

"I can play golf. I just don't like to. So if I list it and end up with some golf lover, he'll want me to play all the time. I'd be bored. And if I'm going to be bored, I may as well be single." I felt my jaw going stern, and I'm sure I was frowning.

Gabby pushed my wineglass closer to my hand. "Relax, I'm not trying to pick on you. I just feel like it's my duty to warn you that this profile is going to land you on some dullsville dates."

"No, it won't. It's scientific, Gabby. That's the beauty of the computerized profile. It's like my weighted list of criteria, only even better. It's a carefully crafted algorithm designed to find me men I have things in common with. Like . . . guys who realize golf is boring."

Gabby rolled her shoulders and rubbed out a knot with her hand. "Yes, fine. I get that. You need things in common, but you also need a little razzle-dazzle. A little humina, humina, humina, you know? Seriously, you ranked sense of humor as irrelevant and civic awareness as essential. Are you looking for someone exciting to date or someone you can vote for?"

I reached up and rubbed my own neck, because this husband hunting was starting to become physically painful. "First of all, I would never date a politician. And second, I'm looking for a guy who's right for me in a big-picture scenario. Somebody who I'll still want to hang around with once we're old and gray. Well, he can go gray. I never will. But I want a guy who likes me for who I really am, so I'm not going to pretend to be something I'm not."

She looked at me with an expression I'd seen on colleagues' faces when a patient's test results were ominous. But I knew what I was doing. I was going to be honest and trust the data. I was going to go about this methodically and logically. I wasn't going to put my future into the hands of something as intangible as chemistry or as whimsical as fate. Fate was for people without a plan. The Bell Harbor Singles website was scientific.

"All right," she said after a moment. "We'll try it your way, but I hope you can do CPR on yourself, because these guys are going to bore you to frickin' death."

She turned back to the computer and typed. I couldn't see the screen now. The wine had made my vision a little blurry. "What are you putting on there?"

"That you like piña coladas and getting caught in the rain."

"Very funny. And thanks, because now I'm going to have that song stuck in my head."

"Serves you right." She typed for another minute and then turned back to me. "OK, are you ready for the moment of truth? Once I push this button, your profile goes live and they can see you, and we can start searching the database for your Mr. Rhoades."

I gulped down the last bit of wine in my glass and hiccupped. "Yep. I'm ready."

There should have been a drum roll or something, but all we had was the tiny, almost silent, click of a keystroke.

We leaned in together as a scattered assembly of pictures filled the screen with squares of text beneath each one.

"Are those all matches?" I asked, amazed at my good fortune. This was a jackpot! There were so many. Then I looked a little closer.

Tobias Fitzhammer, forty-seven, exterminator's junior assistant. Eugene VanderBosch, forty-four, Reiki master and martial artist. Franklin Bluth, fifty-seven, sex god.

"Does that say *sex god* as his occupation?" I asked, blinking to clear my vision.

"Yes. It does. And is that . . ." Gabby adjusted her glasses. "Is that a monkey on his shoulder?"

It was. A monkey wearing a sombrero. There were men in mesh tank tops, men holding various animals, tools, or sports memorabilia. There was a man in a top hat and tails—which should have made him look dapper, except he was also holding a ventriloquist's dummy. This was not the cream of any crop. Thankfully, the pictures scrambled to bring others to the forefront.

"Oh, wait! Here's one. He's cute." Gabby moved the mouse and clicked on the picture to bring up a full profile before I could object.

David Hill, forty-one, architect. Silver hair. Brownish eyes. I didn't find him that physically appealing, but he had a nice smile, and he wasn't holding a monkey or a dummy and he was wearing a real shirt, so that put him at the top of the list thus far.

We went through a dozen or so profiles until the second bottle of wine was gone, and so was I. I never could hold my liquor. It was time to call it a night.

"Take two ibuprofen, a B-12, and drink a big glass of water before you go to bed," Gabby said as she got up to leave. "You'll be fine. Tomorrow, with any luck you'll have e-mails from some hot prospects. *Boa noite.*"

"What?"

"That's Portuguese for good night," she said, picking up her purse and fishing out her keys.

"No, I mean the other thing you said. About the e-mails."

"Oh, well, now that your profile is live, you should start getting e-mails from interested men. That's the fun part. It's like shopping."

E-mails? From total strangers? Total strangers with names like Jeremy Laramey, Chuck Luckey, and Khaled Formichelli-Pugliese? Men who thought we might be suitable life partners? Oh, no. What had I done?

My stomach roiled, and I wasn't sure if it was the wine rebelling or my sense of hope circling the drain.

Chapter 8

"IT'S LIKE WE'RE NOT EVEN friends anymore. Why are you keeping so many secrets from me?"

Hilary was back in my office, another enormous coffee in her hand, and from the stern expression on her face, she'd obviously heard all about my visit to Bellharborsingles.com.

"I tried to tell you the other day, but you had to leave for surgery." My voice was petulant. My head was still aching from the wine I'd drunk last night, and her scolding did not help, but I was glad she was there. I had eleven e-mails waiting in my dating profile that I'd been too chicken to open without someone holding my hand.

Hilary sat down in the chair, careful not to spill any of her daily caffeine. "Well, you should have made me listen so you didn't have to go to Gabby. My God, Evie, if you follow her advice, you'll end up with some tattooed biker dude or a starving artist sculptor who sells his plasma to buy groceries. She has terrible taste in men. Hers is even worse than yours."

Now I was less glad she was here. "I don't have terrible taste in men."

"Well, maybe not technically, because you avoid them altogether. But when you do pick one, it's always somebody who's grossly inadequate, and then you just let the relationship die of natural causes. You're a classic commitment-phobe."

I'd heard this song a dozen times before. Hilary was convinced my lack of matrimonial interest was pathologic in nature. Not just a healthy decision based on my needs at any given stage of my life.

"You know, as much as I enjoy these little pep talks," I said, bristling, "I'm clearly demonstrating an effort here. A little support might be nice."

She nodded once, conceding my point. "You have my full support. I'm just wondering why you asked Gabby for help instead of me." She got that sad, wounded look in her eyes again. The same one she'd had when saying her husband wanted a fresher model, and I realized I'd hurt her feelings. I'd spent more time with her sister lately than I had with her. No wonder she was feeling left out.

The apology was evident in my tone. "I'm sorry, Hil. I just knew you were busy with family stuff, so I didn't want to pester you. But you'd be proud of me. I made a list of criteria just so I *wouldn't* fall for the wrong guy."

"You made one of your infamous lists? Let's see it." Now she sounded more amused than supportive. Apparently, no one trusted me to know what I wanted, or what I needed.

A fast knock sounded on my office door, interrupting my response, and Gabby joined us, bright in a sunshine-yellow maxi dress.

"Hey. Good morning. Do you have any messages in your profile mailbox, Ev?" She took the coffee from Hilary's hand and tasted it. They both looked at me expectantly. Waiting. Wondering. Hoping. Their eyes were practically watering in suspense.

"I do," I answered reverently. "Eleven of them." It suddenly felt like some sort of score, and maybe I should have gotten more. More was always better, right?

But Gabby smiled. "That's a good start. Any promising ones?"

Hilary moved forward to the edge of her chair. "Yes, any good ones?"

A whoosh of anxiety and exhilaration flooded my senses. The point of no return.

"I'm not sure yet. I haven't opened them."

"What? Why?" Hilary demanded, any residual hurt feelings swept away by impatience.

"I was waiting for you guys." I didn't explain I was actually postponing it out of fear and dread. There was no harm in letting them think I just wanted to include them in this glorious experiment I was performing.

"Well, open them," Hilary urged. "Let's see what your list of criteria buys these days."

"And hurry up. We've got patients showing up in about fifteen minutes," Gabby added, closing my office door as if we were about to surf for porn.

I stared back at my computer and swallowed down a football-sized lump. My fingers twitched as I logged on to the website.

Hilary caught sight of the bubblegum-pink screen and chuckled. "Oh, wow," she whispered.

"Shut up," I murmured back. "You're already married. Desperate times call for desperate measures."

She drowned out the next chuckle with her coffee.

My pulse sped up while my breathing seemed to halt altogether. I clicked on the first message.

Phil Carter. That name seemed innocuous enough. His picture came up with his note, and I recalled seeing him last night, although the wine had fogged my memory. He was nice looking, in a soft, middle-management kind of way. A little frayed around the edges, but being a plastic surgeon, I was hypersensitive to that sort of thing.

"He's cute. Ish," Gabby said.

"He's cute-adjacent," Hilary said. "Is that a bowling trophy he's holding?"

"It looks like it," I answered. I wasn't much of a bowler, but just because he was didn't mean we wouldn't have other things in common. Right? At least he wasn't holding a golf club.

"Read the note," Gabby whispered, as if asking me to chant some magical incantation.

I took a big breath and blew it out.

Hi, Evelyn. I see you are new to BHS.

Using an acronym for Bell Harbor Singles was worrisome, indicating he'd been at this rodeo for a while, but I kept on reading.

Your profile is a seventy-two percent match to mine. I've found that anything less than seventy-five percent is not a good fit but I think we should meet and see if we can beat the odds. You're very pretty. I hope you look like your picture. Would you like to meet for dinner at six o'clock at Arno's today? Let me know.

"Today? He wants to meet today? That seems kind of rushed and desperate, doesn't it?" I looked at them over the desk. Hilary took a sip of her coffee and avoided eye contact, but Gabby was more enthusiastic.

"Don't be silly. It means he likes what he sees and he's decisive. Just like you," she said. "And that perspective on percentages sounds good, right? I bet this guy has a weighted criteria list too."

I looked back at his picture. "I guess so. I'll think about this one. Maybe."

I clicked on the next message, and the three of us gasped in unilateral horror at a photo of a very chubby man in a very tiny thong. At least I think it was a thong.

Hey, baby. U R one hot babe. Let's hook up and—

Click. Instant delete.

"I feel dirty," Hilary whispered.

Gabby flicked her on the arm. "Give it a chance, OK? This isn't like shopping at a boutique. Some of us have to sort through a lot of tacky stuff at the discount store to find something good."

Great. I was looking for a man at T.J.Maxx. I selected the next message and prayed the photo would be less offensive. It was. In fact, this guy was kind of cute, in a Matt-Damon-wearing-glasses kind of way. He was wearing a green shirt and sitting on a sunny patio.

Gabby and Hilary both leaned forward as I read.

Hello, Evelyn. I am new to the Bell Harbor area having just returned from being stationed overseas. I haven't lived in the United States for a couple of years and so I'm looking to get reacquainted with old friends, and hopefully make some new ones, too. I'm thirty-nine, and now own a landscape design firm. If you'd like to meet, send me a note. I hope to hear from you.

Sincerely, Zach Parker

"Not bad," Hilary said, nodding with enthusiasm. "A soldier and a businessman. This guy has some potential."

He did. My optimism took a leap from dismal to definitely, maybe.

A loud knock at the door made the three of us jump and then giggle like preteens at a slumber party telling scary stories.

Delle's voice penetrated through the wood. "Dr. Rhoades? Dr. Pullman? Patients are arriving."

Hilary stood up and pointed at my computer screen. "Give that guy a go, for sure. But if it were me, I'd stay away from the other two. Especially the lard-ass in the tiny underwear."

—⎍⋀⎍— —⎍⋀⎍—

The day went by painfully slowly. I was double booked for most of it, and the wine hangover didn't help. Neither did the fact that I had more e-mails coming in and no time to check them. The curiosity was killing me, although I couldn't ignore the irony. Men were suddenly distracting me from my job. That's exactly the reason I hadn't dated before—because I wanted to focus on my patients. Maybe this whole Bell Harbor Singles thing was a big mistake. Maybe the reason I was thirty-five and single was because I liked it that way. I was satisfied with my life. Most of the time, and right now, these men were taking time away from my career.

I'd nearly decided to scrap the whole thing when Gabby approached me in the hall. It was nearly closing time for the surgery center, and all I wanted to do was to go home, take a hot bath in my tiny apartment tub, and read some medical journals until I fell asleep.

"Great news, Ev," she said, grinning with unrestrained glee. "I made a date for you. Tonight."

I skidded to a halt. "You what?"

"I made a date for you with the percentages guy. He's expecting you at six o'clock at Arno's."

"Why? Why would you do that?" My pulse sputtered and jumped like I'd been zapped with resuscitation paddles.

"Because you have to get this first one out of the way. This is your practice date."

I shook my head. "What are you talking about?"

"When's the last time you were on a date? Like, a year ago? Longer? You need a refresher, and this guy is perfect. He's available, he wasn't naked in his profile picture, and you'll get a nice dinner out of it."

I tried to walk away, but she followed me like a bad aroma.

"I'm not going out with him tonight, Gabby. Call and cancel."

"I can't. It's nearly six now. You've got just enough time to freshen up and get to the restaurant. I'm doing you a favor, Ev. You asked me to help you find a man, and that's what I'm doing. Pushing you from the nest, baby bird. *Voe para longe.* Fly away." She gestured with her hands, shoving me from her imaginary nest.

"I can't do it. I'm exhausted."

She turned to walk back to her own office. "Yes, you can. Stay for at least one drink. You'll be fine. And you'll thank me for this later, Ev. I promise."

—◯/◯— —◯/◯—

I would not thank her for this. Not ever. Not under any circumstances. My date, Phil Carter of the 72 percent, sat across from me at Arno's restaurant wearing an orange-and-yellow striped shirt that reminded me very much of a circus tent, and since his bulbous nose was bright red with rosacea, he looked just like a clown to go with it. I bet he even drove a tiny little car.

My distaste wasn't a product of his appearance, though, nor was it because his eyebrows looked as if they could take wing at any moment and lift off in flight. No, it was because he was an insufferable bore, chewed with his mouth open, and never stopped talking. I wasn't sure I'd even introduced myself yet, but I knew all about him. He made quite a production of informing me his family had been in the Michigan lumber business, as if that was supposed to mean something to me.

It didn't.

"I'm into plastics manufacturing these days, though," he said, stuffing a hunk of rump roast the size of my fist into his cavernous mouth. "Toilet seats, to be exact. We use a new polymer that's indestructible. You can bet your ass our seats will never break. They could survive a nuclear blast."

He caught his own inadvertent play on words and laughed uproariously.

I picked up my steak knife and considered slicing my wrists. Gabby was right about one thing. People do lie on their applications. Or at least exaggerate. That photo of him must have been decades old.

"Where did you go to school, Phil?" I spoke loud enough to be heard over his laughter and his chewing.

"School? Case Western. PhD in engineering. Didn't you read my profile? I read yours. Plastic surgeon, huh? You must be very confident."

"Confident?" I was, of course, but it seemed a peculiar point for him to land on.

He stuffed another bite of meat in his mouth and talked around it. "Yes. I mean it takes a pretty confident woman to spend her life making other women more beautiful. I really respect that. And thanks, by the way. Too bad all homely women can't afford plastic surgery." He laughed again. "Have you had work done yourself? Those look pretty real."

He pointed his fork toward my breasts.

Oh.

No.

We were done here. I'd kept my promise to Gabby to stay for at least one drink. I'd even ordered dinner, although watching him chew had ruined my appetite. It was time for an extreme tactical maneuver. I reached down and pulled my phone from my purse.

"Sorry, I have to take this call. It's from the hospital."

"I didn't hear it ring."

"It's on vibrate."

I put the phone to my ear and pretended to answer a nonexistent emergency summons. "Hello. This is Dr. Rhoades."

While I fake listened to my fake caller, I plotted my escape route. Twenty steps, right out the front door. A front door that was opening as if my eyes were willing it to let me out.

My imaginary Tyler Connelly walked in and . . . wait . . . that was not my imagination!

I sat motionless as the very real and very symmetrically gifted Tyler Connelly strolled in through the door and sauntered over to the bar.

Chapter 9

HE WAS TAN AS EVER and wearing charcoal-gray pants and a white dress shirt with the cuffs rolled up. Damn, he looked better in person than in my imagination. How was that even possible?

He shook hands with the bartender, then eased onto a stool. For so many reasons I didn't dare examine, I did not want him to see me with Phil the circus clown.

"An emergency, you say?" I said to no one on the phone. "Stabilize the patient. I'll be there right away."

I dropped my phone back into my purse. "Sorry, Phil. I have to go back to the hospital. Best to you and the toilet seat business."

He wiped his mouth with the back of his hand. "You're leaving? We're in the middle of dinner." His voice rose.

I sighed. "No, not really. You're in the middle of a monologue."

He frowned. "Well, that's all kinds of rude, don't you think?"

Yes, it was. But I was tired and cranky, and I'd done my due diligence to this farce of a date. And Phil was an asshole.

"Yes, it was rude. So is monopolizing the conversation and pointing at my breasts." This night was on a collision course anyway. I may as well let it crash and burn.

His cheeks were chipmunk round, full of gargantuan bites of roast. "That was a compliment. Those boobs look real even though they're big." He gestured with his hands, as if cupping his own impressive mammary glands.

"I have to go." I reached down to grab the handle of my purse.

"But what about dinner?" His voice rose even higher. My skin started to heat with the flush of embarrassment.

"You'll just have to eat without me. Sorry."

"No, I mean who's going to pay for yours? Not me. Not if you leave right in the middle of it."

I just wanted to get out of there as quickly and as surreptitiously as possible, but his voice carried like the screech of a seagull, and all the people within a three-table radius turned our way. So did all the people at the bar.

Including Tyler Connelly.

"You're a classy guy, you know that, Phil?" I pulled my wallet from my purse and opened it, praying I had cash. Of course I didn't, because I never have cash. I yanked out my debit card instead. I was going to have to wait here while the waiter cashed me out. Unbefuckinglievable.

I looked around, hoping to catch the server's eye.

I caught Tyler's instead.

He had the good manners not to smirk. He picked up the beer that the bartender had just set in front of him, and he took a sip. Watching.

"I know you're new to the Bell Harbor Singles scene," Phil said, still not modulating his voice in the slightest. "So I understand this is all a little overwhelming, but you can't just walk out on a date. Word gets around."

"Does it?" If that were true, I would have been forewarned about him.

"Yes, it does, and men aren't interested in dick teases."

I felt my mouth go slack and my mind go blank. Well, it was blank for a split second. Then it filled with a vision of me clubbing Phil Carter over the cranium with one of his own goddamned toilet seats. Before I could articulate a response scalding enough to do justice to my outrage, Tyler got up from the bar, leaving his beer behind, and walked over to our table.

"Good evening, Dr. Rhoades," Tyler said, no hint of mockery in his voice. "Heading out? I'll walk you to your car."

"Who are you?" Phil asked, pointing with his fork again.

"I'm a friend of Dr. Rhoades's."

He was my friend at the moment. He might be a whiskey-drinking, dog-walking dock demolisher, but under the circumstances, he was the better of my options.

"I have to pay for my meal first." I held up my debit card.

Tyler looked at it for a second, then scowled at my date. "Dude, seriously? Man up." He reached over with both hands to scoot out my chair. I rose instinctively. It seemed we were leaving. I dropped my card back into my purse.

I felt the eyes of the other diners boring into me from every different angle, but when I looked around, everyone seemed to be studiously staring down at their own food.

"Only seventy-two percent," I heard Phil mutter. "It figures."

Tyler's hand was light on the small of my back as we walked to the door. I should have told him I was fine. I didn't need him to escort me out as if I were some damsel in distress. Men like Phil Carter didn't scare me. The only part about this whole fiasco that upset me was how I'd wasted a perfectly good evening. I could have been at home in my fat pants reading about advancements in rhinoplasty instead of watching that slob gobble up his food like a pelican.

We left the restaurant, and as soon as we'd moved past the windows, I stepped away from Tyler's side and stopped walking.

"Thank you. That was very thoughtful, and I appreciate your assistance. I could have handled him myself, though."

"I'm sure you could have, but he was an asshole."

"Yes, he was." I sighed and slung my purse over my shoulder, crossing the strap in front of me, and started walking again.

Tyler fell into step next to me. "So why were you with him?"

I smiled tightly. "Long story, but I've got it from here. I'm good. Thank you."

It crossed my mind just then that there was a downside to walking places. I had no car to jump into to whisk me away. I'd walked to work that morning and had planned to walk home from the restaurant. I'd lived in Chicago long enough to know how to get myself safely from point A to point B. I had my whistle and my mace, and in a pinch, I could throw an elbow and run pretty fast too, but none of those things would help me get away from Tyler Connelly if he was set on going full white knight on my behalf. I could hardly knee him in the groin for being interested in my welfare.

"It looked like a date," he said. Curiosity curled around his syllables.

"It was a date. An accidental date." I started walking faster.

He kept pace. "How do you end up on an accidental date?"

I really didn't want to talk about this. Not with him. He looked so good in that white shirt it simply wasn't fair. Especially after the nightmarish forty-five minutes I'd just spent watching Phil Carter grind up his food.

"How did I end up on an accidental date? I'd imagine about the same way you accidentally end up on a stolen Jet Ski. Shit just happens sometimes, doesn't it?" I should be laughing, but it didn't feel that funny. Or maybe I should be angry, but mostly I just felt tired. Phil Carter was already history. But Tyler Connelly was right here, right now. And I needed him to be someplace else before I started feeling . . . appreciative.

He stopped walking, and foolishly, so did I. We were standing on the corner now, near Jasper's restaurant. Yellow lights shimmered through the window, splashing in patterns against the brick sidewalk. Music played from outdoor speakers, something jazzy and mellow.

Tyler slid his hands into the pockets of his charcoal pants. I wanted to ask him where he'd been that he'd gotten dressed up, but more answers would only lead to more questions. And more attraction. I couldn't deny that something about him stirred me, but I also couldn't deny it was pointless to pursue it. Hilary would tell me he was the wrong kind of man, and she'd be right. Nothing he had to offer was on my list of requirements.

"Yes, shit just happens sometimes." He nodded slowly, not taking his eyes off me.

I wondered if he was having illicit thoughts about me just then. I was feminine enough to hope so. List or no list.

"Well, thank you again." I turned to leave.

"I sacrificed a beer," he said, his voice following me as I tried to retreat to the safety of my solitude.

I turned back, like Alice looking down the rabbit hole, knowing I shouldn't. "What?"

"I had a full beer waiting for me at that other restaurant, but I'll look kind of foolish if I go back there now. So, I guess I'll just go into Jasper's and order another one." He tipped his head toward the nearby doorway.

"Are you suggesting I owe you a beer?" He clearly was, and I bit back a smile.

His smile, on the other hand, was broad. "Of course not. I would never suggest such a thing. Good night, Dr. Rhoades." This time he said my name as if it were my 1-800 moniker. How did he manage to make *Dr. Rhoades* sound so very naughty?

He turned, walked inside, and left me alone on the sidewalk clutching my purse as if it were a life preserver. Did he think I'd follow him in there? *Should* I follow him in there? My brain said no, but then again, my brain always said no.

Hilary thought I should loosen up and have more fun. But Hilary also thought I fell for unsuitable men. On purpose. Apparently I was going to get it wrong either way. So in that case, what the hell?

Tonight, I'd give my brain the evening off and finally listen to another part of my anatomy.

Chapter 10

TYLER WAS SITTING IN A booth rather than at the bar. Arrogant bastard. He'd known I'd come in there. I dropped my purse into the seat and sat down with a plunk.

"One drink." I held up my index finger. "One drink, and I want to know why you didn't tell the police you were returning the Jet Ski."

He stared back for what felt like a full minute but was probably ten seconds. "Two drinks, and you tell me how you ended up on a date with that douche bag."

I shook my head and smiled. "No, we're not negotiating. I set the terms."

"Why should I agree to that?" He leaned back and rested one arm along the back of the seat, the picture of nonchalance.

"Because you're the one who asked me out to dinner."

"This isn't dinner. This is *you* following *me* into a bar. I set the terms."

He'd tricked me. This *was* me following him into a bar. I nearly giggled. And I am not a giggler.

"One drink," I said. "And I'll answer all your questions. Two drinks and I'm liable to tell you where the bodies are hidden." I never could hold my liquor.

He laughed at that, making all of the tight spots inside me loosen and all the loose spots tighten. I never should have come in here, but I was still glad I did.

A dark-haired waitress in a crisp white shirt came over to take our order. I asked for a martini, not to be elegant, but because I loathe gin. It was the only surefire way to make sure I didn't drink too much, too fast, and accidentally go all Stella trying to get her groove back. Tyler ordered a beer and the waitress left.

I tapped my fingers on the table and looked around. A dozen or so couples were in here tonight. Candles glowed in every nook, and the air was heavy with the scent of warm cinnamon bread. This place spelled intimate with a capital *INT*. I tapped louder.

He laughed again. "Nervous much?"

I looked back at him. "I'm not nervous. Should I be? Why? Are you an ax murderer or something?" I said it too fast. Maybe I was nervous. A little nervous.

"I'm not the one talking about hidden bodies. Maybe I should be nervous about you," he said.

Realistically, he should be. I had almost eight years of wisdom and life experience on this young gun. Just because he had perfect white teeth and shoulders wide enough to block traffic, that was no reason for me to be the least bit intimidated. I was in charge here.

"Bell Harbor Singles," I said with falsely defiant confidence.

"What?"

"That's where the douche bag came from. An online dating service. So far I don't recommend it." I folded my hands in front of me.

Tyler's smile blossomed slowly but completely. "Why on earth would a woman like you need a dating service?"

That was a compliment in there, plain and simple. And I liked it. I decided to reward it with bold, straight-up honesty. That would save us both a lot of trouble in the long run anyway. "Because I work all the time and rarely date, but my parents have reunited after a twenty-three-year divorce and now they think I should find myself a husband." I leaned forward for emphasis. "Are you prepared to marry me, Mr. Connelly? Because if you're not, and I assume you're not, then there's not much point in taking me out to dinner."

I'd kept my tone light and playful, but his eyes rounded in surprise, and I heard him inhale sharply.

"Wow. Jesus. When you decide to set the terms, you really set them, don't you? Now I see why there are bodies." He chuckled self-consciously and turned to see the waitress coming with our drinks. He reached for his and took a swallow. A big swallow.

Now who was nervous?

She set my drink in front of me on a square cocktail napkin.

"Will you two be having dinner this evening?" she asked innocently.

I smiled at him expectantly, batting my lashes. "Are we having dinner, Mr. Connelly?"

He blinked fast, as if sleet were zinging him in the face. As if the waitress had asked, "Will you be fornicating this evening as a prelude to marriage, or were you hoping to just fuck around?"

"No dinner. Just drinks," he said emphatically, but he smiled. And I smiled back.

"Very good." She took our menus and walked away.

I sat back and lifted my very strong martini. "To just drinks, then."

He clinked his mug against my delicate glass, and took another hearty chug.

"Marriage, huh?" he said, after setting down his beer.

"Yep. Why? Are you not a fan?" I was flirting. Hilary would be so proud of me.

Tyler chuckled. "Um, I'm not opposed to it. In a global sense. I just, uh, haven't given it much thought."

"Truthfully? Neither have I. But this last birthday catapulted me into all sorts of things I've never thought about before." There was no way the gin had already gone to my head, so why I was being so forthright was a mystery. Maybe it's because I had nothing to lose. Tyler was adorable, and sexy as hell, but this really was *just drinks*. Now that I'd decided to look for a real boyfriend, that's what I wanted to find. *A real boyfriend*, not some random scuffle between the sheets. Regardless of how enjoyable it might be, Tyler was a detour I didn't have time to take.

He rubbed his thumb across his jaw, right where I'd given him stitches. "Catapulted into what sort of things?" he asked.

"Things like marriage. And . . . family." I'd very nearly said *children*, but that was just too much. I couldn't expect any man to relax with all that on the table. I was amazed he hadn't bolted already. He must really want that beer.

"Well, that's, ah . . . huh. That's intense stuff."

I laughed at his very appropriate reaction.

Sure, I was being honest, but I was also teasing him, trying to see how far I could push. "So, you see, Mr. Connelly, I really have been trying to do you a favor. I'm trying to save you time and energy. You don't want to take me out to dinner."

"I don't?"

I shook my head. "No, because, as I said, I'm looking for a husband."

His eyes filled with mischief. "Well, maybe I could be your last hurrah before marriage."

Everything inside me lit up like Christmas morning. Oh, Lord. Maybe he could be. Now he was flirting back, and I was drowning in those Caribbean-blue eyes. This wouldn't do. This wouldn't do at all.

"Let's talk about you," I said, deftly steering the conversation to shallower waters. "First of all, tell me about the guy in the bathrobe."

Tyler chuckled and shook his head, leaning back against the booth. "That's Carl, my mother's third husband. She won him in Vegas."

"Won him?"

"Yeah, not really. She went to Vegas with some cash in her pocket and came home with him. Not much of a prize, but he's a good enough guy. He puts up with my mom. That's not easy." His tone was a mixture of affection and frustration. I recognized that because it was the tone I used when discussing my own parents.

"What about your father?" I took another sip of bitter martini.

Tyler's smile turned down. "Husband number one. Good man. Great dad. Lived on his own terms." That had a ring of finality to it.

"What happened to him?"

"Iraq war."

"Oh, I'm sorry." I'd done reconstructive surgery on some veterans, and every single one of them was politely tough, doggedly pragmatic, and all any of them seemed concerned about was getting back to their job.

"Yeah, well, you know. Shit happens." He took a big gulp from his beer, then set it back on the table and shrugged off his momentary wistfulness. "So anyway, after my dad died, husband number two came and went. He didn't last long, and now we have Carl."

"Who's we?"

"Me, my mom, my little brother, Scotty, and my sisters, Aimee and Wendy. I have an older brother too, but he's off in New Zealand or somewhere. He's a cameraman for a wilderness TV show, so we don't see much of him."

"That's too bad," I said, although he didn't seem particularly upset about it.

Tyler's shrug was minuscule. "Not really. He's kind of an ass."

"Hm, too bad. So, tell me about the day you got arrested."

Tyler stretched, raising his arms up over his head and treating me to a vision of muscles flexing beneath a nice shirt. He really was a hunka hunka something yummy. Damn, if I were ten years younger. Or seven. Or even five . . .

"The short version is Scotty likes to borrow stuff that doesn't belong to him."

"You mean steal things?"

"No, I mean borrow without asking. He always intends to take it back."

Scotty didn't sound very bright. "OK, what's the longer version?"

"The longer version is pretty long. It's going to require a second drink." He signaled for the waitress to bring him another beer. He pointed at my nearly full martini glass and cocked a quizzical brow, but I shook my head. The gin was burning right through my esophagus. I could almost feel it soaking into my blouse. One of these cocktails would be plenty.

Tyler set his forearms on the table. "OK, well, the day I got arrested had started off pretty good. I was on a boat, hanging out at the marina with some friends, just having a few drinks. It was early, but most of us were coming off a week of night shifts, so it felt late to us. And then—"

"Night shifts?" I interrupted him.

"Yeah, and my friend says—"

"Night shifts from where?"

He looked at me as if the question made no sense.

"MedPro Ambulance. I'm an EMT."

"You are?" Surprise sent my voice two octaves higher. And it wasn't flattering. "I didn't realize you were an EMT. Your patient chart said you were unemployed." All this time I'd thought he was a deadbeat dog walker, but all this time he'd actually been working. At a real job. A hard job. Tyler Connelly was an EMT? Damn.

He shook his head slowly, chagrined by my reaction. "Yeah, well, here's the thing about patient registration paperwork. Those questions are a lot harder to answer when you're drunk. Especially if you think your arm might be broken."

I thought back to that day, but nothing about his demeanor suggested medical training. Then again, I'd been so distracted by the physicality of him, I would have missed it anyway.

"So, anyway," he continued on, "we're sitting at the marina and my buddy says, 'Hey, isn't that your brother?' And there's Scotty pulling up to one of the docks on somebody's Jet Ski and he's . . . freaking out."

The waitress arrived and set down another beer. Tyler eyed it, as if he could see the reflection of his memory on the surface. He pushed it to the side.

"Why was he freaking out?" I asked as soon as she'd walked away.

Tyler rubbed a hand over his jaw, his facial muscles tensing. He looked around the restaurant, then back to me, and leaned in. I found myself mimicking his motions until our faces were just inches apart. The bronze light fixture dangling above our booth cast a warm glow over this intimate scene, but Tyler's eyes were dark with shadows.

"This is the part you can't tell anyone," he said in a husky whisper. "Scotty has been working with a couple of house painters, and they were at this cottage on the waterway. But the owners weren't home, so Scotty, being the rocket scientist that he is, he figures he can just take a quick ride on the Jet Ski during his break and not get caught. Only he's such a dumbass, he doesn't check the gauge first, and he almost runs out of gas. He was closer to the marina than he was to the cottage, and he knew I was there, so that's where he came."

"But how did you end up on the Jet Ski?" I whispered, loving the clandestine nature of our conversation.

Tyler's eyes held mine, as if gauging my trustworthiness. "Scotty was in a panic because he had to get back to work, but he didn't have any money for gas, so I told him to just take my Jeep, and I'd fill up the Jet Ski's fuel tank and ride it back to the house. Stupid of me, but I figured by the time I'd gotten the gas, I'd be sober enough to drive. Only I guess I wasn't, because that's how I misjudged the distance. I didn't turn sharp enough, and that's when I smashed into the boat dock. You know, with my face?"

I nodded. That part had been obvious.

Tyler took a big breath and exhaled slowly. "So I'm lying there, half in the water, half on the dock, bleeding and clueless, and the next thing I know, Scotty is dragging me into my own Jeep. Then he dumps me at the hospital and leaves. But apparently one of the neighbors saw the whole thing, got my license plate number, and naturally called the police. That's why I got arrested."

I sat up. "But why didn't you tell them you were returning it for your brother?"

He looked me straight in the eye, as if I might challenge his answer.

"Because he's my brother."

I paused to let that sink in. I understood it from a theoretical standpoint, but from a practical and a moral standpoint, I didn't get it.

"And you're *his* brother. He should have told the police himself what happened and not let you take the blame."

Tyler shook his head and frowned at me, his voice low. "No, he shouldn't have. And you can't tell anyone either."

"Well . . . I won't, but I'm still confused."

Tyler sat back, his expression grim. "Scotty is already on probation. Two guys jumped him in a bar last year, but he knocked one of them out and got charged with assault. If he can stay out of trouble until he turns twenty-one, that previous offense is gone, like it never happened. But if he gets arrested for anything, even a traffic violation, it all goes on his permanent record."

"But now you've got it on your record."

"These charges aren't going to stick. I'll plead it down and pay restitution, and it'll all go away. But Scotty couldn't take that chance. If he gets stuck with that old assault charge, he can't enlist. And being a soldier, like our dad, is the only thing he's ever wanted to do."

The pieces had finally formed a picture, but not at all the picture I'd expected. "You pled guilty to something you didn't do just so your brother could enlist?"

He pressed an index finger against his mouth. "Shh. That's the secret."

My senses stirred. This was either the most selfless thing I'd ever heard, or the stupidest. Or, quite possibly, both.

"That's a huge risk you took on his behalf."

"Well, like I said, he's my little brother. If I don't take care of him, who will? Our dad's gone, Carl is a stooge, and my mother? Well, she's not so good in a crisis. She doesn't know anything about this. That's the other reason I'm trying to keep it a secret. Plus if Scotty's probation officer catches wind of it, he's screwed."

I had thought there'd be some funny anecdote about drunken antics on a boat or a comedy of errors and misunderstandings that led to the Jet Ski incident. Not a tale of brother sacrificing for brother. It made me see Tyler in a whole new light, which was not necessarily a good thing, because he was still too young for me.

"Tyler?"

I heard a man's voice from over my shoulder and looked up to see Jasper walk up to our table. "Hey, I thought that was you. Good to see you, Ty."

Tyler stood up and they did the he-man, A-frame hug with requisite back thumping while I wondered if Jasper had overheard any of our conversation.

"How are you, Jas? This is your place, isn't it?" Tyler asked. His smile was relaxed, and I felt that momentary tension leave. If he wasn't worried, I guess I shouldn't worry.

"Yep, all mine." Jasper nodded and turned toward me. Surprise quirked his features. "Well, hello. Evelyn, isn't it?"

"Hello, Jasper." I waved like a pageant queen.

"You two know each other?" Tyler asked.

Jasper nodded. "Evelyn works with Gabby Linton. Remember her? Blonde hair. Tie-dye. Drama club."

"Kind of. She was a year older, right?"

I winced. Everyone around here had attended Bell Harbor High School, but that comment was a harsh reminder that while I was graduating from Northwestern University, Tyler was here, struggling with tenth-grade geometry.

Jasper nodded. "Yeah, that's Gabby. She looks exactly the same except now the hair is kind of pink. So what are you up to these days, Ty? Got your boat in the water yet?"

Tyler hesitated. "No, not yet."

"It'll happen. I never thought I'd have this place either, but somehow it all worked out. How's your family doing?" Jasper gripped the back of a nearby chair and leaned.

"Oh, you know." Tyler shrugged. "Same old, same old. Everybody's misbehaving."

"That sounds about right." Jasper laughed and bobbed his head. "Hey, if either of your sisters are looking for a job, though, tell them to come see me. Like, tomorrow. I'm desperate for a couple more waitresses, especially since we've started doing deliveries too."

Tyler hesitated again. "All right. Yeah, I will."

"Great. Hey, did you guys have dinner?"

Tyler cast a glance my way.

"Just drinks," I said. "It turns out Tyler wasn't ready for dinner."

"What?" Jasper's frown was exaggerated. "How could you come here and not eat? I'm insulted. At least let me get you some dessert. On the house."

"Oh, that's not necessary—" But Jasper was already holding out his hand to shut me up.

"I'll be right back," he said, turning toward the kitchen.

Tyler slid back into the seat. "Dessert, huh? Where does that fall into the scheme of drinks but no dinner?"

Hmm. Dessert. The sweet, forbidden ending.

I wasn't normally a self-indulgent woman, but maybe tonight I could make an exception.

Jasper was back minutes later with one plate and two forks. Fantastic. Because that wasn't at all provocative, sharing a moist, gooey dessert. He set the plate between us. It was some kind of chocolate mousse surrounded by an artful arrangement of berries and a deep red sauce.

"There you go. Enjoy! Hope to see you here again soon."

He walked away, and we stared at the plate as if waiting for it to hatch. Tyler ruffled the back of his hair.

"That looks good," he said, nodding at the dessert.

"Yes, it does." I picked up a fork. "I feel guilty already."

Chapter 11

THE DESSERT WAS DELICIOUS, AND so was the conversation. We moved on from his adventures in crime and talked about other things—like how ridiculous he'd felt trying to navigate all those teensy little dogs through the park, and how embarrassed he'd been to see me there. Then I confessed I'd once known how to twirl a baton.

"You could probably still do it, don't you think?" he asked.

I sensed a dare coming on, but I wasn't going to fall for it. "Probably, but I'll never show you."

His smile brightened, and I wondered if he fully comprehended how marvelously attractive he was.

"Did you have a sparkly costume with red, white, and blue stripes? I bet you did." His teasing was dangerously addictive. I could get used to it. But then I'd just want more and more, until there wasn't any left. Still, he persisted.

"You did have a costume! I can tell. Did it say *Dr. Rhoades* right here?" He pointed to a spot right over his heart.

I laughed along with him. "No, it did not say *Dr. Rhoades*. It said Evie."

"Evie." He said my name as if it were a revelation. I wanted him to say it again.

And he did.

"Evie. I like that. Evelyn seemed a little formal."

I straightened my spine and tried to stare him down, but I'd polished off that martini and felt more tipsy than threatening. Nonetheless, I was determined to make my point.

"I'm a formal kind of person." My declaration was ruined by a hiccup.

"I can see that," he answered.

On a scale of tepid to scorching, his gaze registered at slightly hotter than platonic, and his charm was a tangible web surrounding me. But the hour was getting late. Late by my standards, at least. I sighed and leaned back against the seat cushion. "I should go home. I have surgery in the morning."

His smile faded, his gaze cooled to companionable resignation. "Yeah, and I have to walk the dogs. Will you be in the park?"

I wanted to be. I wanted to walk alongside him and those silly little dogs. Too bad for me. "No, surgery days start too early for walking."

He looked down, then reached back to pull his wallet from his pocket.

I was faster and tugged my wallet from my purse. "No, these drinks are on me. My thanks to you for rescuing me from the toilet seat salesman."

He pulled out his own wallet out anyway. "I don't think so. I got them."

"At least let me pay for my own."

A matching pair of lines formed between his furrowed brows. "No." He pulled out some bills and tucked them into the leather folio left earlier by the waitress.

"I'm the one who followed you in here," I said.

"Exactly. That's why I'll pay for the drinks."

His logic made no sense, but then again, he was a man, so I shouldn't expect it to. I could see I wasn't going to win this one.

"Well. Thank you."

"You're welcome."

I didn't know what to say after that. I didn't particularly want this night to end, but it had to. And Tyler had an unnerving habit of maintaining eye contact without blinking, as if we were having some sort of contest and I just didn't realize it. I always seemed to be the one to look away first. I resisted the urge to tap my fingers on the tabletop.

"Well," I said again, "I guess I'll . . . see you around."

"I'll walk you to your car." His tone was as certain as it had been when he'd said "no" about the drinks.

"I don't have a car. I walked."

"From home?"

"From my apartment, yes. It's only about six blocks from here." My intention was to prove I could get home quite safely on my own, but he didn't seem to pick up on that.

"Then I'll walk you," he said.

"It's really quite close."

His smile was honey sweet. "Then it shouldn't take us very long."

We paid the bill, waved to Jasper, who was behind the bar, and walked out into the Bell Harbor evening. It was still warm, and the crickets were loud. Off in the distance I could hear the lake. The moon was a sliver, but the streetlamps lit our way.

"I really will be fine, you know," I said one last time.

"I know," he said, with no hint of giving up.

Having him walk me home to keep me safe was the height of irony. Sure, I'd be protected from muggers and vagrants, which

I wasn't sure this town even had, but Tyler was a whole different kind of dangerous. He was the sexy kind, with big, tan hands and a mouth that managed to be both masculine and beautiful at the same time.

A mouth I wanted to kiss.

I wanted to kiss him in the same desperate way I'd wanted to taste that dessert, knowing the sensation would start out on my tongue but spread out deliciously through the rest of me, pushed by the pulse of my heart. This was a problem. A big problem.

While science made sense to me, human nature was imprecise and spontaneous. Emotions were unpredictable. Tonight was the perfect example. Everything I knew to be true about myself provided evidence that Tyler Connelly was a high-risk, low-return gamble, but my body didn't care. My body wasn't using logic. My body was falling back on neuron patterns formed during the caveman days when women needed a club-wielding he-man who could wrestle a wooly mammoth to the ground. But Bell Harbor didn't have an unruly wooly mammoth population, so why did I feel so fluttery and feminine with Tyler by my side? Was it because he moved around to my left when we crossed the street so he was consistently between me and traffic? Was it because he smelled so damn good? Was it because my DNA sensed that his DNA would make a superior baby?

Whatever the reasons, if I wasn't careful, my hormones would flood me with mood-altering endorphins and trick me into thinking this man was right for me.

He wasn't. Being with him would be like shooting a flare gun. Once I'd pulled the trigger, there'd be no stopping the fireworks. It would light up the sky for a minute or two, but then it would be over, as if it had never happened at all.

"So," he said after we'd walked a moment in silence. "Are you pretty set on this marriage thing, or are you just trying to scare me away?"

My voice sounded a little resigned. "Both, I guess."

"Why?"

"Simplicity. Expediency."

"Is that why you're using a dating service? For simplicity and expediency?"

I nodded. "Yes. I don't have time to waste on the wrong kind of man."

He scoffed and stopped walking, and I realized how insulting that had sounded. I flushed with remorse and turned to face him. "I didn't mean it like that. I only meant I don't have time for, you know . . . a last hurrah. It's not that I wouldn't enjoy one. But I'm looking for something more. And my guess is, you're looking for something . . . less."

Tyler didn't say anything. He just stood there with his hands in his pockets and a frown on his face. I'd offended him with my very unpoetic explanation. Obviously that hadn't been my intention, but maybe it was for the best. I *was* looking for more, and he *was* looking for less. Neither of us was *wrong*, we were just in very different places, heading in very different directions. He should understand that.

He shifted on his feet. "That's kind of presumptuous, isn't it? To think you know what I'm looking for?" His voice had lost some of its earlier warmth, and the bubble of affection we'd been floating in popped.

"I suppose. I don't mean to be. I just . . ." I let my voice dwindle away. I'd only make it worse if I tried to explain my point of view. Anything I said would make it sound as if I thought he wasn't good enough for me. And this wasn't about that. It was about age and timing and phases of life. "Well, anyway, thanks for walking me home." I pointed to the two-story Victorian house on the next corner. "My apartment is right there. I can manage from here."

He rolled his eyes and started walking again, determined to get me right up to my front door, in spite of my insults and assumptions. I reached into my purse to get my keys as we headed up the sidewalk and onto the little front porch. There were lights on either side of my door with moths and all sorts of flighty little bugs buzzing around them. Definitely not a romantic place to stand, which, again, was probably for the best.

I put my key into the lock and twisted, popping open the door. I turned back and he was standing on the top step, a few feet away. Hands still in his pockets, expression neutral.

"Safe and sound," I said, pointing into my dark apartment.

"Yep. Looks like it. I guess this is good night then." He hesitated near the railing, and I knew I could still kiss him. I could reach over and grab the front of that nice white shirt and haul him inside my apartment. He'd get over those hurt feelings if I showed him my breasts. I knew enough about men to be certain of that.

But I didn't. I just said, "Thanks again. Good night." And walked inside alone.

I regretted it instantly. I was an idiot.

I should have kissed him.

Chapter 12

HILARY WALKED INTO MY OFFICE first, but her sister was close on her heels. They shut the door and locked it. Gabby's smile was suspiciously bright as she sat down in the chair across from my desk and placed a six-gallon latte in front of me as if the scent of mochaccino-hazelnutty goodness would make up for the fact that she'd sent me on a date with a trash-talking toilet seat maker.

"So," Gabby said, crossing her arms with dramatic flair. "Would you like to explain how it is I sent you out to dinner with Phil Carter and yet you ended up licking frosting off a plate at Jasper's with some guy I know from high school?"

Damn her and her Bell Harbor connections. I should have realized I couldn't spend two hours chatting with Tyler in a public restaurant without the town criers catching wind of it. I glanced at Hilary, who was leaning against my filing cabinet, staring at me enigmatically over her own coffee.

"There was no licking of frosting, from a plate or from anywhere else. It was all completely innocent."

"Well, then that's a waste of good frosting, but how the hell do you know Tyler Connelly?" Gabby picked up a stack of patient files from my desk and moved them to the side to clear her line of vision.

I very deliberately moved them back. "I have a filing system here. Don't mess it up."

"Stacking isn't a system. And stop changing the subject. Tell me about you and Tyler."

"Yes," said Hilary, "tell us about you and Tyler." Her tone was benign enough, but the look on her face said *what the hell are you doing?*

"There is no me and Tyler. I gave him stitches in the ED on my birthday, and he thought we should have dinner. Last night I was just trying to convince him otherwise."

"By having martinis and mousse instead? Good plan," Hilary muttered. Sarcasm was not a good color on her, but she wore it often.

I shook my head definitively. "It wasn't like that. Tyler just happened to be at the restaurant to witness that debacle of a date Gabby sent me on." I jabbed a pointer finger in her direction. "Phil Carter was an asshat, by the way, and Tyler decided to rescue me." I air quoted the word "rescue" to ensure they both understood my complete dismissal of needing assistance. "So I bought Tyler a beer just to say thanks. How well do you know him, anyway?"

Hilary huffed at my question, but Gabby leaned forward.

"Well, I never dated him, but my friend Patty went to prom with him, and he totally broke her heart."

"Prom?" Hilary said, exasperation popping from her voice. "How about something a little more recent? And relevant? Like the fact that everyone knows he just got arrested for stealing a Jet Ski?"

"He didn't—" I stopped myself. I'd been sworn to secrecy. "That situation is not exactly what it appears to be."

"What the heck is that supposed to mean?" Hilary asked, her perfect eyebrows slanting together.

"Yes, what does that mean?" Gabby's tone was much more conversational, and I knew if I shared these details, she'd have it posted on Twitter before I'd finished my sentence. This wasn't my truth to tell.

"Nothing. And anyway, it doesn't matter. We had a drink and that was it. Let's talk about Bell Harbor Singles. I have sixteen new e-mails. Who wants to see them?"

I wasn't at all in the mood to talk about Tyler, or the other men, for that matter. But I especially didn't want to talk about Tyler.

"But that wasn't it," Gabby said. "He walked you home, right? What happened after that?"

Damnation! Her network of informants was vast. I should have stayed in Chicago, where a girl could maintain some privacy.

"Are you spying on me?"

She giggled. "No, but your waitress at Jasper's is our cousin. She said Tyler was totally into you and very insistent that you let him take you home."

"He was. And he did. And he left me on my front porch, where we said good night."

"So that's it?" Gabby's disappointment marred her expression. "Why the hell didn't you invite him in?"

Hilary crossed her arms. "Because he's a loser, Gabby. He stole a Jet Ski. That whole family is a fucking train wreck. His younger brother assaulted some guy in a bar, his older brother just disappeared off the planet one day, and his mother is a shoplifter. And if I'm not mistaken, she has a gambling problem too."

My lungs felt kicked and stomped on. With cleats. "How do you know all that?"

She paused, as if reluctant to say.

"Hilary?"

"Steve is their family lawyer," she finally blurted out. "I know all about them. I'm not supposed to say anything, but God, Evie. Please tell me you're not involved with this guy. He is bad, bad news."

Boy, I sure did know how to pick them, didn't I? Tyler might not be directly involved with any of that, but it was his family. He was guilty by association. No wonder he thought he had to keep them out of trouble. I picked up my latte.

"I'm not involved with him." I said it calmly, as if none of this really mattered. And it shouldn't. I *wasn't* involved with him. And yet, it did matter. I felt it, deep inside.

Gabby flopped back against her seat. "Well, that is a huge disappointment, because Tyler Connelly is sexy time with sexy sauce on top. What a waste. Well, at least I've got you set up for a few more dates."

I set my coffee down so hard it splashed onto my lab coat. "What? Stop doing that, Gabby. I only meant for you to help me with the profile."

Hilary automatically went into mom mode and pulled an alcohol wipe from her pocket. She tore open the packet and came around to my side of the desk to dab at the stain.

"I can't help it," Gabby responded. "It's fun. If I can't get Mike to marry me, maybe I can at least get someone to marry you."

I leaned around Hilary to glare at her sister. "Let me pick them this time."

"It's too late. I've triple booked you for Thursday night."

"Triple booked?" I gasped. "Are you kidding me? How am I supposed to be on three dates at once?"

"You're all about being scientific, so I decided to make the most of the time you had and give you a nice cross-section of bachelors. You've got drinks at five with Beau Maloney, appetizers at six thirty with Sebastian Clark, then a late supper at eight thirty with Marty Cable."

I looked back at Hilary. "She's killing me with this."

"You could have just let me fix you up with one of Steve's friends, you know," she replied.

"Does Steve have any single friends?"

She thought about this for a second. "No, but for you, he'd be willing to make some."

"Well, tell him to get right on that, would you? Before your sister marries me off to a toilet maker?"

"Mwah-hah-hah," Gabby said. "Just leave it to me. I'll have you sharing that sexy six-headed shower before you can say *slippery when wet.*"

My sexy, sudsy shower for two would have to wait indefinitely if these last three dates were any indication of the rest of my life.

Bachelor number one had been nice in a *let-me-do-your-taxes* kind of way, but even with lifts in his shoes, he was shorter than me. While I would never judge a man for being vertically challenged, I do judge a man who finds being eye level with my breasts too much of a distraction. Even when we sat down and could have been eye to eye, it was too late. He was already mentally motorboating me. I could tell from the sheen of perspiration covering his nearly hairless scalp.

Bachelor number two, on the other hand, had a full head of glorious hair and a Texas machismo rarely seen this far north. He was a cowboy, right down to the snakeskin boots and the ten-gallon hat. He was articulate, charming with a good ole boy mannerism, and he loved his momma. This I know because he talked about her and her recent hysterectomy for forty-five minutes. Then he said, "But you're a right fine little filly. I'm fixin' to take you home to my stable." At that point I resorted to my fake emergency phone call trick so I could ride into the sunset without him.

Now here I was in the lobby of Jasper's place for a late supper with Marty Cable.

"It's pronounced Ka-BALL-ee," he told the dainty blonde hostess as she checked the list of available tables. His breath was uncomfortably moist as he turned to whisper in my ear.

"If they think we're Italian, we'll get a better seat. Connected, you know what I'm talkin' about?" He held his hand out for a fist bump. I pretended not to see it.

No. I didn't know what he was talking about. I also didn't know how anyone's breath could be so wet without them actually spitting. And I didn't know if I could go through with another date tonight. A night that started out bad had deteriorated into the fifth circle of hell.

Marty Cable, a man who may or may not have been a member of the Gambino crime family, had black, slicked-back hair, giving him a reptilian profile. His suit was shiny, and so were his shoes. And I couldn't be certain, but that tie might just have been a clip-on. Considering how he was dressed, if he was connected, it was through some distant third cousin who everyone called Vito but was actually named John.

"Yes, Mr. Cable (Ka-BALL-ee), your table is right this way," said the hostess.

He let me go first and pressed a proprietary hand against the curve of my waist as we made our way to the booth. It was the same one I'd sat in a few nights ago and shared a gooey dessert. I should ask to sit someplace else. It was already impossible to not compare the charisma of these other guys to Tyler's, and every last one of them came up lacking.

"You thinking about parking it, sweetheart?" Marty pointed to the seat across from him. "Or are you gonna stand there all night so I can gawk at you?"

I sat down, lowering both myself and my standards. I silently offered up a little prayer to the patron saint of awful dates that this would not get uglier. Of course, I wasn't a Catholic and had no idea if there even was a patron saint of bad dates, but if there were, I bet she'd been out with lots of guys like Marty Cable. I mean . . . Ka-BALL-ee.

"Your server will be with you shortly," said the hostess, handing us the menus.

My head ached, my shoes pinched, and the area south of my waistband was ready for an autopsy. Cause of death: prolonged atrophy.

"So, a doctor, huh?" Marty nodded his head, which must have been no easy feat considering the amount of fleshy adipose tissue around his jowls. He looked like a hound dog.

"Yes, a plastic surgeon. And tell me again what it is you do? I'm afraid it slipped my mind." Date number one had designed security systems for bank vaults. Number two was, not surprisingly, in the cattle business, and if I remembered my notes correctly, Marty here did something with shipping or cargo.

"I'm the senior manager at Winchester Storage, the largest storage unit company in southwest Michigan."

"Oh, yes. Storage." I nodded. Now it was coming back to me. I'd done a little Google search earlier in preparation for these dates and learned that "largest in southwest Michigan" meant not very big at all.

Marty leaned closer. "You know those TV shows? That, whatcha call it? *Storage Wars*? Yeah, that was totally my idea. But some other yay-hoo is getting the credit. It's all about who you know, right?"

So much for being connected.

I just smiled and nodded. There was no point in telling Marty that your place in life had nothing to do with who you knew. It was about planning, hard work, tenacity, and talent. Master something and it will lead to success. I hadn't relied on my parents' great reputations to get me through medical school. I had gotten to where I was by doing the work.

Marty continued talking, as I assumed he would. "But you'd be amazed at the stuff people put in storage and then forget about."

I picked up the menu but didn't look at it. I was too busy doing a mental makeover of my date. If Marty washed his hair, he might not be *that* bad looking. He had kind of a hook nose, but I'd seen much worse. I could even fix it. Fewer spritzes of man-musk cologne would help too, but his eyes were a nice, rich brown, and his teeth were in pretty good shape. Maybe he just needed some restyling from a woman. Maybe I needed to be more open-minded about this whole dating process and give Marty a chance.

"Like what kind of stuff do they forget about?" I asked.

"Porn, baby! Tons of porn. If people still watched DVDs instead of ordering everything online, I'd be a flippin' millionaire."

What was that sound?

Oh. Yes. It was the final, tiny blip of my optimism flatlining. Time of death, 7:33 p.m.

"That is a shame." I shook my head. "I hate to see good porn go to waste."

"Welcome to Jasper's."

I jumped at the voice. First of all, because I hadn't realized our waiter had arrived. Second, because I was embarrassed that someone just overheard my sarcastic remark about porn.

And third, because our waiter was Tyler Connelly.

Chapter 13

TYLER WAS STANDING AT THE edge of the table wearing a white shirt, black pants, and a short black waiter's apron. He held a tablet in his hand, his pen poised and at the ready.

"How are you this evening?" His voice was as bland as toast, as if he'd never seen me before. As if we hadn't shared a dessert in this very booth. As if he'd never stood on my front porch making me want to kiss him.

"Can I get you something to drink?" he asked. "Beer. Wine. *Martini.*"

He locked his gaze on me when he said that last word, as if what he wanted to say was "Really? I'm not good enough, and yet you're out with another douche bag?"

My insides curled and shrank like a plastic dish left too long in a microwave.

"I'll have a martini," Marty said, not waiting for me to go first. "And make it dirty. The dirtier the better."

He snickered at his own innuendo.

Tyler turned his head and cleared his throat, although I could have sworn I heard him cough out the word "Pervert." Then his eyes were back to me, alight with challenge, a tight smile tilting just the corners of his lips. "And you, *ma'am*? Can I interest you in something a little dirty?"

When, when, when, and how, how, how did he start working here? I'd been looking for that small-town feel when I chose Bell Harbor, but I had underestimated what a tiny village this really was. Slides under a microscope had more privacy.

"I'll have a club soda with lemon, please," I said.

Marty frowned, his thick, dark brows nearly crossing in the process. Clearly loading me up with alcohol was paramount to his dating strategy, but no amount of gin was going to gain him access to any part of me. A dozen Ambien wouldn't make me loose enough at this point. This date was already over. He just didn't know it yet.

"Excellent." Tyler turned and walked away, giving me my first really good look at his ass. I'd always been facing him or next to him. Now I knew that even in restaurant-quality chinos, his gluteus maximus was on par with the rest of him. Muscular, defined, pleasant to the eye. Probably pretty pleasant to the touch as well. My hands flexed of their own accord and my dead zone reawakened.

Marty went on talking, but I didn't pay much attention. All roads seemed to lead back to the old porn loitering unviewed in his storage units. The unspoken invitation was there. *Come to my pad and we'll watch* Debbie Does Dallas.

Maybe I should've listened to him more carefully, engaged him more actively, directed the conversation to things worth talking about. But the truth was, my mind was on Tyler. And Tyler's ass.

The object of my obsession returned as Tyler brought us our drinks. He gave a nearly silent sigh as he set mine down, just loud enough for me to hear.

Marty was studying the menu. "You got any specials, kid?"

Tyler looked at me and sighed again. Audibly this time.

"Sure." He flipped through his little notepad, his irritation palpable. "There's salmon with ginger sauce, lobster ravioli, and risotto that looks like it might have bacon and peas in it. I don't know. I didn't taste it."

I bit my lip. Clearly it was not his intention to dazzle us with superior customer service. I could hardly blame him. This was patently awkward.

Marty's eyebrows rose and fell at Tyler's attitude.

"I'll have the risotto," I blurted out.

Both men looked at me so fast it was as if I'd said, "Do you think this blouse is too low-cut?"

"What?" I snapped in response, my glare trying to capture them both at once. "I'm starving. I'll have a salad with vinaigrette dressing too, please."

My patient appointments had run long, so I'd missed lunch; I'd let date number two snarf down all the appetizers hoping they'd distract him from telling me all about his mother's post-hysterectomy recovery; and I had expected a nice dinner here at Jasper's. Oh, how naive could I be?

I wanted to pull the plug on this entire misadventure, but I had no food at my apartment. My best option was to eat here, eat fast, and get this date over with before Tyler got fired for being rude.

Marty nodded at me, jowls jiggling. "You're decisive. OK. I can roll with that. I'll have the steak, bloody. Baked potato, loaded. Garlic-ranch dressing on the salad."

"Garlic-ranch? Excellent choice," Tyler said, the implication being garlic ranch = skunky breath = no kissy, kissy from me. As if there were any chance of that.

Tyler flicked me with another *if-this-is-what-you-want* glance, then turned and walked back to the kitchen.

Dinner progressed. Tyler brought our food in a moderately courteous manner but didn't say much. Not that he could have, what with Marty's constant anecdotes about the seedy underbelly of storage unit politics. In between stories, my date would ask questions, such as "how many gallons" was the largest breast implant I'd ever given a woman?

"You know," Marty said, screeching his knife across the plate as he carved up his virtually raw steak, "that gives me a phenomenal idea. You and I could team up on this and make a killing."

Typically, as a doctor, I tried to avoid that phrase. "Really, and what's that?"

He leaned forward, his face serious as bad news. "Saline-filled testicular implants. Boom!" He smacked his hands down on the table and sat up straight. "Think of it. Just like boob implants, only for the balls. 'Cause women like a good set of stones. Am I right?"

No.

He was wrong.

No woman ever was attracted to a man because of his gargantuan balls.

"This could be a huge moneymaker," Marty said.

I burst out laughing. The carbs had gone to my head, and the absurdity of his suggestion was the *second*-funniest thing ever—the first thing being that I was out on a date with this moron.

Thank goodness my risotto was delicious, because if it weren't, this night would have been a total loss.

"You like the idea?" Marty asked, smiling big and revealing a gap in the back of his teeth I hadn't noticed before.

I shook my head and swallowed down my next wave of laughter.

"No, I don't like the idea. And I hate to tell you this, Marty, but someone has beaten you to it. No pun intended."

His smile waned, his jowls drooped . . . like a pair of saggy balls. "Testicular implants are already available," I said. "Although they're typically reserved for reconstructive surgery rather than cosmetic enlargement." I hadn't done any myself. Something like that would most likely be handled by a urologist, but there was no point in explaining that to Marty. I'd already crushed his dreams, and I also knew his night was not going to improve.

I caught a glimpse of Tyler in my peripheral vision. He was holding a tray and waiting for the bartender to fill it up with drinks. And he was frowning. At me. Because he thought I was having fun.

I wasn't.

I was having a good chuckle because Marty Cable was pretentious in the most misguided and undignified manner, but so far my scientific attempts at finding the perfect man were falling far short of the mark. So, no. I wasn't enjoying myself.

"Are you sure they're already invented? Seems like I'd have heard something about that if they were," Marty argued.

Really? Were we still talking about this?

"Testicular implants aren't exactly something you'd see advertised on an infomercial. Most doctors would only mention something like that to patients who needed them due to a medical condition."

Marty's chest puffed up, his jaw jutted forward. He looked like an American eagle—a cartoon version of an American eagle. Wearing a shiny suit from the Men's Wearhouse.

"Well, that's why I've never heard of them, then," he blustered. "Because I can assure you, I'm in perfect physical health."

"I'm sure you are." Both hemispheres of my brain were firing neurons frantically at the moment, trying to eliminate any image of Marty's testicles. Or testicles in general. Thank goodness I was done eating.

My risotto was only half finished, but I was full, and these leftovers would make an excellent lunch for tomorrow. So all I needed now was a box to take it home. Unfortunately, for that I'd need Tyler, and he'd been fairly negligent. It wasn't because he was a bad waiter. I'd watched him charm his way around the dining room for the last hour. He was very attentive to his other customers, smiling and chatting. It seemed to be just me and Marty-of-the-inferior-nut-sack he was ignoring.

I let my gaze wander back over toward the bar, and Tyler was still there. He was talking to the bartender, but after a few seconds, he turned and caught me staring.

I crooked my finger at him. *Come here.*

He pointed to the tray of drinks he was about to deliver. *You'll just have to wait.*

"Give me the chance between some sheets, Evelyn," Marty insisted, "and I'll prove to you I'm in excellent health."

I looked back to Marty as he wiped his napkin across his lips and chin. A dark spot, which all evening I'd thought was a benign little mole, was swept away along with the cloth.

No.

Really?

That little dot had been a scab over a pimple?

Yes.

And now it was bleeding. Only Marty didn't know it.

He started talking about his fitness regimen, and how he could bench press three hundred pounds, and how he ran six miles a day and had amazing stamina. On and on he went, but all I could do was stare at that speck as fresh blood oozed to the surface and began to form a droplet. I should tell him what was happening. That blood was going to drip any second now, but it was hypnotic, watching it grow. I felt like a Cullen.

Tyler showed up right about then, the bill for our dinner in his hand. He set it on the table and did a double-take at my date. With a blink, humor chased away the surprise from Tyler's face. He looked at me and folded his arms. *Are you going to tell him or can I?*

I gave the most infinitesimal tilt to my head.

"Um, hey, man. You've got a little something, right there." Tyler tapped his own chin.

"What?" Marty wiped at his face with his bare fingers, smearing blood across his hand and jaw. "What?" he said again, looking at the crimson stain. He picked up his napkin and pressed it against his mouth. "Am I bleeding?"

"It appears you are," I said.

"Maybe you should go to the men's room," Tyler suggested.

"Excuse me." Marty lurched from his seat and hurried across the dining room.

Tyler looked down on me. Literally and figuratively. His voice was quiet but inquisitive. "What are you doing, Evie?"

"Me? What am I doing? I'm on a date. What are you doing? When did you start working here?" I had no right to be irritated, but I was.

"Jasper said he needed servers, remember? My sisters both have jobs right now, and I've got legal fees to pay for, so here I am, earning a little extra money." His arms spread, emphasizing his location, right here, right now.

"So, you're an EMT and a waiter?"

"Technically I'm an EMT and a bartender, but times are hard, so I fill in wherever somebody needs me."

He pointed his thumb back toward the restrooms. "But it looks like you don't need me. You've found yourself another winner."

I couldn't argue with him about that. "My computerized dating profile won't work if the applicants lie."

"You think?" Tyler slid into the booth opposite me, pushing Marty's plate to the side. His presence was like static electricity, pulling me close and certain to create a spark.

"Maybe you should just meet somebody the old-fashioned way." A mischievous glint brightened in his eyes. "You know, like, by giving them stitches."

Reality-blinding endorphins flooded through all my systems, just as I'd worried they would. I could only hope to fend them off with logic and persistence.

"Tyler, I admit it. I find you very attractive, and I suspect you're a wonderful person, but you're not what I'm looking for."

He shook his head slow, his eyes never leaving mine. "You're right. If oozing and crude is what you're after, I guess your fiancé is in the men's room right now, dealing with his scabs."

A chuff of laughter escaped me. I couldn't help it.

Tyler reached across the table and lightly tapped his fingers against mine. "Come on, Evie. Go out with me. I promise you'll have fun."

My pulse went tachycardic at his touch.

"I'm not looking for fun. I'm looking for a husband."

The one-two punch of his burst of laughter and unrepentant smile knocked me senseless. Damn, he was sexy.

"Well, I'm no expert on marriage," he said, "but I think the whole idea of finding a partner to share your life with is supposed to be fun. Not a research experiment."

I pulled my hand back and let it fall to my lap. "But I'm a scientist. That's the only way I know how to approach things. In a linear fashion, moving from point A to point B."

"Yeah, so point A is meeting someone, point B is spending time with them, and point C is . . ." He paused to chuckle again. "Well, point C is still up to you at this point."

"Why do you even want to go out with me, Tyler? Because you think I'm pretty? That's not enough of a reason." My voice hitched.

"First of all, yes it is. That's how I approach things. But the other reasons, well, I guess I'm just intrigued by you. I like how you try to be all businesslike. But I can tell you're not really all business all the time, or you wouldn't blush so much. And quite frankly, I like the way you keep telling me I'm not for you. Every time you say that it just makes me want to prove to you that I am."

"But that doesn't make any sense. You know we want different things."

He laughed again, his voice going husky. "Quit telling me what I want, Evelyn. I know what I want."

His gaze locked on mine, turning me to a useless puddle of estrogen. He was talking about me. He wanted me. Maybe only for a little while, but the compliment went straight to my . . . vanity.

"I'll think about it." *Damn it, who said that?*

He straightened in his seat. "You will?"

Oh, crap. It was me.

"Yes, I'll think about it, but no promises. And you need to move now, because if you sit here any longer, Jasper will fire you."

"It would be worth it." His smile was ridiculously broad.

"I doubt that. Plus my date's coming back." I tipped my head toward Marty's approaching form. He had a little piece of paper towel stuck to his chin. That was klassy with a capital K. He watched with furrowed suspicion as Tyler move out of his spot.

"Could I have this wrapped up to take home?" I pointed to my leftovers and tried to sound nonchalant, as if my waiters always sat down with me.

"Certainly." Tyler took my plate and pointed at Marty's cold steak. "Did you want to take that home?"

"I'm not finished."

"Mm, I think you are." Tyler picked up the plate and took it with him, and I bit back my guilty smile.

Marty glared at me. "That kid is the worst fucking waiter ever."

Yeah, he was. But I was starting to like him anyway.

Chapter 14

"ARE YOU SURE ABOUT THIS, Mom?"

My mother was standing on a carpeted pedestal in a champagne-colored chiffon dress, eyeing herself in a gilded three-way mirror. As promised, I'd driven to Ann Arbor so we could spend the weekend together and go wedding dress shopping. This was the fifteenth or sixteenth gown she'd tried on. We'd been in this bridal salon for so long I think the shop had changed owners since we'd arrived.

She turned to see the reflection of her backside. "What? Do you think the color is bad on me? I rather like it."

"No, the color is fine. I like that one. I'm talking about the wedding. Maybe the reason you can't choose a dress is because you're not sure you want to go through with this."

Her breath expelled in a huff, and she faced me, hands on her hips. "Evelyn Marjorie Rhoades, the only reason I'm having trouble is because I've lost a few pounds since the last time I tried on dresses. Honestly, I had no idea you'd be so resistant to your father and me reconciling. I thought you'd be pleased."

I was being a terrible maid of honor, tossing doubt her way every chance I got. But I couldn't help it. This was my last-ditch effort to prevent her from making a big mistake.

"I'm sorry, Mom. I'm still having trouble figuring this whole situation out. I mean, I'm happy if you're happy, but I'm worried too."

"Why? That's silly. Your father and I are both certain this is the right thing to do."

"See? That right there worries me. Usually when you start a sentence with 'your father and I,' it ends with 'and then we nearly killed each other.'"

My mother chuckled, and I realized how very happy she looked. She looked younger and brighter. That perpetual crease of tension was missing from her forehead. It was as if she'd had work done, but I knew she hadn't. She would have come to me for that.

"I know it's a little strange, darling. But the truth is, we've changed. He's not the same man he was ten years ago. And I'm not the same woman. We've relaxed." She stepped down from her perch and came to sit next to me on the pink satin sofa in the changing room.

"Evie, I'm ready to retire. I want to take time to enjoy my life for a little while. All I've done for the past forty years is work. Now I see you doing the exact same thing, setting up a life full of professional achievements but having no one to share them with. That's why I'm pushing you to find someone special. It's not good to be alone all the time. It makes us brittle."

I looked down as she patted my hand. Hers appeared more delicate now, with veins showing under the surface. But I knew they were still strong, still talented, still resilient. My mother was a brilliant surgeon. Those hands had saved countless lives, and the idea of her retiring was as incomprehensible to me as her being abducted by aliens.

"Retiring, huh? Is Dad retiring too?"

"He's cutting back his hours so we can do some traveling. We're going to Italy for our honeymoon. We'd wanted to go there the first time around, but we both had school loans to pay off. Those were the frugal days." She laughed as if that bleak hardship was a lovely memory.

She adjusted the pillow behind her. "Listen, darling. There's something else I want to tell you. I wasn't going to, but your father thinks I should. I have a little confession."

Confession? Confessions, like apologies, were rare in our family. My body heated with suspense.

"OK?" I said slowly. "What confession?"

She gave a minute shrug of her shoulders, a tiny bob of her head, as if this admission were the most insignificant thing ever.

"Last summer I had a minor cardiac incident. That's how I really reconnected with your father. Not a wine tasting in La Jolla, although that's where things really heated up."

My mouth went dry as gauze as I tried to swallow down my wave of apprehension.

"A minor cardiac incident? Don't use that ambiguous lingo on me, Mom. What exactly are we talking about here? And last summer? Why am I just finding this out now?" My voice squeaked. I was about to have my own cardiac incident, judging from the wild thumping going on in my chest.

"It's nothing." She patted my hand again, but now it felt patronizing, as if I wouldn't understand the implications of what she had to say. Had she conveniently forgotten I went to medical school too?

"I had an arrhythmia," she said. "It ended up being nothing. I think my hormones are out of whack. Goddamn menopause. But I had a little fainting spell in the operating room. I cannot tell you how humiliating that was, passing out like some fragile intern." She scoffed and shook her head. Weakness, physical or mental, wasn't something we tolerated in our family either.

"You fainted?" Maybe it was the power of suggestion, but I felt a little woozy myself. I put a hand to my temple as if that might steady me.

"Oh, I knew I shouldn't have told you."

"Yes, you should! You should've told me when it happened! What if it had been more serious?" Concern over her well-being was replaced with worried annoyance. It was wrong for her to keep this a secret from me!

She waved away my comment with a flick of her wrist. "Well, then I would've told you sooner, but it turned out to be medically insignificant. You know how sometimes these things turn out to be nothing. And Evelyn, in a way, it was the best thing that could have happened. It forced me to reevaluate all my priorities. I have an excellent cardiologist, and since I'm being honest, I also have a therapist now. I unloaded all that rage and resentment I've been hauling around for years, and I feel better than ever. You'd think by my age I would have figured things out, but apparently I was a hot, jumbled mess. I blamed all of that on your father, of course, but apparently some of it was my own fault."

She flipped her hands open in her lap, as if to say, *Huh? Who knew?*

"Your fault?"

"Well, I was pretty mad about the adultery." Her tone was blasé, as if she'd said, *I wish I'd ordered the roast beef.*

"Of course you were mad, Mom. He cheated on you." I felt some of my own latent resentment rising to the surface. He'd been nearly as lousy a father as he was a husband.

My mother stood up and walked toward the mirror, the dress swishing around her legs. She got close, looking at her reflection as if she were seeing it for the first time. Her voice remained utterly matter-of-fact.

"Yes, he cheated on me, and that was his weakness. But I wasn't entirely blameless. It was never enough for me to be as good a surgeon as he was. I wanted to be better. But the male ego is a delicate thing, Evie. He went after those vapid women because he needed to take care of someone, and I never let him do that for me. I should have given him a dragon to slay once in a while, instead of always being the dragon."

The room tilted. Maybe my mother *had* been abducted by aliens, and this was just the shell of her body being manipulated by some extraterrestrial mind-snatcher, because I'd never heard her be so philosophical or reflective. I'd never heard her take ownership of any of her own behavior. What the hell had that therapist prescribed for her?

"You are rocking my world right now, Mom." My voice was a breathy whisper.

She smiled at herself and then turned back around. "This is all supposed to be good news, darling. I'm perfectly healthy and I'm taking better care of myself than ever before. So is your father, and we're both certain we'll get our marriage right this time."

"OK." I said it slow, as if the word might detonate.

There was so much more I should add, and ask, but my mind was like an overstuffed suitcase I was trying to close. I just couldn't cram any more oddities in there for this trip. Cardiac arrhythmias, forgiven adultery, apologies, admissions. Was this the kind of stuff grown-up families dealt with all the time? Maybe that was a healthier way to live, but I couldn't really say I liked it. Denial had its advantages.

"I like that dress," I said instead.

She twirled like a homecoming queen. "Do you? I do too. This might be the one." She sashayed her way over to the couch and sat back down. "I'm very happy, honey. Please be happy for me."

"I am. I really am." And I realized then, I really was. Who's to say she and my dad couldn't make a go of it? Lord knew they were both stubborn enough to stick with it this time, if they wanted to.

"Do you suppose that store clerk is ever coming back?" My mother looked over her shoulder for the salon attendant.

"We've been here so long I think they've all gone to lunch." My stomach rumbled at the mention of it. "And I'm starving."

"Good. I'll take you to a nice restaurant after this. In the meantime, tell me what you've been up to. You said you had someone in mind to bring to the wedding." She leaned back against the sofa. "Is he special?"

Special? Hmm. That word had all sorts of connotations, and Tyler Connelly could fit several of them.

"Let's just say I've met some very interesting men lately, and I have been making an effort."

Her eyes went twinkly. "And?"

I could tell her about Bell Harbor Singles, but so far that had proven disastrous. And I could tell her about Tyler, but I knew when she said *someone special*, she meant someone with true marriage potential, someone wearing scrubs or an expensive suit and tie. My mother wasn't a snob, per se, but her expectations tended to be very specific.

"And you'll just have to trust me."

Chapter 15

NEVER HAVING FOOD IN MY apartment was a terrible habit, but I just never thought of it until I was hungry, and then it was too late to go to the store. So I was thrilled Sunday evening to open my refrigerator and find the leftovers container from Jasper's. My risotto! Hallelujah! I'd forgotten all about that.

I pulled the container from the shelf and opened it. Written inside the lid was a note. A fun and flirty little note from Tyler. My nerves did a spontaneous little jiggety-jig of joy.

"Don't forget to think about it." And then he'd scrawled his phone number.

Oh, I had thought about it.

A lot.

During the long drive from Bell Harbor to Ann Arbor, I'd thought about it. And on the long drive from Ann Arbor back to Bell Harbor, I'd thought about it some more. Sitting there with my mother, watching rays of sunshiney love streaming out of her, I'd thought about him, about the way he made me feel, all gooey and young and full of girlish hope. If that's what my mother had going on, maybe I could understand why she was willing to give my idiot father another chance.

But then I thought about what Hilary and Gabby had said. *He's bad, bad news, Evie. His family is a fucking train wreck. He took my friend to prom and totally broke her heart.*

OK, the prom thing I could ignore. High school boys were not known for their sensitivity. But then again, neither were most grown men. Intellectually I knew the futility of having a relationship with him, long or short. He was infatuated with me because I'd presented a challenge. If I gave him what he wanted, he'd probably just take it and leave.

But even if this was nothing more than just a last hurrah, what was the harm? A little *foda pena* for Evie. I could sure do worse than Tyler Connelly.

I picked up my cell phone and dialed his number.

"Hello?"

"Tyler?"

"Yeah?"

"Someone left a phone number in my risotto."

There was a pause, and then a soft chuckle. "Evie? Oh, shoot. I meant to give my number to the dude."

Laughter blossomed in my throat. "Oh, wow. Sorry. You got me instead. But I'll be sure to let him know you're interested. He likes porn, by the way."

"Excellent." Tyler's voice was low, as if he were trying to be extra quiet. "Where are you?" he asked.

"Home. I just got back from Ann Arbor. Where are you?"

"Call room at the MedPro station. I'm on until six a.m. But I'm walking the dogs in the morning. You should come with me." His voice sank lower and tumbled into sexy. "You know you want to."

Damn it. He was right. I did want to.

Hilary might think Tyler was a bad news kind of guy, but inviting me to go strolling in the park at sunrise was chapter one in the Nice Guy Handbook. Whatever the dysfunction in his family, Tyler seemed determined to rise above it. I respected him for that. And in spite of all the reasons I should probably say no, I very much wanted to say yes.

And so I did.

"Yes, I would like to go dog walking with you in the morning."

"You would?" His voice lifted, then he cleared his throat and it returned to studied nonchalance. "Great. I guess I'll see you in the morning then."

Yes, he would.

I rounded the corner before reaching the entranceway to the park and spotted Tyler sitting on a bench. He was leaning back, one arm stretched out on the back while the other hand was petting today's dog du jour. The herd of furballs had been replaced by a big, gangly black-and-tan fellow with wavy fur. A cross between a German shepherd, a sheepdog, and maybe a little Chewbacca. His head was resting in Tyler's lap as he gazed up at him adoringly.

I might understand how that dog felt.

"You're not a very good dog walker if all you do is sit there," I said.

Tyler turned and pushed his sunglasses to the top of his head. I wished he wouldn't do that. I could focus better when not blinded by those eyes, or his ultrabright smile. But I was suddenly facing down all of that.

The dog stood up and wagged its tail so fast and furious I could feel the breeze from three feet away.

"It's about time you got here. We've been waiting." He patted the spot on the bench next to him. "Sit."

Both the dog and I complied, but instantly the pooch moved closer to nuzzle up between us. I scratched his head. His tail whumped against the ground.

"Who's this guy?" I asked.

"Panzer."

"Like the tank?"

"Yeah, but he's sweet. Aren't you, boy?" Tyler scratched him under the chin, and the dog snuffled closer still. "Too bad today is his last day."

A cloud passed overhead, dimming the already overcast sky. "His last day? Why?"

"If he doesn't get adopted by tomorrow, he's a goner. He's been at the shelter, but nobody wants him because he's so old. He lived with the same lady since he was a puppy, but she just went to a nursing home and couldn't take him. She thinks her son is keeping him, but he dumped Panzer off at the animal shelter instead."

"Oh, that's so sad." Poor dog. And poor little old lady.

"I know. I wish I could get him adopted." We sat in silence for a few seconds, each of us playing with one of Panzer's ears while the dog sighed in doggy bliss, ignorant of his impending demise.

Tyler turned to me after a moment, his eyes growing brighter. "Hey, are you in the market for a dog?"

"Me? What? Oh, hell no. I can't take a dog. My apartment is the size of a laptop."

"Yeah, but you're moving soon, right?" His tone was hopeful, leaving me to feel like a troll under the bridge. Because no way was I taking this dog, no matter how sad his end-of-life story was, and no matter how endearingly either of them was gazing at me.

"No. I'm never home. It wouldn't be fair to the dog. He'd be alone all the time."

Tyler's shoulders slumped. "OK. That's no good then. Let's walk." He stood up and moved through the entrance of the park with the big mutt loping alongside him.

I stood too, but guilt weighed me down. "I'm sorry I can't help."

I'm not sure if I was saying that to the nearly dearly departed dog or to the very-much-alive man.

"That's OK. Just thought I'd ask. Come on." He kept moving down the path, and I hurried to catch up as my mind filled with all the reasons why I could not have a dog.

I'd never even had a dog. I wouldn't know how to take care of him. Even if he was the world's best slipper-retrieving, newspaper-fetching, toe-warming superdog, I still didn't have a place in my life for a pet.

We trudged along the path, gravel crunching.

"I really can't take a dog," I said decisively.

Tyler chuckled. "I know. Don't worry about it."

"But you're not saying anything."

He smiled down at me. "I'm sorry. I'm exhausted. Tough shift last night."

"Are you sure that's it? You're not upset about the dog?"

He stopped walking. Panzer sat down, his big pink tongue lolling out to the side. "Of course not. I didn't mean to put you on the spot. It was a spontaneous suggestion."

I frowned. "OK, but now I feel bad. Like I should help him."

"Evie, he's no worse off now than he was five minutes ago. You don't have anything to feel bad about."

"But I do." I actually felt a little misty. What the hell was the matter with me, getting all sentimental about a dog I'd known for two minutes?

Tyler reached out and slid his hand down my arm until his fingers twined with mine. "Well, don't feel bad. Come on, let's walk. I need to get home and get some sleep."

We started walking, and I tried to remember the last time I'd held hands with someone. It was nice, and our silence became companionable instead of stifling. Still, Panzer's fate followed us like a Dementor.

"How old is he?" I asked after a minute. I looked at Panzer, and I'll be damned if that dog didn't bat his lashes at me.

Tyler's laughter was breathy. He wore a pale blue T-shirt today. Did he deliberately wear blue just to make his eye color pop? It was manipulative as hell and totally unfair.

"I'm not even going to tell you, Evie. This dog is not your problem. Come on. Let's talk about something else."

"How old is he?" I asked again. "The least I can do is ask around at the office today and see if anyone else is interested in him."

He thought on that a minute. "OK, that might be helpful. He's fifteen. That's pretty old for a dog of his size. He's probably only got a year or two left as it is."

"All right. Well, if I hear of anyone looking for an old dog, I'll call you. I have your number, you know." I tried to sound flirty, and Tyler smirked, so I must have succeeded.

We walked farther along the path until it forked, with half going off toward the beach but the other staying in the park. We kept to that one, letting Panzer set the pace as he sniffed every single tree and waved his tail like a flag. The breeze picked up, rustling leaves and making me wish I'd brought a jacket. Off to the west, dark clouds were rolling in, looking as ominous as Panzer's future.

"How often does a dog like this need to be let outside?" I asked as Panzer snuffled his wet nose against the palm of my hand.

Tyler stared at me, his eyes sleepy. "I'm not letting you take this dog." His tone invited no debate, but I debated anyway.

"Just answer the question. How much attention does a dog this size and age require?" I was only trying to get my facts straight so I could pass that information on to my colleagues. Surely one of them could take this dog. Hilary could handle him. One more dog? She wouldn't even notice.

"More time and energy than you've got, if you have to ask that," Tyler said. "Trust me, I'll figure something out."

Of course he would. Rescuing and caretaking were his hobbies.

"You do that a lot, don't you?" I said.

"What?"

"Figure something out? Come to the rescue? Like you did for your brother? And me."

He shrugged. "I guess."

"So, who takes care of you?" It was a leading question. An intimate question, and it seemed to stump him.

"Me," he finally said. "I take care of myself."

That sounded familiar.

It sounded like me.

We walked a little farther, but the sky was getting darker by the minute, heavy, bruise-colored clouds blowing in from over the lake. Just as we turned on the last curve in the path heading back toward the entrance, the first fat droplet pelted my head, and in seconds the rain was coming down in earnest.

We ran like crazy ninjas toward the nearest gazebo, a six-foot round, rickety structure with a roof but no walls. It didn't look sturdy enough to hold us, but if we stood in the center, we might just escape the worst of this storm. Thunder rumbled as my shoe hit the first step, and I jumped up and over like a gazelle. The clumsy, awkward gazelle who all the other gazelles made fun of.

I nearly slipped, but Tyler caught me around the waist and kept me upright.

Panzer ambled up behind us, seemingly indifferent to the storm. A few other walkers were now dashing toward the parking area, but soon it was just us.

"That came up fast," Tyler said, looking out at the sky. His shirt was soaked and clung to his skin in a deliciously indecent way. The rain and the wind gave his hair an adventurous tousle. I was certain I hadn't fared so well and wiped a hand across my wet face. The wind blasted with a sharp edge through our tiny sanctuary. I shivered from the adrenaline, the cold, and the physical proximity of Tyler near me. There was no avoiding him.

We were standing face-to-face inside the little dwelling, our heads bowed a bit to escape the rain riding on the wind. I breathed in, letting the scent of damp cotton from his T-shirt mix with the warmth emanating from his skin. I moved a little closer, and he wrapped his arms around me, just as I'd known he would.

I relaxed into him and let myself enjoy it, this moment of letting go and giving in. Of simply being in a pair of nice strong arms. No thought of big-picture criteria, just immediate need. I was cold, he was warm. It didn't have to be more complicated than that.

Only it was. Because I knew right then and there how very much I wanted him. I could put it off a day, or a week, or maybe even a month, but eventually curiosity and desire would devour me, and I'd have to know what his mouth tasted like, and how those hands, now wrapped so securely around my shoulders, would feel trailing down my legs.

I turned my face to the side and laid it against his chest and wrapped my arms around his waist. He tensed for a moment, as if not certain how to interpret my motions, but after a few seconds, his hands dropped lower on my back, and he pressed me closer.

"I guess it's not such a bad thing after all, getting caught in the rain," he said.

I smiled into his shirt. "I guess not."

Panzer walked around us and sniffed at the air, his wavy coat now bedraggled and dripping. He'd had a rather dignified air to him before. Now he just looked like a wet dog, and my heart broke a little more on his behalf. This was no way for him to spend his last day. It was too unfair, having your life cut short just because you were on the oldish side and no one wanted you.

I looked up at Tyler.

"I'll take the dog," I said.

He shook his head, sending droplets to the floor of the gazebo. "You don't have to do that."

"I know. I want to. I'll figure out a way to make it work."

"Are you sure?"

"Yes."

That earned me the dimples, and my knees turned to water.

"I'll help you with him, you know."

Now it was my turn to smile. "I know you will. Even if I don't ask you to."

It seemed we were agreeing to more than just the dog. We were making a pact, forming a frail sort of union, entwining our lives, if only for the moment.

This was my point of no return. If I was going to step away, this was the time.

But I didn't.

And he knew I wouldn't.

Tyler's hands moved slowly up my back and over my shoulders until his fingers cupped my face, as if I were as fragile as I felt. I was a bubble about to burst, but his lips were soft, grazing over mine in a tease more than a kiss. I sighed, a feminine little flutter of breath I couldn't hold back. And then he did kiss me. Really kissed me, with pressure, and certainty, and a confidence that made me forget my own name.

I kissed him back, not caring that we were standing in a public park where anyone could see. Not caring that he was too young for me. Not even caring that he'd never marry me. For right now, I just wanted him to keep kissing me.

And he did.

Chapter 16

"I HAVE THE PERFECT MAN for you," Hilary said, pulling me into her office. "If I wasn't married, I'd take him myself."

She shut her office door and practically pushed me into a chair.

"Good morning, Hilary," I said sardonically. "I'm fine, thanks. How are you?"

I'd only been in the office for five minutes. My hair was still wet from my walk in the rain, but nothing could dampen my spirits—except maybe having to tell Hilary that I'd just played tonsil hockey with Tyler Connelly in the public park. Perhaps I'd keep that little secret to myself for a while.

"Good morning. Yes. Whatever. We don't have time for that. Here, read this." She shoved a stack of papers into my hands. "His name is Chris Beaumont, and seriously, this guy looks like a keeper. And thankfully, he's got nothing to do with that cheeseball website."

I looked down. Stapled to the corner of the papers was a picture of a very handsome man with thick dark hair and chocolate-brown eyes. Next to that were the words *curriculum vitae*. I flipped through the stack.

"This isn't a dating profile, Hilary. This is somebody's résumé and credentialing paperwork."

She grinned like one of those animated dogs on a commercial with oversized human teeth. I hate those commercials.

"I know," Hilary said. "Score for me, huh? He's applied for privileges at the hospital because he just joined a dermatology practice in Bell Harbor. He's single, grew up in Grand Rapids, and he wants to settle down here and start a family. I tell you, Evie, he's perfect for you."

I looked at the paper again. He was strikingly handsome, and he certainly had nice stats. So why did my stomach drop as if I were staring at a photo of a swastika?

"How did you get this? What makes you even think he's interested in dating?"

"I got the full scoop from Reilly Peters. She's that slutty physician recruiter. Remember her? Honestly, three cosmopolitans and that woman will tell you anything. Don't ever ask about her trip to Jamaica."

Duly noted. "She had no business sharing his personal data with you. It's inappropriate," I said.

"So is bringing wine to an intervention, but she did that once too. She said it was rude to show up empty-handed."

That sounded like the Reilly I knew.

Hilary shrugged and leaned back against her desk. "Yeah, OK, so she's not particularly bright, but in this case, I think her intel is dependable. I mean, look at this guy, Evie. He graduated from University of Michigan, did his residency at Stanford, and now he's here looking for a wife. He'd have regular office hours, little or no call, and he'll make a shitload of money."

"It's not all about money."

"That's easier to say when you've got some. But either way, this guy has the whole package, including the actual package." She giggled at her own joke. "Gabby showed me your list. You want intellectual compatibility, economic equality, and sperm. This guy has all that."

I looked at his picture again. Even if he was only half as good-looking as the photo suggested, he'd still be damn good-looking. At first glance, he certainly met my criteria.

Hilary eyed me suspiciously. "I don't get it. What's the hesitation? I thought you'd be elated."

Ruh-roh. I brushed the hair back from my face.

"Um, no hesitation. He looks great. It's just, how am I supposed to meet him if he's not actually a part of Bell Harbor Singles?"

That wasn't my only hesitation, of course. There was the little matter of Tyler. My lips still tingled from his kiss, and I was fairly certain that tonight when he came over to bring me my dog, there might be some *unleashing*.

Hilary made a checkmark in the air with her index finger. "Already handled. You're having lunch with him next Tuesday."

"What?" The floor beneath me wobbled. These sisters were driving me crazy. First Gabby, and now Hilary.

"Yep, at Jasper's. You're welcome." Hilary's smile was smug.

"Tuesday's not going to work," I blurted out.

"Why? I checked your calendar. You have patients until one, and then you're off for the afternoon."

Think fast, Evie. Think fast.

"Exactly, I'm off for the afternoon because I'm meeting some new decorator at my house. I want to get it painted before I move in." Maybe I should just admit to her about Tyler, but I wasn't ready, and it wasn't even really *a thing*, so there was nothing to tell. What would I say? *I'd like to take a break from husband hunting to fool around with a man young enough to be my yard boy?*

"Who's your decorator?" She said it as if she didn't believe me.

"Some guy named Fontaine Baker. I got his name from one of my patients."

"That's not until four o'clock. I told you, I checked your schedule. And by the way, I know Fontaine. I hope you like feathers and animal prints."

"Animal prints?"

"Yes, but don't change the subject. You can do a late lunch on Tuesday, right?"

"Um . . . ?"

Damn it! I had no explicable reason to say no. This Chris Beaumont looked like the real deal. And maybe a date with a decent guy would help me see Tyler Connelly for the speed bump that he was. He was slowing me down from my real destination. Marriage. A husband, some kids, a real, grown-up relationship.

"Yeah, OK. I think I can manage lunch. But could you change it to that sushi place on the corner? I've been craving sushi."

I wasn't, of course. But I couldn't risk lunch at Jasper's. If Tyler had been upset about Marty Cable, he certainly wouldn't be happy about this guy.

Chapter 17

TYLER WAS BRINGING PANZER TO my apartment, and they should arrive any minute. I'd rushed around for the last half hour tidying things up, but in the scheme of messes, the figurative one I was making was far worse. I had stopped at the shelter at lunch and filled out all the adoption forms. Now all there was left to do was wait. Officially, the dog was mine. And unofficially, so was Tyler.

Earlier this morning, standing in rain, I'd been so certain of my decision. Taking in the dog had seemed like the right thing to do. I'd felt a rush of altruism and good-deedliness. I was saving a life. We doctors love that sort of thing.

I'd been certain about Tyler too. The wind and the storm and his arms and his mouth. It had all proven too irresistible. Even now, the thought of him sent blood whooshing to every erogenous zone on my body.

But this afternoon, I'd taken some time to look over Chris Beaumont's credentials, and that had caused a little whooshing as well. Everything Hilary had said about him seemed true. The only part she'd left out of her description was his dedication to charity work, his multiple awards and publications, and the fact that he was the child of two physicians, just like me. I did want to meet him. And I had every right to meet him.

Tyler and I weren't *a thing*. We were hardly even a fling. Maybe I should just take my dog and say good night. For both our sakes, maybe I should end this road trip before it even began, before our emotions got tangled up in the bedsheets, and each good-bye felt like the final one.

I jumped like a hot kernel of popcorn when my doorbell rang. They were here. I was ridiculously nervous, as if the dog might reject me and not want to live here. Or even worse, he'd love it and want to stay. And so would Tyler. What was I doing?

I wiped my palms over the front of my shorts. I'd put on a sundress after work, but moments earlier had changed into navy-blue shorts. With a belt. A complicated belt. It had three prongs and two loops. If Tyler was going to get to me, he was going to have to work for it.

I breathed deep and slow, trying to recall what my yoga instructor had taught me. Then I remembered—I'd never taken yoga. That's how rattled I was right now. I made a mental note to give yoga a try—because clearly I needed to learn its relaxation properties—and then I opened the door.

There they were, all sunshiney and happy bright. Panzer's tail was wagging as if he knew I'd saved his life. Tyler leaned over and kissed my cheek, a natural gesture, as if we'd been easy lovers for a decade instead of virtual strangers with barely twenty hours of conversation between us. Somehow it felt like more. My left ventricle slammed twice as hard as normal against the right as the two sides tried to regulate.

I pulled the door open wider. "Come on in."

Tyler was carrying a couple of white grocery bags. The plastic crinkled as he set them on my counter. "I have some other things for you in the car. Some dog food and bowls, stuff like that."

Dog food? Bowls? I hadn't thought of that. See? That's how bad I was going to be at taking care of this animal. I wasn't prepared for this at all. Not for any of it. But my Boy Scout was. He made two more trips in and out of my apartment, bringing in various canine necessities, including a fresh new doggy bed made of Sherpa material.

"Where do you want this?" he asked.

"Um, in my bedroom, I guess."

His smile was equal parts sexy and playful. "Lucky dog."

I pointed to the bedroom door, trying to look unfazed and probably failing. I followed behind him, noticing his nice, broad back in the process. "Put it in the corner, please."

He set down the bed and patted it. Panzer strolled over, sniffed it, and then made three circles before settling down with a *wumpf* and a doggy sigh.

Tyler turned to me, bright and satisfied. He brushed his palms together and stood up. "Well, he's all moved in."

"I guess so." I tapped my hands against my thighs. This was when I should tell him thanks very much and buh-bye. He'd done his good deed for the day, and so had I. Now I needed to nip this budding romance right in the . . . well, in the bud.

"Want some wine?" I asked instead.

Excellent, Evelyn. Alcohol is definitely the way to shore up those defenses.

Tyler stepped a little closer. His gaze dropped to my mouth and lingered so long it nearly felt like a kiss. I wondered if anyone had ever burst into flames from the heat of his stare. Something indefinable about him set off reactions in me I'd never felt before. I understood biology well enough, but none of this made sense. It was like when I'd tried ice-skating as a child and had no control over where my feet went. No control over the slip-slide of my body. The lack of certainty over where I was headed felt like falling. Endlessly.

He took another slow step and rested his hands on my hips, tugging me gently toward him. I had the resistance of a magnet.

"Wine sounds good." His voice had gone all husky, in that *I'm-about-to-kiss-you-blissful* tone.

Run away. I should run away.

My head knew it, but the message went no farther. My hands eased up his arms and slipped naturally around his shoulders, drawing him near when I should be doing just the opposite. Wherever we were headed was a dead-end road. There was no future for the two of us. But Tyler Connelly seemed like a worthy destination all on his own. An all-inclusive resort, and suddenly I needed a vacation.

I lifted up on my toes, rubbing against him as I rose and enjoying his sharp intake of breath. I wasn't completely without wiles.

"We should have wine," I whispered, my lips so close to his I could already taste him.

He nodded. "Later." He hands moved fast, wrapping all the way around me until I was tight in his embrace, and then he kissed me, thoroughly.

All the certainty I'd felt this morning came crashing back, a tidal wave of desire nearly drowning me. I wanted him. All of him. It had been two years—two years since I'd been kissed at all, and a lifetime since I'd been kissed so well.

This was about to become a very, very good night.

Light from the setting sun cast golden rays around the room, creating patterns across the bed as I pulled Tyler toward it.

Yes, we should have wine first.

I knew that.

I was familiar with the protocol. A little wine. A little conversation. A little bob and weave while we pretended this wasn't a sure thing. But we'd done that, in our way, and my partner didn't seem to mind the rush.

As soon as the backs of my legs tapped against the edge of the mattress, down we went. I'm not sure if he pushed or I pulled, but it didn't really matter. Kisses scattered everywhere. He grazed his mouth across my neck, pressing here and there, biting just a little. I arched to grant him access gladly. The bed creaked as we moved, as if even my furniture was out of practice, but Tyler skimmed his warm hands over my warmer skin, and knowledge I hadn't used in a while all came rushing back. This was just like riding a bike. Only so much better. I tugged his T-shirt up and over his head and thought my pulse might exceed my heart's ability.

Tyler in a shirt was a delicious vision.

Tyler without one was a work of art.

Impatient now, I pushed at his shoulders to roll him to his back. He laughed, but his humor turned into a throaty growl as I kissed my way from his navel up toward his chest. His hands tangled in my hair, tugging, caressing. I was alive, in the moment, with every nerve ending in my body shouting to be touched.

Pheromones didn't care about tomorrow. They didn't care about education or employment or age. Their only job was clearly defined, and ours were working overtime.

Tyler let me have my way for a minute, but then I was on my back again as he tugged at my intricate belt. I should've worn the sundress.

"Damn it, Evie. Is this thing locked?"

I giggled low, a sexy, sultry purr I'd never heard from my own throat before.

"It only unlocks if you brought protection. Please tell me you brought protection along with all those dog toys."

"I brought protection."

"Thank God."

Tyler laughed at my demonstrable relief, and so did I. Then I reached down to help him set me free of the belt, and free of any residual reservations.

Laughter faded as tussling gave way to rolling waves, and flutters turned to long, sure strokes. I was hyperfocused on sensations, giving and receiving. I was happy.

And then I was soaring.

And then I was blissful.

And then I was laughing, because when all was said and done, when the loving was over and our pulses had returned to almost normal, Tyler lifted his tranquil face from my shoulder and said, "Now will you go out with me?"

—∿— —∿—

"What's this tattoo supposed to mean?" I traced my fingertips over Tyler's deltoid as we lingered under the covers of my bed. The markings on his arm were a little harder to make out now that the sun had set sometime during the midst of round two.

Tyler tucked his other arm up under the pillow as we faced each other.

"Just my dad's initials with some extra swirls."

My euphoria dimmed. I wished I hadn't asked him, but the topic was out there now.

"That's sweet. How old were you when he died?" I rested my palm against the ink.

"Sixteen. Grant and I both got them the day after the funeral. My mom was furious."

"Because it's your father's initials?" Surprise pitched my voice upward.

He gave a tiny shake of his head, as much as the pillow would allow. "No. No, of course not. When we explained that's what they were, she cried. But she was still mad as hell because she hates tattoos. Plus we took Scotty with us, and he was only ten." He said that last part as if it were inconsequential.

"Ten? What kind of place would agree to give a tattoo to a ten-year-old?"

Tyler smiled, a lazy, sleepy smile. One weighted down by memory. "None, as it turns out. They almost wouldn't do mine except Grant knew the guy." A wistful sigh escaped him, and I recognized the longing. The missing of someone who was out of reach, as my father had often been. In a strange way, this was something we had in common, although my father's absence had been voluntary.

I leaned over and kissed his arm, right over the markings. It was a sentimental thing to do, really not my style, but tonight I was giving in to all my feminine instincts, and in that moment, I wanted to kiss his tattoo.

"Are you hungry?" he asked, his voice a little gruff and abrupt.

I let my head fall back to the pillow. "I am, now that you mention it, but I don't have much to eat here."

"Jasper's delivers. We could order something from there. Or get a pizza."

Pizza delivery. On a Friday night. With a guy and my dog. This should feel utterly average and mundane, but my heart brightened like the lighting of a sparkler. I wasn't going to question why. I was enjoying myself. No sense in ruining it with overanalysis.

"Sure. Pizza sounds good."

We each reached around to find our scattered clothing. My shirt was on top of the covers, so I pulled it on, skipping my bra, which seemed acceptable under the circumstances. My shorts were on the floor. I grabbed them next as Tyler found his boxers and pulled them on, followed by his jeans. But my underwear was AWOL. I looked up at the ceiling fan. Maybe it had landed there, since our disrobing had been a little frantic. But no. No underwear up there.

I slid my hand around under the sheets.

"What are you doing?" he asked.

I felt my cheeks heat up. "I can't find my underwear."

Tyler walked around to the other side of the bed and gave a little chuckle. "Um, were these them?"

He pulled a wad of shredded pink satin from Panzer's mouth.

Yes. Those were them.

"Panzer. Bad dog."

He wagged his tail as soon as I looked at him. Obedience training was going to have a steep learning curve for the two of us.

Tyler laughed harder. "I think these are done for." He carried my soggy, chewed-up underwear by his index finger into the bathroom, and I heard them go into the trash basket just before he shut the door. I slid from the bed and grabbed a fresh pair of panties from the drawer, pulling them on, along with my shorts. I tried to fix my hair in the mirror above my dresser, but there was no repairing it.

"So, pizza it is," Tyler said as he came from the bathroom a minute later and we walked into the other room.

Panzer wandered out with us, yawning as if he'd been the one exerting himself. I tossed him a rawhide from the counter. He picked it up and took it over to the other side of the room to gnaw.

"Wish I'd given him that half an hour ago," I said.

Tyler smiled as he dialed his phone. He ordered us food while I unpacked the last bag of dog stuff.

"So you should walk him at least once a day, but twice is even better. I can help with that," Tyler said as soon as he'd hung up.

The offer was thoughtful, and not unexpected, but the sense that we'd agreed to joint custody of this dog created a pressure in my chest. It wasn't necessarily uncomfortable, just . . . foreign.

"Do I need to walk him every time he has to pee?"

"Not a long walk. But he'll need to go outside a couple of times a day. You've had dogs before, right?"

I shook my head. "No."

His motions stilled. He looked stunned, as if I'd just exposed my Borg implant.

"Never? What kind of a miserable childhood did you have?"

His tangible disbelief made me laugh, and the pressure went away.

"I had a perfectly acceptable childhood, but I was busy with school, and piano lessons, and science camp. You know, the usual stuff." I cleared a space off the folding table that served as my dining room and part-time home office.

"Science camp? I think your concept of the usual stuff might be different than mine." He tossed two more dog toys on the floor. There were already five of them lying around for Panzer to choose from. Apparently dogs liked things scattered.

"Why, what was your usual stuff?" I asked.

Tyler hadn't put his shirt back on, and I watched the muscles of his back flex as he reached into a kitchen cabinet to pull out some plates. Even now, in the midst of my postcoital satisfaction, I felt my body responding. Just a little pizza break, then I'd be taking Mr. Connelly back to bed.

"Well, around here it was mostly swimming, fishing, water-skiing. My dad ran a charter fishing company, so Grant and I spent our summers working on the boat."

I set a stack of medical journals on the floor. "Charter fishing company? That's interesting."

Tyler put the plates on the table and came around behind me, wrapping his arms around my waist. "Yep," he said, kissing the side of my neck.

"Stop that." I tilted my head and pressed back against him precisely so he wouldn't stop. If I'd thought that a little sex would ease the longing he'd stirred up in me, I was wrong. Very, very wrong. His touch had only thrown gasoline onto a banked fire, and now I had a real inferno raging. I wanted him now more than ever.

His breath was warm against my skin. "How sturdy is that folding table?" he teased.

Not sturdy enough for what I had in mind. But that would have to wait. Using every ounce of will, I twisted away from him.

"The pizza will be here any minute. Behave yourself." I playfully pushed at his arms. "And put on a shirt. Your chest is distracting me."

His laughter was another warm caress. "Then you'll have to put on a bra, because, trust me, your chest is pretty distracting too."

He reached out, but I evaded him.

"Let's talk about something else. Do you play any musical instruments?"

Tyler burst out laughing. "What?"

I was so confused by all his testosterone, I wasn't making any sense. I have no idea where that gem of a question came from. All I knew was I needed to dial down the sexy factor or we'd be naked again when the pizza arrived.

"It's a legitimate question. I mean, don't you think we should get to know each other a little better? Now that we have, you know, *known* each other."

His head bobbed. "OK. Fair enough. I play a little guitar, but badly. Do you still play piano?"

I found the corkscrew and set it on the counter. "I haven't played in years. I never really enjoyed it, but my parents insisted because it's good for manual dexterity. They started grooming me to be a surgeon by the time I could sit up."

He picked up the corkscrew and looked around for the bottle of wine. "What would you have become if you weren't a doctor?"

I stood still and let the question roll around in my befuddled mind. I'm not sure I'd ever given it any thought before.

"Evie?"

"I don't know. I'm thinking."

His brows lifted. "So, you've always been certain that's what you would do with your life?"

"I guess. I mean, I had a certain level of expectation to live up to. Both my parents are surgeons, so it came pretty naturally to me. What made you decide to be an EMT?"

"Necessity."

Necessity? What kind of an answer was that? I was about to ask him, but he opened the refrigerator door and frowned. "Where is all your food? There's nothing in here except butter and olives."

I stepped up behind him and pointed.

"And yogurt. And wine. See?"

He bent lower. "And yogurt and wine, but where's the rest?"

He squinted as if there were some highly suspicious reason for my lack of produce, and pulled out the chilled bottle of chardonnay.

"I hate to grocery shop. I usually eat at the hospital."

"OK, well, I'm going to write down the number to Jasper's. Call over there next time you're hungry and somebody will bring you something to eat."

God, he was sweet. And thoughtful, and generous. I could gobble him up with a spoon.

This was a problem. A big, big problem, but I could hardly play surprised. Tyler Connelly had been *adorável* since the first moment I'd seen him snoring on that stretcher. Now that I'd had him in my bed, it would be tough to settle for someone else. But I couldn't let my head be ruled by my hormones. If I did, I'd never find myself a decent husband.

Chapter 18

"THIS IS A SEX TOY party? Why the hell didn't you tell me that before we got here?"

Gabby, Hilary, and I stood in the fading sunlight on Delle's bricked front porch between two enormous flowerpots full of red geraniums. As the last chime of the doorbell faded, my annoyance grew louder.

The wicked sisters had tricked me, telling me this was some kind of home merchandise party. I'd thought Delle was selling jewelry, or candles, or those ceramic baking stones that I had no idea how to use, but apparently I was in for something quite a bit spicier than spinach dip and aromatherapy.

Gabby's bright smile was accented by bubblegum-pink lipstick. "I didn't tell you, Dr. McFrigid, because if I had, you might not have come."

"You're right. I wouldn't have."

I had no moral objection to sex toys. Whatever floats the boat. But I did have an objection to sharing my bedtime preferences with a group of women I hardly knew. Or worse yet, women I knew and had to work with. Any second now, my receptionist would fling open that door and display her bagful of conjugal goodies.

This was going to be A . . . W . . . K . . . W . . . A . . . R . . . D. They already talked too much about my sex life. This would only make it worse.

On the bright side, at least I'd finally find out what a Vagazzler looked like.

Gabby tucked a strand of pink-and-blonde hair behind her triple-pierced ear. She was wearing cute jeans and a sparkly tank top. I should've known when I saw her outfit we weren't going to spend the evening talking about pastry dough or how to accessorize with scarves.

Even Hilary was dressed racier than usual, in a silky red top and shorty-shorts. Damn her and her long legs. She took a hold of my shoulders and faced me. She jiggled my arms a little, but I was deliberately stiff.

"If anyone could use a few toys, Evie, it's you. We need to loosen you up before you meet your sexy dermatologist next week. We need to bring out your wild, adventurous side."

I bit back a smile.

These two had no idea my wild, adventurous side had been ridden like an electronic bull not ten hours earlier. Tyler didn't leave my apartment until six o'clock that morning. We'd gotten almost no sleep, and Panzer had eaten two more pairs of my underwear. Every part of my body felt used up and spent in the best possible way, and I was thoroughly enjoying my postcoital hangover.

As if our night of sexual debauchery wasn't decadent enough, Tyler had sent over the delivery boy from Jasper's at lunchtime with a grilled onion cheeseburger. And french fries. Some men might have tried to woo me with flowers. He sent cholesterol-laden ground beef. It was heaven times ten. The taste of it had nearly sent me into another round of orgasms. Thank goodness the delivery kid had left before I ate it.

But they knew none of that, and I wasn't ready to share.

"My adventurous side is primed and ready to go, Hilary. I don't need battery-operated tools to charge it up."

"Primed and ready, huh? Well, even so, a little revving of the engine never did a girl any harm."

"Vroom, vroom," Gabby said enthusiastically.

The door opened, and there was Delle. Her cheeks vasodilated to a bright cherry red, a garish contrast to her lavender-framed glasses.

"Oh, goodness! Dr. Rhoades! And Dr. Pullman. And Gabby. Come on in. Make yourself at home."

She turned with a flourish and led us through the foyer, her floral-print blouse billowing as she went. The house smelled like sugar cookies. And lubricant.

"You know, if I get a toy, I won't need a husband. I can just cuddle up with my inflatable boyfriend," I whispered in Hilary's ear as we walked into Delle's paneled family room.

"Trust me. Even with a man, toys are essential," she whispered back. "Steve couldn't find a G-spot with a map and a compass."

The place was decorated with old lace, an abundance of dried floral arrangements, and Precious Moments figurines. Not exactly sex toy party motif. Family photos abounded, covering every inch of wall and surface.

Wonderful. Just what I wanted. Five hundred more pairs of eyes to watch me shop for dildos.

"Just relax." Gabby squeezed my wrist. "This is going to be fun."

We stepped farther into the room, and I saw several familiar faces. I tugged on her sleeve.

"There's hospital staff here. Don't you think they'll talk about seeing us here?"

She rolled her shoulders in a careless shrug. "So? It's a bonding thing. Seeing you here will make them like you better."

"People like me just fine now."

"Sure they do. But sometimes you're a little edgy. And not trendy edgy. Edgy like you need to get laid. Consider this a long-overdue intervention. So sit down, have a glass of wine, and look through this catalog."

She pushed me into a folding chair and handed me a shiny red brochure with a virtually naked woman on the cover. I stared at it, noting the poorly done augmentation of the vixeny cover model. Her implants were too big, and too round to look natural. But then again, she was arched over a black leather sofa wearing a red thong, a white mask, and cowboy boots with spurs. That didn't look very natural either.

Hilary and Gabby set their purses on the chairs on either side of me and turned away.

"Where are you guys going?" I practically hissed the question.

They laughed out loud. Not with me. At me.

"I'm getting wine for me, and for you, a Valium," Hilary answered.

"You're hilarious."

They walked toward the kitchen as I glanced around the room to see who I recognized. Susie from the emergency department waved at me. I waved back. She had on cute low-cut jeans and a hot-pink top. Her hair was loose and wavy. She looked ten years younger than she did at work.

I looked down at my own basic black capris and my light blue blouse. I was the only one here not wearing something cute and sassy. All my clothes were work clothes. But now that I was dating, I needed some new, more sultry outfits. And didn't I deserve it? I worked hard. Of course, my sudden interest in fashion had nothing to do with Tyler, or any desire to look younger, hipper, sexier. I just hadn't treated myself to a shopping spree in a long time, and I needed some new clothes. There was nothing more to it than that.

It had nothing to do with him . . .

Seriously. I was a terrible liar, even when I was the only one who could hear me.

Gabby came back and handed me a glass filled to the brim with a frothy, peach-colored drink.

"Try this. It's good."

I took a sip. She was right. It was fruity and delicious.

"What is it?" I asked, taking another big swallow.

She waited until I had a mouthful. "It's a penis colada."

I coughed and nearly spit it out through my nostrils. It burned. This was going to be a long, long night.

She sat down, and Hilary joined us, holding a glass of white wine.

"Anything interesting in the catalog?" she asked.

I hadn't had the nerve to open it, but it was now or never.

Oh. I should have stuck with never.

I always felt obligated to purchase something at these home parties, but I wasn't in the market for see-through baby-doll pajamas, furry handcuffs, or nipple ring charms. Hopefully I could find a nice body lotion or something. But no. There was nothing that was remotely nonsexual in this entire thirty-page brochure. Thumbing through it, I discovered instruments I had never even imagined. Things with prongs, whirligigs, spirals, spangles, ears, and tails. Things with batteries and chargers and assorted attachments. I elbowed Gabby and pointed at the pinkish monstrosity on page eleven.

"Is that what it looks like?" I whispered.

She leaned in close. "Do you think it looks like a giant, battery-operated, rubber tongue?"

"Yep."

"Then yes, it is what you think it is."

"Ladies, if I could have your attention for just a moment," Delle said, mopping perspiration away from her forehead with a tissue. "Thank you all for coming. This is Scarlett, our pleasure guide for the evening."

She put her fleshy arm around a thin but muscular woman dressed in a crimson bustier and pleather pants. I had to admit it. Scarlett did look kind of sexy, but those pants must be hotter than hell. And not hot in a sexy way, but hot in the *my-legs-are-drenched-with-sweat* kind of way.

"But before we get started," Delle continued, "I think we should start our evening off on the right note by introducing ourselves by our stripper name."

Everyone laughed except for me. "Our stripper name?"

"Yes." Delle's fleshy cheeks bounced as she nodded enthusiastically. "Take the name of your first pet and add it to the street you grew up on."

Really?

See, this was the kind of stuff I missed out on by always studying or working. All this time I'd had a secret stripper name and hadn't even known it.

We worked our way around the room, making introductions. Susie's name was Mittens Hightower. The woman next to her was Gypsy Main, and so it went. Jinx Belmont. Rosie Leffingwell, Taffy Fulton. Gabby and Hilary became Roxie and Snowball Caravelle. And I was Panzer Mulberry.

"You had a dog named Panzer? That's a cool name," Gabby said, sucking up the last of her drink through a dainty straw.

I squirmed in my chair, not certain I wanted to delve into this.

But the penis colada had loosened my tongue. My real tongue. Not the rubber one on page eleven.

"I have a dog named Panzer right now. I got him yesterday."

Hilary turned in her chair. "You got a dog yesterday? Yet another secret? How the heck did I not know about this?"

"It was sort of spontaneous." I wondered if my four-legged spontaneous decision was at my apartment right now trying to pry open my underwear drawer to find a snack.

Hilary's eyes narrowed. She was winding up for an interrogation, but Scarlett interrupted.

"As Delle mentioned, my name is Scarlett, and I'm your guide to total sexual fulfillment, either with a partner, in a group, or through self-love. Now, is anyone here uncomfortable talking about masturbation?"

Oh, crap.

The night went downhill from there, although I will say Scarlett was well versed in anatomy. I learned more from her than I had in medical school. I also learned about *pleasure enhancers* such as the Pocket Rocket, the Venus Butterfly, the Happy Rabbit, and the infamous Vagazzler. It looked like something Panzer might want to play fetch with, but certainly not something I wanted anywhere near my tender bits. I'm all for innovation and variety, but any gizmo with ten speeds and five attachments seems risky.

"Here. Try this." Gabby handed me another drink. This one was just as frothy as the first, but dark pink.

I accepted it with caution. "What is it?"

She grinned. "A strawberry dickery. So drink it and tell me about this new dog of yours. Where'd you get him?"

Careful, Evie. Careful what you say here.

"He was from the animal shelter, and if no one adopted him,

he was going to be put to sleep. He had such a sweet face, I just couldn't let him down."

Of course, when I said *sweet face*, I wasn't only thinking of the dog.

Susie came over and sat beside us. I hadn't worked with her since the day we'd watched Tyler being carted away in handcuffs. Regular handcuffs. Not the furry kind like on page nineteen.

"Did I hear you say you just got a dog? What kind?"

I was about to be squeezed in a vise of questioning.

"Um, I'm not sure. He's big, and furry, very sweet. But he likes to eat underwear."

"Oh," Delle exclaimed, stepping over to us. "There's edible underwear on page seventeen. Cherry, blueberry, peach, and green apple. I don't recommend the green apple, though. That's not a flattering color on anyone."

"Well, I'm glad you got a dog," Gabby said, ignoring Delle. "It's a good first step toward committing to a relationship."

"First step?" Susie asked.

I felt the veins in my head start to pulse. I didn't need all the nurses in the emergency department knowing I was on the prowl for a husband. And I was more than afraid this conversation would somehow come around to Tyler. I tried to use pure energy to will Gabby to keep her mouth shut, but she'd had about nine strawberry dickeries. If the alcohol didn't set her off, the sugar certainly would.

"Evie has finally dived into the dating pool and decided she wants to get married. I've found her the perfect man," Hilary said, leaning forward into the group.

"The Perfect Man is on page twelve," Delle said, waving around the catalog. "He's a bestseller, but don't forget he needs D-cell batteries."

We all stopped and stared at her. Unfazed, she shook the catalog again. "D-cell batteries. Six of them. He's a high-voltage toy."

After a pause, I turned back to Susie. "I'm just making more of an effort to be social," I said as if this was not a big deal. Because it wasn't. Women went on dates and found husbands all the time. I was nothing special.

"Good for you," Susie said. "For what it's worth, Dr. Hoover from the emergency department thinks you're hot. He'd go out with you in a heartbeat."

"Dr. Hoover?"

Susie nodded and took a long, noisy drink from her straw, draining the glass. Geez, these women could certainly put away the dickeries.

"Frank Hoover. Tall guy, receding hairline. Not bad-looking, but he's kind of full of himself. Plus his wife left him financially broke. And emotionally broken. Come to think of it, you probably shouldn't go out with him."

Broke and broken? That did not sound appealing.

What did sound appealing right about now was a big dose of Tyler. It was impossible not to think of him while talking about men. And while looking at all this carnal merchandise. My libido had lain dormant for too long. Now that Tyler had tapped *me*, he'd tapped *it*. The seal was broken, and all I wanted to do was climb back into bed with my twenty-seven-year-old lover, pull the covers over our heads, and—what was it Scarlett the pleasure guide had said?—give in to our basest nature? Yes. That's what I wanted to do.

"By the way," Delle interjected again, "these furry handcuffs are actually quite comfortable. See?" She clicked one onto Gabby's wrist. "Ronald got quite a blister when we tried real handcuffs. These are much better."

Gabby stroked the fur. "Mike would love these. And they are quite soft. *E muito* sexy. That's Portuguese for very sexy."

Susie poked me with her elbow. "Hey, speaking of very sexy and handcuffs, what do you suppose ever happened with that Jet Ski guy? Do you think he was able to charm his way out of going to jail?"

I stared down into my drink but felt telltale heat in my cheeks.

"That was Tyler Connelly," Gabby said. "I went to high school with him."

"Was that the *adorável* young man who came into the office to have his stitches removed?" Delle asked. "He was quite insistent about seeing Dr. Rhoades instead of one of the nurses."

Shit.

"So you've seen him again?" Susie asked.

"Yes, she has," Hilary said, her voice a little slurry. "But I've warned her off him. He may be cute as hell, but he and his family are all about one foot from jail time. Lucky for them my husband is such a good lawyer."

Hilary was drunk. I could hear it in the pace and curl of her words. If I was going to tell any of them about Tyler, now was not the time. I needed to change the subject, and fast. I set down my drink and picked up the catalog.

"Well, that's enough about that. The real question is, are we going to sit here chatting all night, or are we going to buy some sex toys?"

Chapter 19

CHRIS BEAUMONT WAS JUST AS good-looking in person as he was in his picture. Maybe better when you added his friendly smile and a nice tan, accented by his pale yellow shirt.

"Evelyn?" he asked, standing up when I walked into the lobby of Mutsusaka's sushi restaurant. He extended his hand, but as I reached out, we both leaned in and had that awkward *are-we-hugging-or-just-shaking-hands* moment. He laughed and kind of patted my arm, opting out of the full-fledged embrace.

"It's nice to meet you. Chris, right?"

"Right." He nodded a little too rapidly.

He was nervous, which helped put me at ease. I was nervous too. I had tried everything I could think of to get out of this lunch date. But Hilary wouldn't budge, and I couldn't explain why I wanted to avoid it. She had too many bad things to say about Tyler and his family of gypsies, tramps, and thieves for me to admit I was involved with him.

And it's not as if we were exclusive. We'd had one night. One incredibly fantabulous night of mind-blowing sex. I hadn't seen him since he'd left my apartment that morning because he'd been working. We'd exchanged a few naughty text messages, but that was about it. So I had every right to be on a lunch date with another man.

But I still felt guilty. Dating multiple men was something I'd have to get used to if I was still looking for that long-term, grown-up husband. Somehow the whole idea had lost a little of its luster, and yet there was no denying Chris met several of my most important criteria. If I had to guess, I'd say he was about an 80 percent match. I didn't want to think too much about where Tyler would score.

"Dr. Beaumont, your table is right this way." A slender hostess approached us. She was reed thin with jet-black hair. I brushed my own copper strands away from my shoulder and wondered if this Chris liked red. I knew Tyler liked it. He'd told me so. Whispered about it right into my ear.

The hostess led us to a quaint little table between a window and a bubbling fountain. Chris pulled out my chair and earned a point for being a gentleman. Regardless of how he might compare to Tyler, he was certainly ahead of my Bell Harbor Singles dates so far. Although that wasn't much of a challenge. Unless he started cleaning his ears at the table, he'd have those guys beat. By about 1,000 percent.

Chris took his own seat and the hostess handed us menus.

"Please enjoy your lunch," she said and wafted away on delicate little ankles.

"Have you eaten here before?" he asked.

"A few times. You?"

He shook his head. "Nope, first time. But I'm always up for something new."

We exchanged some idle chitchat about food preferences and favorite restaurants, and the waitress came and took our order. The conversation was comfortable, even if it wasn't very exciting.

It was hard to get too worked up in the middle of the day while sipping iced tea, even if he was handsome.

"So, your friend Hilary seemed nice on the phone. It's kind of interesting she sets up dates for you." He posed it like a statement but the implied question was *why didn't you call me yourself?*

"Hilary and I have been friends since our internship year. Sometimes she has a little difficulty remembering boundaries."

"Oh, really. How so?" His eyes were a rich, warm chocolate brown, but as with most people, his were not perfectly symmetrical. Something only I would notice. But I did notice.

"How does she forget boundaries?" I said. "Well, how about this? The other night she and her sister tricked me into going to a sex toy party." It was a bold thing to share but would tell me right away if Chris had a sense of humor.

Apparently, he did. He smiled wide and leaned forward. "Really? Did you buy anything?" His demeanor was purely playful, and I'd pretty much set myself up for him to ask.

"I won a door prize, but I'm a little afraid to open the box. Anyway, let's talk about you. Did I read somewhere you're from Grand Rapids?"

He rolled easily with the change in subject. "I am. Where did you read that?"

Whoops.

"Um . . . probably not on your credentialing paperwork from the hospital." I was completely in the wrong here. It was quite possible I was about to accidentally get recruiter Reilly Peters fired.

His brows lifted, and he leaned back. "You know what? You're the first one to actually admit that."

"Admit it? What are you talking about?"

His posture was relaxed as he rested his hands on the table. "Today is the fifth date I've been on since handing over that paperwork to Reilly. She gives recruiting a whole new meaning. I think she's got a computer dating service on the side."

I squirmed in my chair. Now did not seem like the time to admit my association with Bell Harbor Singles.

"Fifth date? I'm suddenly not feeling very special."

"I didn't feel very special being contacted by your friend on your behalf, either. But here we are. And I'm glad. It's very nice getting to know you." He seemed sincere.

And it was nice getting to know him too.

"In my defense, Hilary set up this date before I'd even had a chance to call you. I hope that makes you feel a little bit better? Does it?"

"So much better." His smile made his eyes crinkle, and a warmth settled low in my stomach. Chris Beaumont had some husband potential. There was no denying it. His manner was calm but energetic, his smile genuine. And he was very easy to look at. He wasn't as attractive as Tyler, but still, I could see myself falling for a guy like him. Probably.

Our sushi came, and the conversation continued. We swapped tales from medical school and laughed. We talked about interesting cases, and colleagues, and laughed some more. I was amazed by how fast the time went and what a nice lunch we were having.

"So my secret inside source says both your parents are physicians, right?" I asked, popping a final piece of sushi into my mouth.

Chris wiped his hands on his napkin and gave a nod of his head. "Yes. My dad is an allergist and my mom's a pediatrician. They both work part-time now. A few summers ago they bought a Winnebago, and now they spend a few weeks out of every year driving around to tourist traps. I think they're going for a Guinness world record for most truck-stop breakfasts eaten or something equally mundane."

"That's very cute."

"Cute, eccentric, whatever. They're happy. And at least while they're gone, they're not pestering me about getting married."

I laughed too loud and slapped my hand over my mouth. "Yours too? What is it with parents these days?"

"I know. Exactly. What's the rush? I'm only thirty-six years old." He laughed as he said it, obviously realizing that was plenty old enough. "How old are you?"

I tried to frown around my smile. "You're not supposed to ask a woman that."

"You're not supposed to read my confidential paperwork."

Touché. He had me there. "True. I'm thirty-five. But just barely."

"So why haven't you gotten married?" The question was more conversational than accusatory.

I could say that no one had asked, but the truth was, I'd never given anyone a chance. "Busy working, I guess. Honestly, I hadn't really thought about marriage much until recently, but I just had a birthday, and now my parents are getting remarried."

"Both of them?"

"Yes. To each other, after being happily divorced for twenty-three years." I shook my head and gave a little sigh, as if to say again *parents these days!*

"I think there must be an interesting story there," Chris said, pulling out his wallet. "I'd like to hear more about it, but I'm afraid I have to get back to the office. How would you feel about finishing this conversation over dinner some night?"

Dinner? Dinner was a bigger deal than lunch. But not *that much* bigger. Even so, imaginary Tyler popped up with arms crossed and a scowl on his face. Apparently he didn't find Chris nearly as entertaining as I did. But too bad for figment boy. I had no reason to say no to this dinner invitation.

"I'd like that," I said and realized it was true. I would like to know him better. Chris Beaumont was appealing, and he met all the proper requirements. He was handsome, intelligent, employed, available. Sure, he didn't make my body tingle or my skin flush the way Tyler did, and I hadn't given much thought to tearing off his clothes, but we'd had a lovely, pleasant lunch. "I'll have Hilary call you to set it up."

I was teasing, but this time he missed the joke.

"Uh-uh," he said, pulling a card from his wallet and scribbling something on the back. He pushed it toward me over the surface of the table. "That's my private number. If you want to see me, make a little effort. I really hope you do. You're in the top five dates I've had lately."

Was he teasing? I picked the pen up from the table and wrote my number on the back of the restaurant receipt and slid it over to him. "Tell you what. Top five seems a little crowded. How about you call me when you've whittled it down to just two or three contestants? That's my private number."

He took the slip of paper. "Fair enough. Let me put this into my contact list right now." He pulled out his phone and pushed a few buttons. Seconds later, mine was ringing.

It was him. I smiled and answered. "Hello?"

"How's next Tuesday?"

The warmth inside began to lift, like dough rising. Slow and purposefully. Tyler Connelly was a spark and a bright flame, but Chris Beaumont just might be a lit fuse leading up to something more.

—√ᴧᴧ— —√ᴧᴧ—

"Evelyn, this new house of yours is to die for, but egad, what were they thinking with this schizophrenic color palette? It's like Sherwin Williams and Benjamin Moore had a wild sex orgy in here."

Fontaine Baker was as loud and eccentric as his mother, Dody. I should have predicted that when she'd told me he was an interior designer, but everyone in town said he was cheap and he was available. In fact, I got the distinct impression he was cheap and available with regard to most things.

"Yes, it definitely needs paint," I said. "I'm going to need furniture too. All I have is a couch and a bed."

Fontaine rubbed his hands together gleefully. "Furniture too? Oh, we're going to have so much fun."

He said fun, but what I heard was cha-ching, cha-ching. Even if Fontaine was cheap, it was going to cost me some serious coinage to get this place furnished. I hadn't really thought that through before I'd bought this great big house. I'd been too distracted by the image of Tyler in that damn shower. And in the kitchen. And in the bedrooms.

All of them.

"Let's go look upstairs," Fontaine said as if reading my mind. "The kitchen may be the heart of the home, but the master bedroom is where pulses race." He turned his dark, glossy head my way and grinned like a game show host. "Do you like that analogy? I tried to make it sound medical-like because you're, you know, a doctor."

"Um, thank you?"

We reached the door to the bedroom and Fontaine gasped. "Oh, no, no, no. This won't do. This won't do at all. This room doesn't say make mad, passionate love. This room says blah-blah-blah-snoresville. We can do so much better."

He walked in and spread out his arms, twirling slowly. "What's your favorite color?"

"My favorite color? Um, green, I guess."

"Wrong! It's purple. Picture this room a deep, sultry purple. Almost an eggplant but without the icky taste. Then add a few red and gold accents and lots of mirrors. Like a sultan's harem. We can do a four-poster bed with lots of sheer draperies and fabulous silk linens. Do you love it? Tell me you love it."

His hands went to his hips as he stared me down.

"I was thinking something more soothing and maybe cottagey?"

"Wrong again! That is so, so boring! Just because you live on a lake doesn't mean it has to look like every other house on a lake. If you tell me you want nautical decor, I'm going to cut myself."

"I don't want nautical, but I don't think I'm much of a sultan's harem kind of person either."

He giggled and waved his delicate hand at me. "Oh, I was just kidding with that. No sultan's harem. But I do think this room should have dark purple walls. Nothing too girly in here. You want Tyler to feel comfortable too."

I gasped. "Tyler? What would make you say something like that?" How the hell did this guy know about Tyler?

"Oh, sorry," Fontaine whispered, covering his lips with two fingers. "Is that a secret? My brother said you'd been banging it out with Tyler Connelly. Excellent choice, by the way. Love the whole EMT, run-toward-danger thing. Very sexy."

The floor starting spinning, and all that white carpet seemed to be getting closer. I reached out to grasp the door frame. "Your brother? Who's your brother?"

"Jasper Baker, of course."

Of course. Another link in the Bell Harbor chain of incessant information sharing. One night with Tyler and the news had spread like Nutella over a warm toaster waffle. There were no secrets in this town, no concept of privacy. My personal data would continue to bubble out like water from a leaky sprinkler head, and once the information was out, there was no containing it. What was the point in even trying?

Chapter 20

AN EARLY SUSHI LUNCH AND an emotional meeting with my flamboyant decorator had left me starving and exhausted. It was nearly six by the time I'd finished listening to Fontaine pitch one outrageous idea after another. If I gave him free rein, my house would end up looking like something Picasso had painted. But we'd reached a comfortable middle ground, and after convincing him I did not want a Cirque du Soleil–themed living room, I think we'd come up with some good design compromises.

Now, at last, I was home, the dog was walked, and I was in for the night. I kicked off my shoes and padded over to the refrigerator, hoping the grocery fairies had filled it with food. No such luck. I shut the door and saw the note from Tyler with the number to Jasper's. My mouth watered, and before I could even swallow, I'd picked up the phone to order myself some dinner.

I'd just slipped into some pajama pants and a tank top when the delivery boy rang my doorbell.

Only it wasn't a delivery boy.

It was Tyler.

Panzer barked a greeting and thumped his tail against the floor. If I had a tail, I'd have done the same thing. Thoughts of

Chris Beaumont dimmed as I stared into the brightness that was Tyler. The surprise of him being there only added to the swell of my attraction. Maybe we'd only shared one night, but it had been one fantabulous night. Way better than a sushi lunch.

Tyler held up a brown paper bag with the logo for Jasper's restaurant emblazoned on the side.

"Hi!" My voice squeaked. So much for playing it cool.

"Hi, yourself. Hungry?" He strolled in as if he owned the place and set the bag down on my kitchen counter, unloading the contents. Then he opened my utensil drawer and pulled out a knife and fork.

"I didn't realize you did the deliveries." I walked over and stood next to him, wondering how I could be so hungry, have food right there in front of me, but suddenly be thinking of postponing this meal for a little hanky-panky.

He turned so we were facing each other, toe to toe, chest to chest, bits to bits.

"I was done with my shift and offered to drop this off." His voice lowered along with his gaze. I wasn't wearing a bra. He noticed, and we both smiled.

"So, you're finished for the night, then?" I asked, trying to sound as if it didn't matter much.

He looped a finger around the strap of my tank top. "I'm done working for the night. But I'm by no means finished."

He leaned down and kissed me, and life was good.

Chris was a nice guy. Maybe even a great guy. And I should get to know him better. But Tyler was here, and he was now. All my senses soaked him in and reveled. My gaze followed my hands, traveling over his shoulders, my nose teased by the sweet-spicy scent of his cologne, and my mouth tasting mint and pleasure. I could do this all night.

But he ended that kiss far too soon and started taking the foil top off the food container. "Here. Eat this manicotti while it's still warm. And I have a question for you."

I scooped up a bite. I didn't think anything could be as pleasurable as that kiss, but this was a close second. I carried the plate over to the couch and sat down, and Tyler joined me.

"What question?" I asked between bites.

"How would you feel about going to a bonfire tonight? Some friends of mine are having a little beach party."

A beach party? On a Tuesday night? That sounded . . . youthful. I shook my head. "I think I should pass on that one. I don't want to impose."

Tyler's laugh rolled around my apartment. "You can't impose on a bonfire, Evie. Come on. It'll be fun. You can meet some of my friends."

That's kind of what I was afraid of. What would they think of me? What would I think of them?

"If we show up together, your friends will think we're dating." I took a bite of manicotti.

"So?" He smiled, which was very unfair, because those dimples of his were about ten feet deep. One of these times I was going to fall in and not be able to climb back out. Chris Beaumont did not have dimples. I hadn't thought about that at lunch. But I thought about it now.

"So, I'm not exactly sure what we're doing," I said. "But whatever it is, I'd like to keep it mostly private. And anyway, I have a huge day tomorrow. I need to be in bed early."

Actually, what I needed, or at least wanted, was to be in bed right now, with Tyler, but it might seem a little desperate and clingy to suggest he miss a party just to go horizontal with me.

"I'll have you back here and in your bed well before you turn into a pumpkin."

"I don't know, Tyler. I might feel a little awkward hanging out on the beach with your friends. You go ahead, though."

His happy expression dimmed. "No, I'll skip it then. I have a week of night shifts coming up, so honestly, I was hoping to spend some time with you. I was planning to text you about the party when your order came in at the restaurant."

"You were?" That felt far better than it should. It's not as if he was inviting me to some exotic location, after all. It was just a bonfire on the beach. With a bunch of twentysomethings.

"Yes, I was," he said, sliding closer to me on the couch. "Because you promised you'd go out with me, remember?"

I did remember. We'd been naked at the time. Naked and in my bed, which is where I wanted to be right now.

But first things first, I guess.

Right now it looked like I was going to a beach party.

—⋀⋁— —⋀⋁—

The setting was picture-perfect. Warm air, cool sand, cloudless night sky full of stars. I'd expected a dozen or so people sitting around a fire pit, maybe roasting marshmallows, probably drinking beer. The only part I got right was the beer. There was plenty of it, just as there were plenty of people; most of them were in various stages of intoxication. I stopped counting, or trying to remember anyone's name, after the first twenty or so.

Tyler knew everyone, and everyone wanted an introduction to me. I hadn't expected such a frenzy of interest. The guys were clearly appraising while the women, girls, really, were either vivaciously overfriendly or reservedly polite. I felt like the new girl arriving on the first day of senior year. The attention and under-current of speculation was unnerving, but I drank my beer and tried to relax. At least it was dark enough now so they wouldn't see I was ten years older than most of them.

Tyler and I found a spot to sit on a big log not too close to the fire, a little pocket of calm in a storm of loud music and unevenly pitched voices. People were dancing and laughing and swapping favorite stories. Two little blondes in bikinis the size of cocktail napkins walked past us toward the lake. They looked like lingerie models. I automatically sucked in my stomach. I was in decent enough shape, but gravity was a bitch who'd slapped me a few times. And although I might have the surgical skills to make a woman's body look better, even I couldn't lift up an ass the way youth and genetics could. I leaned over to murmur in Tyler's ear, "Some of these girls are a little intimidating."

He looked around. "These girls? Why?"

"They're just so . . . firm."

His burst of laughter turned a few heads. At least the heads that hadn't already been tilted our way. He put his hand on my thigh and gave it a little squeeze. "I wouldn't worry about it," he said.

"You can say that. You're pretty firm too." I realized what I'd said when he laughed even louder. I put my hand over his. "You know what I mean. Your friends are really young."

"Some of them, yeah. But guess how many of them are doctors? None. And besides, they're just girls. I've known most of them all my life. But you're . . . a woman." He sounded smug, as if he had something to do with that.

"I feel like Mrs. Robinson."

"Who?"

"Oh, God." I gulped down the last of my beer. Until tonight, I hadn't really thought about him in his natural habitat, just hanging around with his buddies. I'd let myself think he was usually working, and maybe he was. But even so, these were his peers, with their shaggy hair and board shorts. With their lives entirely open before them, so many options, so much time. I was on the middle of my path, and they were just beginning theirs. I did not fit in with this crowd.

"Hey! Ty!"

A voice called from the other side of the fire, and a lanky blond with buzz-cut hair ambled over. He had beer cans in both hands and seemed to be drinking them both.

Tyler nodded at the cans. "Hey, go easy there, huh?"

"I got it. I got this. It's all good. Who's this?" He nodded at me, and as he turned, the Connelly DNA became obvious. He was a shorter, darker version, but the resemblance was unmistakable. Tyler stood up, pulling me with him.

"Scotty, this is Evie."

Scotty's hooded eyes widened for a second, then he grasped both cans with one hand to reach out and shake mine with his other.

"Evie. Nice to meet you. Heard all about you." He tilted a little to one side and stepped backward. Scotty Connelly was drunk. I shouldn't be surprised. First of all, this was a beach party. Second, he was drinking two beers at once. And third, I'd heard enough about him to know his judgment was deplorable. What kind of man would let his brother get arrested and not have the stones to stand up and do the right thing? I kind of wanted to say that, but I smiled for Tyler's sake and said, "Nice to meet you too."

Scotty listed forward again and turned to his brother. "You going swimming? Let's go swimming."

Tyler glanced at me. "No. We're not staying long. Maybe you should skip it too." He nodded at the beer cans.

Scotty's scowl was exaggerated. "No, man, I'm good. I'm going swimming. It's all good."

"No, it isn't. Sit down. Let me get you a Coke." Tyler put his hand on his brother's shoulder.

"I don't want a Coke," Scotty said but looked around for a seat.

Tyler nudged him down to the log. "Here. Sit with Evie while I find you a Coke."

"Yeah, yeah, OK. How you doing, Evie?" He fell as much as sat on the log.

Tyler looked at me apologetically. "I'll be right back."

"OK. Grab me a Coke too, will you?" No more beer for me. Suddenly the idea of being drunk had lost its appeal.

I sat down next to Scotty, who continued to drink from both cans until one was empty, and he threw it into the fire.

After a minute, he looked at me, his forehead creased in a frown. "So, are you Ty's girlfriend now?"

That was a good, if somewhat abrupt question. "Um, not exactly."

"But you want to get married. Like, right now? Right? And have kids. That's what he said." He punctuated his question with a burp.

"Um, well, I guess, yes, but—"

"He's never had a chance to do his own thing, you know." Scotty leaned forward, put his head between his knees, and swayed a bit.

"I'm not sure what you mean."

His head popped back up. "I mean ever since he dropped out of college he's been working his ass off helping our mom. Trying to keep my sisters in school. Trying to keep me out of jail." In the mercurial way of drunks, he giggled at that and put his head back between his knees.

Dropped out of college? I'd never asked Tyler about school, but realized now I'd secretly hoped he'd had a degree. Maybe that was snobbish of me, but I'd grown up being taught that academic achievement was paramount to success in life.

Scotty burped again and looked at me, his eyes narrowing, his voice slowing down even more, as if each word took concentration. "My big brother likes to fix things, you know? Fix." He moved his hands around as if he was tinkering with something. "Like that bullshit with the Jet Ski. That was my problem. All my problem." He shook his head side to side, like a horse shaking flies from his mane. "But Ty has to fix everything for everybody. So if he thinks you need a husband, that's what he'll try to give you."

I suddenly felt as wobbly as Scotty was. Give me a husband? I wasn't expecting Tyler to step up to that plate. That was ridiculous.

"Scotty, I'm not expecting him to marry me. We're just . . . just spending a little time together."

Scotty's nod was philosophical. "Yeah, that's usually how it starts, but spending time with you has got him all fucked up in the head." He pointed to his temple. "You're pretty as hell, so I get that. But he had plans, and you're messing with them. Plans. My brother will never fix that boat if he's got a wife and babies to support."

Wife and babies to support? Scotty had this all wrong.

"We're not getting married, Scotty. We're not even dating, technically. And nobody supports me except for me. I don't need your brother's help." I kept my voice low but insistent. Not that my words would make much impression. I'd spent enough time in the emergency department to know that trying to communicate with a drunk person was rather pointless.

His body lolled to the side before he righted himself, and he laughed again. "Doesn't matter if you need it. He's just . . . there. Helping. You think I wanted him to take the heat for me in court?

No, sir. Ma'am." Scotty scrubbed a hand over his close-cropped hair, and I felt the first flicker of sympathy for this reckless little brother, but before I could say so, there was Tyler, holding out two cans of Coke.

"What are you two whispering about?"

"Singing your praises, bro. Singing." Scotty took a can and struggled to open it. He finally managed on the third or fourth try. "Did you tell her about Dad's boat, Ty? You should tell her about Dad's boat."

Tyler's sigh was audible. "Not really. Who's driving you home tonight?"

Scotty stood up and looked around, then pointed at the two little blondes in the teeny bikinis. "Them?"

Tyler patted him on the shoulder. "Yeah, that's going to happen. Good luck. Call me if you need a ride. And don't go swimming, OK?"

"Yeah, yeah, yeah." Scotty stumbled away without saying good-bye, and Tyler sat back down, eying me thoughtfully.

"Sorry if my brother was obnoxious. It's a talent he's really cultivated."

"He was fine." That was the universal kind of *fine*. The kind that meant *you'd better ask me again.*

"But?"

I shrugged, hoping I'd sound indifferent even if I didn't *feel* particularly indifferent. I felt unsettled by virtually everything Scotty had said. The college, the boat, the married with children. What the hell had Tyler told him?

"But he said I'm fucking up your head and messing with your plans. What boat is he talking about?"

Tyler wrapped his arm around my waist. "Evie, Scotty is a moron and he talks too much. Don't listen to him."

"What plans?" I prodded. I guess the good news was, at least he had some. But now I was nervous to hear what they were. He scratched his fingers across his jaw. Then he stood up and held out his hand.

"Come on. Let's take a walk."

We strolled down the beach, leaving behind the warmth of the fire and the splashing and laughter of the party. I knew I shouldn't let Scotty's words get under my skin, but they had. They hinted of accusation, as if I was Tyler's biggest problem and not the legal issues he was facing in Scotty's place.

"Have you ever heard that joke about how to make God laugh?" Tyler said after a few minutes. He sounded more contemplative than teasing.

"No. How?"

"You make plans."

I squeezed his hand. "I hadn't pegged you as particularly religious."

He took a drink from the beer he carried. "Twelve years of Catholic school, not that much of it stuck. At any rate, I do make plans, Evie. All the time. Sometimes they work, sometimes they fall through. Then I just make different plans." I sensed an underlying disappointment, though he said this in a casual way, swinging our clasped hands as we walked.

"Like what kind of plans?" I tried to sound casual too. "Like . . . college?"

He looked down at me. "Yep. College was in the plans. What exactly did Scotty tell you?"

"He just mentioned you'd dropped out. Why is that?"

Tyler pointed ahead. "Let's go sit in that lifeguard tower, and I'll tell you my life story, OK?"

We climbed the ladder up to a little five-foot-by-five-foot hut with a built-in bench, three walls, and a roof, a cozy little shelter that hid us from the world. Moonlight splashed against the water, giving us just enough light to see each other and the beach in front of us.

"I had a tennis scholarship to Albion," he said, once we were sitting side by side. He held my hand and toyed with my fingers as he talked. "But I tore my ACL during my junior year and came home for surgery. Funny thing about scholarships. When you can't play the sport, they don't let you keep the money."

"So you couldn't afford to go back?" It was easy to take my education for granted. My parents had paid for medical school, and I'd never wanted for much of anything. Except maybe attention.

"Not really. Plus husband number two was giving my mom a lot of trouble. He'd always made it pretty clear that *her* kids were *her* problem. My older brother had taken off by then; Scotty was acting out. Surprise, surprise. And my sisters were double the bad news, so by the time I came home with a busted knee and needed help, he was done with us. So he left."

Tyler took a drink and paused while I wondered how different my life might have been if either of my parents had married someone I disliked. My father's wives had all been pleasant enough. Indifferent, but pleasant. And my mother hadn't dated at all. She was too busy with her career.

"Him leaving was the best thing for everybody," Tyler continued. "But it was hard on my mom. I didn't feel like I could just pick up and go back to school and let her figure everything out on her own. She's not very . . . dependable. So I got a job at the marina. Remember, my dad used to run a charter boat, so I know my way around. I still go out on runs once in a while, whenever some old friend of my dad's needs an extra set of hands. But I needed something steady, something with some benefits, so that's how I ended up an EMT."

"Do you like being an EMT?" It was a hard job, and not everyone was cut out for the more grueling aspects of it. People tended to love it or hate it.

Tyler nodded. "Yeah, I do. I work with some great people. I like the variety and the pace. I like being useful, helping people."

Scotty's words filtered back to me. *My big brother likes to fix things. He's just there . . . helping.*

Tyler continued, "Being an EMT was never part of my grand master plan, but yeah, I like it."

"So what was the grand master plan?"

He shook his head and gave a rueful chuckle. "If you'd asked me that when I was twenty, I'd have bragged about being a tennis pro. But like I said, plans change. After the knee surgery, I just couldn't get my game back."

I pictured him in the shorts. His injury was a loss for him and for female tennis fans everywhere.

"I'm sorry. That must have been a big disappointment." I felt him shrug next to me.

"Yeah, it was. But I'm sure not the first college athlete who never made it to the big stage. I had a plan B. Sort of."

He paused, taking another quick sip of his beer, then offering it to me.

I shook my head and held up my can of Coke, then twined my other arm around his, pressing a little closer.

"OK, so what was plan B?" I asked.

Another hollow chuckle. "You'll probably laugh if I tell you. It's not a very lucrative plan."

"I won't laugh. Of course I won't."

He rested his head against the back of the bench, staring upward.

"OK. Well, I've told you Scotty always wanted to enlist, right? Be a soldier like our dad? My plan B was to save up enough money and restart his charter fishing company. He told us right before he shipped out that when he got back, we'd go into business together. Connelly and Sons Charter, he said. He loved being out on the water, and I guess I inherited that from him, because I love it too. Really love it. Unfortunately, every time I save up some money and think I'm getting close to making a move, something comes along and screws it up. Like this thing with the Jet Ski and the dock. My dad always used to say, 'Millionaires can afford to have boats, but you'll never make a million dollars by fishing.' And that's the truth. Eight years since I dropped out of college, and I still haven't managed to get that damn boat back in the lake. Right now it's sitting in a barn at my mother's house, and I'm thinking it might be time for a plan C."

Tyler took another long drink. His frustration was evident, though he tried to mask it with another false chuckle, and my heart squeezed tight. I'd had every opportunity available to me, every door opened, while he kept getting slammed by circumstances, mostly created by other people. Wanting to restart his father's business was sweet and nostalgic, and his sense of loss was palpable.

I leaned my head against his shoulder. "I'm sorry it hasn't worked out yet, but it still could, couldn't it? I mean, besides the financing, what things are in your way?" Certainly not me. I was brand-new in his life. But the whisper of Scotty's words repeated in my ear. *He can't do anything if he's got a wife and kids to support.* As if I'd expect him to support me. That was absurd.

Tyler turned and pressed his lips to my forehead in a soft kiss. "Financing is a big enough issue all on its own. Then there's the unpredictability of being successful. The season in Michigan is temporary, so even in the best circumstances, it's only a part-time job. That's why I thought the EMT thing was a good combination. I'm working on some other things right now, though. Things with more potential. More stability."

"Such as?" I wasn't trying to push. I was sincerely interested. Not because I thought I played any role in his future, but because I wanted him to succeed. OK, and because I wanted to push. A little bit.

Tyler slid his arm around behind me. "Just some plans. But I'll tell you about them later. In the meantime"—he pulled me onto his lap—"you're just about to turn into a pumpkin, and I'm not ready to take you home."

"You're not? Why? Do you have plans for me?" The mood in our little lifeguard hut shifted from meaningful discussion to lusty innuendo. I looped my arms around his shoulders, and our concerns about the future melted as the heat from his body warmed me through. His hands were tight around my waist.

"Yes. Big plans. Immediate plans." He moved underneath me, and I laughed at the evidence of that.

"My, what big plans you have."

I thought he'd laugh, but he kissed me instead, and the world disappeared. Breathless, teasing kisses deepened until he started to pull up my shirt. I caught his wrist with my hand.

"Wait. We can't do this here. Let's go back to my place."

He pressed his mouth against my neck and murmured, "Of course we can do this here." He pushed at my shirt again.

"No, we can't. We're outside. Someone will see us."

He tipped back his head. I could make out his face in the glow of the moonlight.

"No one will see us. Everyone is over at the party. Trust me."
His voice was husky but full of mischief.

"But we're outside. I've never . . ." My indoor girl was not
having any of this, but I could tell he was smiling.

"You've never what?"

"I've never fooled around outside," I whispered in his ear.

Laughter shook his whole body. I could tell because I was
sitting on him, and it felt pretty damn good, in spite of the fact
that his humor was at my expense.

"Never? Live a little, Evie. We need to fix that right now."
His effort to remove my shirt increased, and before I could shout
indecent exposure, I was topless. Even my bra had been tossed to
the floor of the little hut.

"Seriously, Tyler. What if someone sees us?" I leaned out to
look around. Thankfully, no one was near us in either direction.
I could see the bonfire far away, but the rest of the beach was
deserted.

"If someone sees us, they'll be very jealous," he said as he pulled
off his own shirt and dropped it on top of mine. His muscles
gleamed in the moonlight.

Live a little? He was right. I should do that.

Starting now.

Chapter 21

THE SISTERS WERE BACK. THIS was getting tedious, but I should have expected it. Hilary stomped into my office already shaking her head, followed by Gabby, who was wearing a lime-green dress and a huge smile. They both sat down, but nobody had brought me coffee this time. I wished they had, because I was exhausted. I'd stayed up with Tyler well past the witching hour and was in surgery by six this morning. Now it was nearly two o'clock in the afternoon, and I was drained.

"I thought we agreed Tyler Connelly was bad news," Hilary said. She was using her mad mom voice. That's how I knew I was in real trouble.

"You may have suggested he was bad news, but I'm not sure we agreed on it." I avoided eye contact. "And anyway, I don't know what you're talking about."

I knew exactly what she was talking about. I should have known I couldn't show up at that bonfire without word getting around. I just didn't think news would spread so fast.

"My cousin said she saw you two at a beach party last night, and then you snuck off into the bushes." Gabby's cheeks were pink with anticipation.

I frowned and started rummaging around in my desk drawers for a granola bar or something. Maybe some food would wake me up. And calm my nerves. I felt an inquisition coming on, and I did not want to face that on an empty stomach. "We did not sneak off into the bushes."

Gabby's face fell, until I added, "We snuck off to a lifeguard tower."

"What?" Hilary's screech was owlish. Mice scurried. I think she may have popped a blood vessel in her eye. "Please start at the beginning, and explain to me how this happened. I thought you had a good time with Chris Beaumont."

"I did. But I tried to get you to cancel that, remember?"

"Yeah, but I didn't realize it was because of Tyler! What are you thinking, Evie?" She'd transitioned to her *I'm-so-disappointed-in-you* mom voice. That one was a drag.

But I was in a damn good mood today, and she wasn't going to change that. Turns out sex outside is delicious, and other than an inconveniently located splinter, my body was still enjoying the memory of it.

"What am I thinking? I'm thinking your advice to me was to have some fun," I said. "Remember? Wasn't that you on my birthday telling me to get a little something-something?"

She rolled her eyes like a preteen drama queen. "Yes, to fun, but why would you waste your time with some doofus like Tyler Connelly when you could have somebody handsome and smart like Chris Beaumont? You said yourself he met most of the requirements on your list. So I don't get it."

"Look," I said, closing the desk drawer. "Don't make a big deal out of this, Hilary. Tyler and I are just . . . ships passing in the night. OK?"

Gabby's phone pinged, and she pulled it from her pocket. "Well, you might try having him dock his dinghy someplace a little more private than a lifeguard tower. This is from a different cousin, and he saw you too."

"Do you have your entire family spying on me?" *God, I wish I had a granola bar.*

Gabby held up the phone and read the message out loud. "Saw hot redhead getting on TC last night. Think it was your boss."

My stomach did the tango from one side of my abdomen to the other. I was a hot redhead?

"Doesn't your family have anything better to do than send you texts about me?"

"Not in this town. Plus I have more bad news. That wasn't a private text. That was Twitter. Hashtag boo-yah-sex-on-the-beach." Gabby giggled.

"Oh, that's just great," Hilary said, crossing her arms and her legs simultaneously. "Your affair with Tyler has gone viral."

"It's not an affair! It's just a . . . it's just . . . well, yeah, I guess it is an affair."

"Yay!" Gabby clapped her hands and tapped her feet on the floor.

"You're doing this on purpose." Hilary's voice rasped with frustration. "You're deliberately choosing the worst possible guy because you know this is going to crash and burn. And you're going to ruin any chance with Chris in the process. You say you want a real, adult relationship, but obviously you don't."

"Why are you getting so mad about this?"

"Because I need you to be part of a couple! I never see you anymore. I can't invite you to any of my dinner parties because you always come alone and it screws up my seating assignments."

"You want me to get married because I'm screwing up your social life?" Something told me there was more to this than table assignments.

Hilary stood up and smoothed the front of her Calvin Klein dress. "Evie, I found you a perfectly acceptable man. If you're going to mess it up on purpose, I can't help you. You're on your own." She sounded more weary than angry, and I found myself wondering why, but she turned and left before I could ask.

Gabby watched her sister leave then swung her gaze back to me. "She'll be all right. She's in some dumb fight with Steve and taking it out on everyone else. She even snapped at Delle. I mean, who does that?"

"What's the fight about?"

In a town of few secrets, Hilary had managed to keep her fears of Steve's infidelity to herself, and I was not going to be the one to spill those adulterous beans.

Gabby fluffed her skirt. "She booked some fancy bed-and-breakfast place for the weekend to surprise him, but then he couldn't go because he had to work. What did she expect? She knows he's working on some big project. Now she just can't let it go."

It looked like Hilary and I were in need of a long-overdue heart-to-heart, like the kind we'd had back in our residency days. I wished I had time right then to perk up her spirits, but I had patients to see. That girl time would have to wait.

"And speaking of not letting go," Gabby said, "why do you say you and Tyler are just ships in the night? Why put an expiration date on it? I mean, maybe he's the one. Maybe he's your Mr. Dr. Evelyn Rhoades."

I swallowed a giggle at the thought of it. "Oh, come on, Gabby. You can't be serious. For starters, he's too young for me. And he . . . um . . ." My mind went blank after that. I knew there were lots of other reasons. Very valid, logical reasons. But they'd scattered like M&M's hitting the floor when the bag rips open. I couldn't retrieve a single one of them.

Gabby leaned forward in her seat. "OK, so he's young, but he'll grow out of that. And in spite of what Steve has told Hilary, everybody else thinks Tyler is a good guy. My cousin Regina, who works at the bank, told me he's been paying his mother's house payments since she lost her job last year. That's a pretty cool thing to do."

I stood up. "Wow. Your cousins are ubiquitous. And I have patients to see." My joke was flip, but my internal reaction was anything but. Tyler Connelly was paying his mother's house payments? Of course he was.

─╴╴ᐯ╲╱ᐯ╴╴─ ─╴╴ᐯ╲╱ᐯ╴╴─

"So I said to myself, 'what's the best way for me to spend this alimony check?' and then it hit me. New boobs. That's going to drive my ex-husband crazy, seeing me strut around town with a couple of C-cups. Serves him right, lying, cheating piece of shit."

My last patient of the day was a beautiful twenty-eight-year-old, fit, trim, full of vitality. She was a perfect candidate for this kind of surgery. Still, I had my job to do.

"Madeline, I think it's important to consider the reasons behind wanting cosmetic surgery. The purpose is to help people develop a healthy self-image and grow their self-esteem. You need to make sure you're doing this for yourself."

"Oh, listen, Dr. Rhoades, this is absolutely for myself. This is the best decision I've ever made. I got rid of one lousy boob of a husband, and now I'm getting two awesome new boobs in his place. I feel fantastic about this. I didn't realize how miserable that slob was making me until he was gone."

Her smile was bright, and I couldn't help but laugh at her enthusiasm.

"OK, then. Let's get you scheduled."

"Great. And do you know any nice single guys?"

I let out an even bigger laugh over that. "You do not want advice from me on that front. Sorry."

I finished with my patient and was packing up my work bag to take home when Hilary shuffled back into my office, shut the door, and slumped down into my chair.

I put my hand on her shoulder and spoke softly. "What's up, Hil? Why the crazy-town lately?"

She looked up, her big brown eyes as sad as Bambi on the first day of hunting season.

"I think Steve is having an affair with the tax-coding whore." And then she burst into tears.

—⎧⎧— —⎧⎧—

Hilary and I sat on the couch at my apartment, sharing a pint of Ben & Jerry's while she filled me in on all of Steve's alleged escapades over the last few weeks. It all sounded pretty circumstantial to me, but I was trying to be supportive.

"They should make a flavor called Cheating Spouse," she said, putting a fist-sized bite into her mouth. "They could fill it with all the stuff women give up eating when they're trying to stay skinny for some jerk of a man. Although I guess that's the definition of all ice cream, isn't it?" Her eyes were still red from thirty minutes of weeping, but at least her sense of humor had begun to resurface.

I took a bite. "I'm still not clear on what you think happened."

"I told you. He's working all these extra hours, he wouldn't go away with me for the weekend, and he's also spending a ton of time at the gym. Who is he getting buffed up for? Not for me."

"How do you know it's not for you? Have you asked him?"

"No. But then there's the fact that he changed his e-mail password. I used to have access and now I don't. What's he hiding?"

"Maybe confidential client information?" It occurred to me then that maybe Steve hadn't told her anything about Tyler at all. Maybe she'd read it in a file. I wasn't certain if that should give me slightly more confidence in him as a lawyer, or less.

Either way, Steve Pullman had a pretty high opinion of himself, but he'd never seemed like the kind of guy who would cheat. And Hilary was a dream wife. If I was going to swing the other way, I'd want to marry her.

"Do you think I should confront him?" Her eyes started to puddle up again.

"Yes, I do. I think rather than driving yourself crazy and getting a tummy tuck that you don't need, you should talk to him. No matter what you find out, it's better than worrying and not knowing."

"I suppose." She took another enormous bite. This was more calories than I'd seen her consume in all of the previous year. "So, what's really up with you and Tyler? I know I haven't been very supportive, but it's only because I don't want to see you waste your time on some deadbeat guy."

I bristled in defense. "He's not a deadbeat. He's the opposite of a deadbeat. Aside from that stupid mishap with the Jet Ski, he's working like crazy to support his family. He's practically Prince Charming."

Hilary quirked an eyebrow.

"OK, maybe a dented, smudgy version of Prince Charming." I took the ice cream container from her.

"I know you, Evie. You are blinded by hormones right now. And even if he's as great as you say, he's not the marrying kind. Not for you. I mean, think about it. You drive a Mercedes. He drives a Jeep POS. He's a college dropout who probably makes thirty-five grand a year if he's lucky, and you make six times that much. Why wouldn't he be hitting on you?"

Irritation shot through me like an electrical shock. "You think he's after my money?"

She reached over and took the ice cream back, taking advantage of my surprise.

"I know that sounds like an insult, and I don't mean it that way. I think he hit on you because you're hot, but the fact that you're about to move into a million-dollar love shack on the beach probably doesn't bother him."

"I hate this conversation. I hate everything about it."

She was trying to bring me down because her own marriage was circling the drain, but I couldn't deny that what she said was valid. Tyler was no stranger to money troubles, and hooking up with me could be the solution to all his problems, but that just didn't seem like him. Not the guy who wouldn't even let me pay for my own drink on the night he'd walked me home.

"You don't know him at all."

Hilary put on her *mother-knows-best* face. "Evie, look. I could be way off base, but I think you panicked a little. You hit thirty-five and jumped on the next guy who came along."

"Oh, and whose fault is that? Yours. You're the one constantly harping on me about finding a man." I hoped I was wearing my *you're-not-the-boss-of-me* face.

"Yes, a *man*. A man with real, honest potential. Hey, I get why Tyler's fun. He's cute and easy and eager to please. That makes you comfortable, and I guess that's fine if it's all you're after, but real relationships have a balance of power. I hate to see you ruin your chance with somebody like Chris just because Tyler got to your panties faster."

I wanted to argue with her, but she was probably right. If I'd met Chris before Tyler, things might feel very differently to me now.

"Why are you so stuck on Chris?" I asked.

"I'm not. I just think he's more worth your time. And as much as I hate to agree with your parents, he's your intellectual and professional equal. Tyler sure isn't."

"You *do* sound like my parents."

"Well, it took them long enough to figure it out, but isn't that what you decided you wanted too?" She handed me the ice cream.

I hated it when she was right. "And didn't you make fun of me for saying that?"

"No, I made fun of you for using that horrible pink website. But listen, do me this favor. Go out with Chris one more time. Give him a fair shot, and if you don't like him, I'll get off your back. You said you had a good time with him, right?"

I did have a good time with Chris. Lunch had been very enjoyable. Not glorious sex in a lifeguard tower kind of enjoyable, but enjoyable enough to give him another chance. I supposed there were worse ways to spend an evening.

Chapter 22

GETTING READY FOR MY DINNER date with Chris Beaumont was like standing in line for an amusement park ride I wasn't sure I wanted to go on. My ambivalence had only grown since telling Hilary I'd see him again. Yes, he'd been funny, and gracious, and appealing at lunch last week, but Tyler was a real factor now, and everything was different.

But nothing was different.

Not really.

I still wanted to get married.

Didn't I? Didn't I still want a family? A grown-up husband with a successful career? Tyler had potential, of course. Someday he'd be a great husband—for someone in his own bracket. But Hilary was right. Everything for us was out of balance. Our ages, finances, education, goals. Taken together, that was too much to overlook. He didn't meet any of my criteria. But Chris did.

So I had to face this date with an open mind.

Just as I'd promised Hilary, I'd give him a fair shot. With any luck, those tiny twinges of attraction I'd felt at lunch would turn into full-fledged throbbing. And if I found myself *wanting* to go to bed with him, it would prove my attraction to Tyler wasn't so special after all. It was just blind biology.

When the doorbell rang at seven sharp, I was ready. It didn't surprise me that Chris was punctual. I wasn't surprised he looked so good in a tan shirt and dark brown pants either.

"Hi. Come on in." I pushed open the door.

His foot hovered for a second over the threshold as Panzer barked and ambled over. He gently sniffed at Chris's hand.

The flinch was ever so subtle, but not so subtle I didn't notice.

"Wow. That's a big dog." He didn't pet him or scratch his head. Panzer still wagged expectantly.

"Go lie down, Panz."

My dog and I had worked out an agreement. I told him what to do, he ignored me, and eventually he would go and lie down. It wasn't that he disobeyed. He was just slow to get to it.

Chris brushed some free-floating fur from those dark brown pants and gave up an awkward laugh. "Sorry. Not a dog person."

"No problem. Oddly enough, I'm not much of a dog person either."

"You're not? Then how'd you end up with that grizzly bear?"

"Saved him from the guillotine."

"Ah," he said.

"Well, I'd invite you in to have a glass of wine, but since Panzer is a third wheel, maybe we should just go to the restaurant."

He laughed again and sounded a little more comfortable. "I think that's a good idea."

We drove to a place about fifteen miles from Bell Harbor, a quaint little bistro type with an arbor-covered patio.

"I hope you like Italian. I guess I should have asked you before we drove out here," he said, pulling his Lexus into the parking spot.

"You're in luck. I love Italian."

"No, you're in luck. Otherwise you'd just have to watch me eat."

I smiled. Chris Beaumont was funny. Gabby had pointed out sense of humor wasn't on my list of husband requirements and should be. Maybe she was right. Although, even if it was, Tyler made me laugh all the time.

Inside we found red-and-white checked tablecloths covering dark wood furniture. The smell of pasta and basil filled the air. My nose twitched. My mouth watered. I hoped the taste lived up to the smell and that the company proved as appetizing as the food.

Chris ordered us a bottle of wine. Both it and the conversation flowed easily, comfortably. As dinner progressed, I decided I did like Chris Beaumont. He was intelligent without seeming pretentious, self-deprecating without being pathetic, and he knew how to tell a good story. He was a pretty good listener too.

"So, you're thirty-six and continue to disappoint your parents by not getting married. What's the holdup?" I asked, tearing a piece of bread off the warm loaf on the table.

"Probably the same holdup you've encountered. Busy with school and then work, plus I guess I never found the right person."

"Define the right person." Did he have a list?

He took his time in answering. "Well, you're familiar with the demands of being in medicine. I guess the right person has to understand that too. I lost a pretty good prospect a few years ago because she couldn't handle my residency schedule. That's partly why I chose dermatology. I like the hours."

"OK. What else? There must be more than just someone willing to accept your schedule."

He tilted his wineglass and watched the liquid moving. "Sure, but I'm not sure I can pinpoint it. Forgive this horrendous analogy, but it's like pornography. I can't describe it, but I know it when I see it."

I swallowed the hunk of bread. "Did you just compare your future wife to pornography?" I couldn't decide if that was clever, funny, or gross. Or all three.

He laughed and set his glass back down. "No, I compared the process of describing something that is intangible and subjective to defining pornography. Totally different thing."

"Yeah, I'm not following."

He crossed his arms on the table. "I've had some very nice girlfriends, and some not very nice girlfriends too. But they were all different. I can't say there was any one trait or characteristic that drew me to them. There was just . . . something."

"No wonder you're not married. You don't have a plan."

His smile grew wide. "A plan? Nope. Just an openness to new relationships. The marriage part will happen when it happens."

"See, that's where men are lucky. No biological clock ticking." Oh, God. Was I really going to talk to him about my ovaries? Just because he was a medical doctor too did not mean he wanted to talk about my ovaries.

"True. Sorry about that. But it sounds like maybe you do have a plan. That's a little bit scary." He didn't look scared. He looked entertained.

"I wouldn't call it a plan so much as a . . . strategy."

"A strategy?"

"I tried a dating service." I wasn't sure why I was telling him this, but like the wine, out it poured. I guess that wasn't any worse than mentioning my aging reproductive organs.

His brows lifted. "A dating service? Really? That's not so unusual these days. Any luck?" His voice was casual but his eyes took on an intensity. If I didn't know better, I might think Chris Beaumont was feeling a little threatened.

I shook my head. "No. Either there was some sort of glitch, or I have terrible taste in men."

"Ah. Lucky for me on so many levels." His smile was wide and confident. Then he laughed, and I wondered what that laugh would sound like if his mouth was just a breath away from the curve of my neck. I wondered what his arms would feel like wrapped around my waist. How it would feel to have my legs tangled up with his. I couldn't be certain, but in that moment, I had the sensation that Chris Beaumont knew his way around a woman's body.

He'd be good in bed, just like he was good at listening, and good at conversation. He was comfortable with himself, and he was comfortable with me. He'd probably make an excellent husband. And we could probably have a nice life. That should be good news, because all signs pointed to him being interested in me too.

And that's what I wanted.

Only it wasn't.

I didn't want Chris Beaumont. I wanted to go find Tyler and bury *my* face against *his* neck and hear *his* laughter in my ear. It didn't make any sense at all. I was letting hormones and emotion trump logic and reason. Hilary was going to be so mad at me. And quite frankly, I was getting mad at myself. What the hell was the matter with me?

We finished dinner, and Chris continued to be charming and engaging, and I tried with all my might to let myself be carried along. I was willing myself to become infatuated. And the harder I tried, the more blocked up I felt.

We talked about our families a little more, and our medical practices. The waitress came and cleared our dishes, and Chris paid the bill.

"So, what now?" he asked. "There's a nice rooftop bar over the old piano factory in Bell Harbor. Feel like a nightcap?"

"The piano factory?"

"It's an old warehouse near the bridge where they used to make—oddly enough—pianos, but it's been converted. Now it has a couple of restaurants, a few shops, and some condos. That's where I live, actually."

He tossed his linen napkin on the table and flicked a crumb off the table, not looking my way as he talked. He was asking me back to his place. He just didn't want to be blatant about it, because Chris Beaumont wasn't the type of guy to be too obvious. No pressure on me to say yes, no foul on him if I said no.

Suddenly, I was cold and clammy all over, as if I'd never been invited to a man's apartment before. As if I'd never said yes. But I had said yes. Recently. I'd said yes to Tyler.

"I think that sounds really nice, Chris. I wish I could, but I have an early patient day tomorrow. Could we make it another time?" My voice was flat and insincere. I should just tell him the truth. That my mind and emotions were tangled up in something else, in some*one* else, and I didn't understand why.

He flicked away another crumb, and his smile seemed forced for the first time all evening. Chris Beaumont might be on to me. "Sure. Rain check, then. You've got my number."

The drive home was quieter. I could chalk it up to us being tired, or full of pasta, or just plain chatted out. I even felt a little queasy and cracked open my window for some fresh air.

"Have you dated many physicians, Chris?" I finally asked, when the silence felt like a burden.

"A couple. Mostly I date pageant queens and swimsuit models." He smiled over at me. "How about you?"

"Astronauts and superheroes, mostly." And EMT-waiters who like dogs and keep their brothers out of jail.

"Ah. Well, I have some very exotic superhero capabilities, but they only work in the dark. Have that drink with me and I can show you."

This guy was smooth. Nice with the old Hail Mary try. Maybe I should have that drink with him. Maybe some perfectly acceptable sex would excise Tyler from my mind. Maybe if Chris Beaumont traveled his way around my body he'd eventually get to my heart.

Probably not, though.

"Another night. OK?" I said.

"Yeah, sure. Of course."

We pulled up in front of my apartment and he got out to open my door. Panzer barked from inside the apartment, and Chris looked toward the windows nervously.

"He's no Cujo. I promise."

Chris nodded and we walked up to the front door. The bugs were all around the lights, and a few tree frogs lingered on the siding waiting for an opportunity to nab a snack.

"Um, I guess I'll say good night out here." Chris pointed at the window where Panzer stood steaming up the glass, and I wondered how anyone could not love that furry face.

"I had a really nice time," he said. "I'd like to see you again."

"That would be nice, Chris."

And it would be.

Nice.

Not fabulous or fantastic or enticing. Just . . . nice. Like root beer floats were nice. And mittens were nice. And cards from your grandmother were nice. I had tried very hard to fall for him tonight. And failed.

"Well, good night." He hesitated for half a second and then abruptly moved in for the kill. No preamble. No breathy hesitation. No long, slow stare. Suddenly he was all up in my mouth, and I squeaked against his lips.

The whole thing went rather awkwardly. Nothing in me stirred, or raced, or thrummed, or heated up. In fact, I felt slightly nauseous and clammy.

Then Chris stepped away, and my imaginary Tyler Connelly stood behind him making a very obscene gesture.

Chapter 23

IT WAS DARK, WELL PAST midnight, when I lurched into the bathroom, getting there just seconds before hurling. Every part of me ached and twitched. Even my skin hurt. I gingerly touched my hand to my forehead, knowing it was impossible to gauge my own temperature but trying to anyway. You'd think being a doctor I'd have a thermometer around somewhere, but I didn't. I guess it didn't really matter if I had a fever. Either way, I felt like shit.

I'd gone straight to bed after Chris dropped me off. I'd tossed and turned and couldn't get comfortable. I'd thought it was just anxiety over my feelings for Tyler. Turns out it was the flu. An easy mistake to make.

I slumped down on the linoleum floor, my head on the bath mat, my energy spent.

I'm not sure how long I lay there. Two minutes. Ten. The space around me was warbly and I couldn't read the bathroom clock. It had to be close to five in the morning, judging from the lightening sky and the damnable chirping of the birds. So irritatingly loud! Their morning joy was an insult to the current near-death drama going on in my bathroom.

Thank God I wasn't due in surgery. I'd never called in sick, but today I was going to have to. I crawled back to bed, literally on my hands and knees. Panzer walked along beside me, pushing his cold, wet nose into my armpit. It would've been funny if it hadn't caused me to seize up in a shivering fit. Using all my reserves, I moved up on the mattress. The sheets felt like sandpaper on my skin.

Panzer whimpered. He needed to go outside, but there was no way I could take him. My stomach rumbled like a cement mixer. This day was going to be ugly.

I lay there for another fifteen minutes, give or take hellish eternity, and finally had the strength to get my phone from the nightstand. I left a message at the office for Gabby, telling her to cancel my appointments. Then I called Tyler.

He answered on the second ring but sounded sleepy.

"Hey," he mumbled. "You're up early."

"Hey. I'm so sorry to wake you up, but I need your help. I'm sick." My head rolled to the side, trapping the phone between the mattress and my cheek. I heard Tyler's muffled response from far away.

"You're sick? What's the matter?"

"I just need you to take Panzer out. Is there any way you could do that?"

"Of course. Do you need anything else? Ginger ale or soup or something?"

"No, just take the dog." I hung up because it was time to puke again.

I made it in time, the determination to not have to clean up after myself propelling me forward. By the time Tyler arrived, I'd managed to put on some pajama pants, realize my period had started, discover I was out of tampons, throw up again, and find some fresh pajama pants. I was in hell.

I must have looked like a zombie when I opened the door.

Tyler literally recoiled when he saw me, and then he chuckled. "You look like you're in a Tim Burton movie."

"Who?"

"Never mind. You just look awful is all. No offense."

I knew that already. And I knew he wasn't trying to be mean, but I started to cry anyway. Big, fat, hot tears. It didn't make him stop chuckling, the bastard.

He put his arm around my waist instead and guided me back to my room. "Let's get you into bed, Morticia."

I lay down and he adjusted the covers. "Are you hot or cold?"

"Yes." My teeth were chattering, but my head was on fire.

He put his hand on my forehead. "You're hot."

"OK."

I think he chuckled again. I'm not sure. Honestly, I wasn't even sure if he was really there. Maybe I was dreaming the whole thing. I could be lying on the bathroom floor right now just hallucinating about him rescuing me.

"I'll take Panzer out and be back in a few minutes, OK?" He leaned over and kissed my forehead. I had the cognizance to hope I hadn't just infected him with Ebola or whatever plague was plaguing me. It was most certainly fatal, whatever the hell it was.

I heard the door open and shut, and then open and shut again. Time must have passed because Panzer came back into my room. Tyler followed right behind him and sat down on the bed. He brushed the hair back from my face.

"Ow."

"So, what's up with you? What's going on?"

I opened my eyes, but focusing on his face required concentration and energy.

"Flu, I guess. Or maybe food poisoning. All I know is I'm

puking up stuff I ate in the third grade. You should get out of here in case I'm contagious. Thanks so much for letting the dog out."

"No problem. I looked in your fridge, though. When are you going to start keeping some food here?"

"Oh, God. Please don't mention food." I rolled to the side and clutched my stomach.

He rubbed my back. "How long have you been feeling like this?"

"Since about three o'clock, I think."

"Oh, that sucks. I'm sorry. But when you start feeling better, you're going to want some soup or Popsicles or something. I have some time now, so I'll run to the store. Can you think of anything that you might need?"

I looked back over my shoulder at him. I was about to cross a boundary no woman ever wanted to cross. "There is, but I just can't ask you."

His smile was patient. "Try me."

"Tampons."

He burst out laughing. The jostling of the mattress made me clutch my gut again. "Stop shaking the bed."

He stood up but leaned over. "OK. What else do you need?"

I rolled to my back and sighed. "Are you really going to go to the store for me?"

"Yeah."

"OK. Then I need toilet paper too. I'm completely out and I used Kleenex this morning before realizing they were mentholated. Oh my God, I cannot tell you what went through my mind when that eucalyptus kicked in."

He laughed again. "You are a hot mess."

I was. "You're finding a lot of humor in my misfortune."

"I'm sorry, Ev. It's lousy that you're so miserable. It makes me sad." He tried to frown.

"I can tell by the way you're laughing."

"It's just to mask the pain."

I might have laughed too, except I was already running on fumes, and I didn't have the energy. I closed my eyes instead, wondering who had put sand under my lids.

Tyler readjusted my covers one more time. "I'll be back as soon as I can. I'll get you some water first, though. I'd make you tea but you don't have any."

I must have fallen asleep, because I woke up when Panzer barked. A glass of water was on my nightstand next to a bottle of ibuprofen, and I could hear sounds coming from the kitchen. Tyler's footsteps. Bags rustling, cupboards clicking shut, items clanking against the refrigerator shelf. My gosh, how much stuff did he buy?

Panzer strolled in with a new toy. Good thing, because I was low on underwear. I slowly rolled over and reached for the water with trembling hands.

Tyler came into my bedroom with two big paper grocery sacks. "Hey. How are you feeling?"

I paused to answer, mostly because my mouth was on a thirty-second delay from my brain. "I don't want to be too hasty, but I think I might be feeling better. What's in the bags?"

He flipped them over and emptied the contents onto the foot of the bed. Boxes upon boxes tumbled out. Boxes of every brand, style, and absorbency variation of tampon.

He looked up at me. "Do you have any idea how many choices there were? Pearl, and super pearl, and gentle glide, and infinity. Seriously? Infinity? And let me tell you, when a dude at the grocery store asks a woman what kind she likes, he is escorted out by security."

Laughter was a painful reminder that all the muscles in my abdomen were sore from puking, but I laughed anyway and covered my face with my hands. "Oh, no. You didn't."

He smiled, and seeing those dimples started to cheer me up.

"No. I didn't, but I thought about it. I just bought one of every kind instead. I even got you some stuff with wings. Not sure what those are for. This was not at all awkward in the checkout line either, by the way."

Awkward, and so sweet of him to do this for me, I started to cry. Again. And he started to laugh. Again.

He came around to the side of the bed to hug me, but my skin still hurt, and my bones felt like they'd been stretched apart.

"Evie, Evie, Evie, you poor thing."

"Please don't touch me. I'll be OK."

"I didn't mean to make you cry."

"I know." I sniffled like a four-year-old, with the little gasping hiccups. "Did you get Popsicles?"

He nodded. "I did. Do you want one?"

"No, but thanks. I'll get one later." I reached for a mentholated tissue to wipe my nose. "Do you suppose you could come by around dinnertime and take Panzer out again? It's OK if you can't."

"No problem. I have to take off now, though, unless you need something. I've got stuff to do. Want these in the bathroom?" He pointed to the three dozen variations of feminine hygiene products.

"Yes, please. And thanks. You're my knight in shining armor."

"Oh, if only slaying dragons were as easy as buying tampons." He scooped all the boxes back into the bag and left, calling out a good-bye. As the door slammed and the sound reverberated, something my mother had said echoed along with it.

*Your father needed to take care of someone, and I never let him do
that for me. I should have given him a dragon to slay once in a while.*

My doorbell rang at four thirty. I was still subhuman but had managed a shower, even eaten a few Popsicles, but mostly I still felt
like shit. I hated having Tyler see me like this, but nothing could
be worse than the crypt keeper he'd seen this morning.

I opened the door. It wasn't him. It was Gabby. She looked
nearly as bad as I felt. Pale skin, red-rimmed eyes. She was wearing
a beige trench coat. I didn't even know she owned anything beige.
She had a canvas shopping bag over her arm, along with her purse.

"Hi," I said.

"Hi. I know you're sick, but I brought you some fruit and
some soup. Can I come in?"

I moved to the side so she could step past me. "Sure, but I don't
recommend touching anything. Whatever I have is vile and nasty."

"So is Mike." She practically flung her stuff onto my card table.

"So is Mike? What does that mean?"

Gabby sniffled and pressed a fist to her mouth. "Mike and I
broke up!" And then she threw herself into my illness-weakened
arms and burst into tears. What the hell was going on with these
sisters? Their relationships were falling apart. And these were the
two I had helping me?

"He says he doesn't want to get married," Gabby said around
her hiccups. "And he doesn't want to live with me either. He's
moving out. How did this happen, Evie?"

I had no idea how it happened and even less of an idea how
to help.

"Have you talked to Hilary?"

"I can't talk to Hilary. She's got something crazy going on with Steve. Has she talked to you about that? It's more than just that weekend he wouldn't go away with her, but she's being very evasive with me."

"Um, not really. But what happened with you and Mike?"

She backed up a little and wiped the tears from her face with her fingertips. "I don't know exactly."

She plopped down on the couch, and I sat next to her. Tyler was going to arrive any minute to walk the dog. I didn't want her here when he showed up, but it seemed there was no avoiding it. I couldn't kick her out when she needed a shoulder to cry on. Even if my shoulders were weak and achy with fever.

"I was showing Mike your husband-hunting list. You know? The one we used for Bell Harbor Singles." She pulled the old crumpled piece of paper from her pocket and handed it back to me. I tossed it toward the coffee table but it bounced to the floor. I should pick that up before the dog ate it, but the idea of leaning over seemed like far too much exertion.

"And Mike says making a list is a pretty smart way to do things. And then we started talking about marriage in general, and then us specifically. And I said I was ready whenever he was." She blinked back another round of tears, and her lips trembled. "But then he got all huffy and said he wasn't ready. So then I got kind of huffy too, and I said, 'Mike, we've been together for four years. How long will it take for you to decide?'"

Her expression was despondent, as if she'd not only lost her puppy, but also discovered it had been eaten by werewolves.

She took a big breath and blew it out in a single puff. "So then Mike says. 'I guess I have decided. I think we should break up.'"

She didn't even try to hold the tears back then. It was Niagara Falls all down her face.

In all the months I'd been living in Bell Harbor, I'd never met Mike. He wasn't remotely social, and I had the sneaking suspicion that Gabby was far better off without him, but telling her that probably wouldn't make her feel better.

You've just wasted four years of your life. But at least the bum is gone now.

"I'm really sorry, sweetie. I wish I could fix this." I moved closer and patted her back. Panzer must have heard the familiar sound. He wandered out from the bedroom to investigate who was horning in on his patting action.

Gabby hiccupped. "Oh, is that your dog?"

She held out her arms. He ambled into her embrace and she hugged him tight, crying all over his fur. He was probably better at comforting her than any trite phrase I might come up with, so I let them have their moment. Plus I didn't want to breathe on her. I got up and walked into the kitchen to get her a glass of water, and me more ibuprofen. My body still ached, and I was starting to get the chills again.

The front door rattled, and then opened. Tyler's eyes lit up when he spotted me upright.

"Hey, you look better than you did this morning. Here's another box of tampons. They fell out in my car." He walked in and set them on the counter, kissing me on the cheek as he passed.

Gabby lifted her face from Panzer's fur and hiccupped again.

Tyler looked toward the noise, and red stained his cheeks as he saw her sitting on the sofa. "I didn't realize you had company."

Gabby's red-rimmed eyes blinked. She gave him a lopsided smile and a wave. "Hi, Tyler. Remember me? Gabby Linton."

He waved back. "I remember. Bell Harbor High. How are you?"

She sniffled and hiccupped. "F-f-fine."

Tyler's gaze slammed back to me. "OK, well. Good to see you. Evie, I'll just take Panzer for a walk and be back in about half an hour. OK?"

He'd already dealt with me crying today. Apparently Gabby's tears exceeded his quota. He grabbed the leash from the hook next to the front door where it hung.

"Panzer. Let's go."

Gabby lifted her arms and the dog trotted over to the door. They were gone faster than a couple of Olympic sprinters.

I looked over at Gabby. She stood up, wiped away a tear, and hiccupped. "Ships passing in the night, huh? That seemed pretty cozy."

"He's just helping me with the dog because I have the flu. Remember? I have the flu? You do not want to catch this." I didn't want her to think she should leave, except that I was desperate for her to leave. I couldn't help her with Mike, not in my present condition. She needed to go find her sister or one of her eight hundred cousins.

She walked into the kitchen and picked up the box of tampons. "This is pretty personal, if you ask me."

I gently took the box back. "Yes, it's personal. So could you please keep this between us, Gabby? What's going on with Tyler and me is private."

She nodded and wiped away another errant tear. "Can I at least tell Delle?"

"No."

She heaved a big sigh. "Well, I'm glad you have something nice going on. I have to go home to my lonely apartment. Do you have any D-cell batteries?"

Chapter 24

GABBY HAD GONE BY THE time Tyler came back with the dog, and I'm not sure who was more relieved, me, him, or the exhausted Panzer.

"You've been gone quite a while," I said as he hung up the leash.

Panzer walked into the bedroom. I heard him snuffle around until he settled into his Sherpa mattress with a happy, doggy sigh.

"We were in the mood for a long walk." Tyler peeked surreptitiously at the sofa. "Is Gabby still here?"

"No, it's just us. Thanks for buying me this soup. Do you want some?"

He came into the kitchen where I was heating it up in a pot.

"I can do that for you. Go sit down." He pointed to the couch. I was tired enough not to argue.

"What was she so upset about?" he asked as he opened my cupboard and pulled out two bowls.

"Her boyfriend dumped her. Mike somebody."

"Oh, yeah. Mike Peabody. Guy's an asshole. She's better off."

"That's kind of what I wanted to tell her, but it's too soon." I moved the pillows on the sofa and thought about lying down. Ten minutes of standing up in the kitchen had done me in.

Tyler brought the soup over to the coffee table and handed me a spoon. Then he brought me something blue with ice in it.

"What's this?"

"Gatorade."

How *adorável* was that? He was giving me electrolytes because I had puked. No one had taken care of me during an illness since I was a child. And even then, my parents had mostly told me to just suck it up. I smiled over at him as he sat down, a rush of warmth and affection cascading over me.

"What?" He looked around.

"I bet you are a really good EMT," I said softly.

He blushed and adjusted a sofa pillow behind his back. "Because I carried the soup all the way from the kitchen to the table?"

I felt my eyes start to puddle again, and my voice warbled. "No, because you rushed over here as soon as I called, and you took out the dog, and you bought me all that food and feminine hygiene products, and then here you are again, bringing me soup." My voice hitched, and I let a tear slip out, and Tyler burst out laughing.

He wrapped his arm around my shoulders and pulled me in for a hug. "Oh my God, Evelyn, this flu has made you a crazy person."

I shook my head. "No, it hasn't. I'm just being honest." More tears slipped out. OK, maybe I was feeling a little crazy. Whatever had taken over my body was obviously messing with my composure too.

He patted my back. "OK. OK. If you say so. Now eat your soup."

I obediently took a bite. "I really bet you are, though. How long have you been on the job?"

He looked upward, as if tabulating. "Almost three years, but I was the FNG for almost half that."

"FNG?"

"Fucking new guy." His half smile suggested being FNG wasn't all that bad. "That's your title until they hire somebody new. The FNG gets stuck with all the crap jobs no one else wants to do. You know, extra cleaning and stocking the rig and such. And you're the target of every prank."

He sounded like a pretty good sport about it, and that didn't surprise me. "What kind of pranks?"

He pondered some more, apparently scrolling through memories. "The usual stuff. Rubber snake under your pillow in the call room, KY jelly on the Hail Mary bars in the back of the ambulance when you're on practice rides, stuff like that. The driver gets points for every body part he can make you smack."

"That's not very nice." Not nice at all, but it did sound funny.

"Well, when you're pulling a double or triple shift, those kinds of things can really lighten the mood. I've been picking up a lot of those lately to earn some extra cash."

Additional call shifts to earn extra money? Just like me. Only I took call so I could pay a decorator to load up my plush new house with plush new furniture, and Tyler was doing it so Scotty wouldn't go to jail and his mother's place wouldn't go into foreclosure. I suddenly felt overly indulgent. I worked hard to have the things I had, but Tyler worked hard too. It didn't seem fair. It made my eyes water again, and if I kept on crying, he was going to sedate me.

"What's your craziest patient story?" I asked instead, hoping to elevate my own mood. Everyone in medicine has crazy patient stories. Boob-flashing Dody Baker was at the top of my list.

"So many to choose from," he answered. "But let's see. I guess the most recent is this one old guy who keeps calling us for the same issue. We keep telling him he's fine, but every time we have to take him into the ED anyway." He set his soup bowl down on the table and ran a hand through his hair.

"What's his issue?"

"Beets."

"Beets?"

"Yeah, apparently he keeps stealing beets from his neighbor's garden and they turn his pee bright pink. He thinks he's dying. But no, it's just the beets. Last time we were there, the neighbor came running after him with a rake. Funniest thing ever, watching two eighty-year-old dudes trying to wrestle each other to the ground."

He laughed at the memory, and I wondered if either of those old guys had noticed how debilitatingly attractive Tyler's dimples were.

Probably not.

"Dr. Andrews said if we brought him into her ED again she'd hit him with a rake herself."

I sat up a little straighter. "Dr. Andrews?" Suddenly I wondered if this Dr. Andrews had noticed the dimples.

"Yeah, over at Trinity Health. That's where we usually go since our area is east of Bell Harbor. I don't make it to your hospital very often. Unless I'm a patient, I guess."

That explained why I'd never seen him in the department before. If I had, I'd have remembered. And so would most of the nurses.

"I didn't realize you were over near Trinity. How are you managing that? Working all those hours for MedPro and then serving at Jasper's? Aren't you exhausted?"

He shrugged. "I guess I'm used to it." He took the empty bowl from my hands and set it next to his. Then he leaned back and stretched his arm over the back of the sofa toward me. "Honestly, the hardest part isn't being busy. I like that. But lately I find myself . . . wondering . . . what you're up to. Where you are. Wishing we were in the same place."

His voice had gone all warm and bedroomy. He must be catching my fever, because he couldn't be gazing at me with such infatuation given how horrendous I looked. I was wearing gray sweats and an extra-large, extra-faded Northwestern T-shirt. But his expression said I was beautiful. Yes, he was definitely catching my delusional fever.

"I like you, Evie. A lot. That's probably obvious, but in case there was any doubt, I thought you should know." He didn't seem to be teasing. Or febrile.

I reached out my hand, entwining my fingers with his. "I like you too. In case it isn't obvious."

He looked down for a second, just long enough for me to realize he was winding up for something big, then his eyes were back on me. Bright. Sincere.

"It's not obvious," he said.

"It isn't? Do you think I fool around in lifeguard huts all the time?" I was trying to make a joke, but he didn't go for it. His jaw set, twin lines creased between his furrowed brows.

"Look, I know you're doing this computer dating thing. And I can't really ask you not to because I know you've got this husband and kids thing on your mind. I also happen to know you went out with some other guy last night. Word travels. But Evie, I'm not big on sharing."

"Sharing?" Suddenly this conversation had taken a turn toward Seriousville.

Tyler clutched my hand a little tighter. "I'm not the type to make promises I can't keep, and I don't know what's in store for me in the next year or so, but the bottom line is, if you sleep with some other guy, I'm out of here."

—⁄⁄⁄⁄— —⁄⁄⁄⁄—

"He said that?" Gabby's face lit up as if she held a winning lottery ticket. "How utterly romantic."

"How is that romantic? He's just marking his territory," Hilary answered.

The two of them were in my office once again. I really needed to get a lock for that door, because as much as I enjoyed these daily dissections of my love life, we'd been discussing this latest milestone in my nonmarital status for almost half an hour, and it was nearly time for me to start seeing patients.

Gabby waved her sister's words away with a flick of her fingers. "Not marking his territory. He's saying she's important to him. So what did you say back?"

"I said OK. And then I went to bed alone because I still had the flu." It wasn't quite as romantic as Gabby seemed to think, and yet . . . it was. Because he *wasn't* just marking his territory. He *was* saying I was important to him. And I hadn't been important to someone in a very long time.

"So that's it then?" Hilary wiped lipstick off the lid of her coffee cup and didn't look at me. "No more husband hunting? No more *I think I want a baby*? You're just going to have playtime with Tyler and forget the rest? That's kind of rash, don't you think?"

This news was proving hard for Hilary, and I wasn't entirely sure why.

"It's not so much that I'm done husband hunting. I'm just postponing all the marriage and baby stuff for a while. I mean, I've waited this long, so what's a few more months? Or even a year? I mean, who knows how long this thing with Tyler will last?"

She looked at me now, her eyes sad. "But what if it does last? Let's say you guys are still together in five years. All that time, will you be longing for children? I know this is pure selfishness on my part, but I'd like your kids to play with my kids. And I don't know about you, but forty and pregnant doesn't sound that fun to me."

"Forty in general doesn't sound that fun," Gabby murmured, earning her a glare from both of us. Hilary and I were a lot closer to the F-word than she was. The F-word being, in this case of course, *forty.*

"Honestly, Hil, at the moment, I don't have an answer for that. This is new territory for me. All I agreed to was to not fool around with anybody else, which was pretty easy to do because I don't want to fool around with anybody else."

Gabby raised her hand. "Can I have Chris Beaumont, then? I'm available." She was bouncing back nicely from her breakup with Mike. She'd even colored her hair a warm honey brown. No more pink tips. If nothing else good came from her heartbreak, at least it was good for her hair.

The copy of Chris's credentialing paperwork was still sitting somewhere on my desk. I rummaged around for it and then handed it to her. "Be my guest. He likes Italian food and he's afraid of dogs. But he's very nice."

I felt a minuscule twinge of remorse as she took the papers, not because I wanted to see him again, but because there'd been no good reason to not fall for him. Except, as Hilary had so eloquently put it, Tyler had gotten to my panties first. I had to believe it was more than that. I had to hope it was more than that.

"I feel like I should call Chris, though," I said, gazing at them. "You know, just to say, 'um, I won't be calling you.' What's the protocol here?" I was completely out of my element in this scenario.

I didn't want to be rude, or presumptuous. I could just wait to see if he called me.

Hilary shook her head. "Don't look at me. I haven't been on a date since I got married. Not sure I can say the same for Steve, of course."

I stole a glance at Gabby and she rolled her eyes. We'd both been pushing Hilary to confront her husband, but so far she wasn't moving on it. She'd taken, instead, to muttering disparaging comments and didn't want to hear our advice.

"So, are you taking Tyler to your parents' wedding? That's coming up pretty soon, isn't it?" Gabby asked, redirecting the conversation.

"Oh, thank you for reminding me. I have to call my mother about my dress." I grabbed a piece of paper and scribbled myself a note. "I haven't asked him. That's a big step, introducing him to my parents and taking him to the wedding. They're not going to be thrilled with his background."

"Or his future?" Hilary muttered. The snark was starting to show a little around her roots today, but I decided to ignore it for the sake of civility. She'd snap out of this funk. I knew she would.

"In the meantime," I said instead, "we're going to Jasper and Beth Baker's baby shower because Jasper invited him, and sometime after that I should be able to move into my house. I haven't been inside since the painting started. My decorator said he wants to do a big reveal."

"Didn't you tell me your decorator is Fontaine Baker?" Gabby asked.

I nodded.

"OK, well, let's hope when he said *big reveal*, he meant your house."

Chapter 25

DES McKNIGHT'S HOUSE WAS LOCATED just a few miles from my new place, on a quaint little street full of picturesque houses with meticulous landscaping. Tyler had arrived at my apartment in plenty of time, but I'd stalled getting ready until he'd finally insisted we leave. We were headed to the baby shower for Jasper and his wife. A baby shower that was sure to be full of hospital staff, a multitude of Gabby and Hilary's cousins, and heaven only knew who else.

I should be fine. All of this should be fine. But the truth was, I was nervous as hell about showing up at this party together. I couldn't imagine there was anyone in Bell Harbor who hadn't heard about us. They'd certainly all discussed my private life before. But being whispered about was one thing. Boldly walking down the red carpet together for all the Bell Harbor paparazzi to see was something else entirely. I was about to make a public declaration. Yes, I was officially *involved* with Tyler Connelly. His ultimatum two weeks ago had pretty much cemented that.

We stood on the brick front step until the door to Dr. McKnight's house swung open and a pretty little girl smiled at us from the other side. "Are you here for the baby's shower?"

"We are. Is this the right place?" Tyler said.

"Yep." She nodded, sending a wave of curls around her face. "I'm Paige. Come on in."

I spotted Mrs. Baker immediately. Of course she'd be here. She was the soon-to-be grandmother. That frothy, pale pink chiffon number she wore looked like it had been whipped up on a cotton candy machine. Des was next to her, holding a tiny baby. My heart gave a little hop, skip, and a flutter. Not because he was handsome, although he was, but because of the sweet bundle in his arms. A precious little junior McKnight all snuggled up right in the crook of his elbow. The pretty brunette next to him must be his wife, Sadie. Fontaine had mentioned her several times, saying they worked together when she wasn't—as he put it—*breeding*. She was holding a baby too.

Twins. Oh, yes, of course. Dody had told me about the twins. My uterus clanged a Tibetan gong, sending out a particularly hollow sound in the cavern of my abdomen. I'd squashed most thoughts of babies lately, knowing that the SS *Fertility* was sailing off without me. Since I'd halted my husband hunt, that illusory dream of motherhood was fading away. With some effort on my part.

"Evelyn, hello and salutations!" Fontaine fluttered over, wearing white pants and a lavender-striped shirt. "How are you, darling?" He air kissed me on both cheeks and then stepped back.

"Oh! And how are *you*?" His voice went husky and dropped two octaves when he spotted my date. Tyler did look particularly fine tonight in a blue linen shirt and nice khaki pants. My decorator obviously approved.

"Fontaine, this is Tyler."

"Yes, I know." He smiled psychopathically, then leaned in and whispered, "Coo-coo cachou, you lucky little cougar."

Oh, no. I was a cougar?

Fontaine grabbed my wrist and pulled me farther inside. "Do you love what I've done here? Tell me you love it. My partner and I decorate for parties too. You'll have to let us plan the first soiree in your new house. Your furniture will arrive any day now, by the way. When do you want to move in?"

"As soon as possible. I've been waiting forever."

"I know, baby girl. I'm getting things done as fast as I can, but artistry like mine can't be rushed."

We took another step forward and I saw . . . pink. Lots and lots and lots of pink. Bright pink vases, crimson flowers, cherry-colored balloons, even maroon lampshades. It was like the Cat in the Hat had thrown up in here.

"It's remarkable," I said.

"Oh, my stars! Is that my Dr. Rhoades?" An operatic voice cut through the mellow din of conversation as Mrs. Baker turned and saw me. She moved like a fluffy tornado, coming straight at us.

"Oh, it's simply delightful to see you, dear. Fontaine, darling, get Dr. Rhoades and her escort some of that yummy punch."

"It's lovely to see you, Mrs. Baker."

"Pish-posh, call me Dody. We don't stand on ceremony around here. And who is this delectable fellow?" She flipped open a plastic fan and began to wave it at her flushed cheeks while her gaze roved over Tyler like he was a centerfold.

He smiled his flirty smile, which was to say, his normal, everyday smile. "So nice to meet you. I'm Tyler."

"Oh, why yes. Of course you are. I've seen you at Jasper's restaurant. You're very handsome."

He blushed adorably. She and I nearly swooned in unison.

"Thank you, Mrs. Baker," he said.

"Oh, gracious. You can call me Dody. Or you can call me, maybe." She held an imaginary telephone to her ear and Tyler laughed.

Fontaine came back with glasses of cherry-red punch. I almost asked if it was a strawberry dickery but immediately saw that conversation veering off in an irreparable direction. I took a sip and looked around instead. There must be close to thirty people here, chatting and laughing, and most of them were holding children at some stage of development. Tiny ones, bigger ones, wiggly ones, sleeping ones.

"You didn't tell me this party was BYOB," I whispered to Tyler.

"BYOB?"

"Bring your own baby?" I suddenly felt empty-handed and out of place. I should have anticipated a Bell Harbor baby shower would be full of babies.

"Have you met my niece? Come and meet my niece." Dody pulled on my arm, almost causing me to spill the punch as we worked our way through the crowd. Tyler tagged along behind us, an amused smile on his face.

If Des McKnight was surprised to see me there, he didn't show it. His wife gave me a warm smile too.

"Look who I found." Dody's singsong voice reverberated through the crowd. She'd make a good auctioneer.

"Evelyn, hi," Des said. "Tyler. Glad you guys could make it."

Tyler blushed as they shook hands, and I realized they'd met once before under less auspicious circumstances, when Des treated him in the ED. Des's manner gave no indication he was thinking of that, though.

"Thanks for having us," Tyler answered.

"Our pleasure." Des leaned forward. "Please understand our house is not usually this pink. Fontaine had a theme, and there is no going against him."

Sadie nodded in agreement. "My cousin was in charge of decorations. Don't judge us."

Don't judge them? I nodded and smiled, feeling more at ease already. I slipped my arm through Tyler's. "I've worked with Fontaine. He is tenacious with his motifs. He thinks my bedroom should look like a sultan's harem."

"Well,"—Dody stepped up closer—"I think it looks simply delightful in here. Lots of pink for a baby girl. They're having a girl, don't you know? Another girl, just like these two beauties." She pointed at the twins. "This one is Shelby, and that one is Sydney." Then she scratched her head furiously. "Oh, or is that one Sydney and this one Shelby? I can never tell."

"I've got Shelby," Des answered. Then he looked at his wife. "Right?"

She slapped him playfully. "Stop pretending like you can't tell them apart. It's not funny."

His glance at me told me he wasn't kidding. I hid my smile behind a sip of punch.

"Dr. Rhoades is going to do my surgery soon, but of course you already knew that. Aren't I lucky to have the best surgeon in all of Bell Harbor?"

"That's very kind of you to say, Dody, but I'm sure there are lots of great surgeons in town," I said.

"Oh, pish-posh. I know how good you are. You needn't be so self-defecating."

Des burst out laughing and Sadie gasped. I heard Tyler chuckling beside me.

"I think you meant self-deprecating, Mom," Fontaine called from over her shoulder.

"I do? Why? What did I say? Oh my goodness! That damned Anita Parker is stealing all the thin mints. Anita!"

Dody bustled away, on a mission. A whirlwind in pink fabric.

"So how old are these two?" Tyler asked, reaching out and squeezing a pudgy baby foot.

"Almost five weeks. And still completely nocturnal," Sadie answered.

"I imagine with twins your hands are pretty full." He nodded as if he knew anything at all about babies.

"They are," she said, "but our older kids help."

Des chuckled. "*Help* being relative. The other day our son wanted to put the babies in his wagon and pull them around behind his bike. I stopped that joyride in the nick of time."

Sadie laughed. "Where was I?"

"Taking a shower. It all went down pretty fast."

She pressed a hand against her face in false chagrin. "I'm just not as sharp as I used to be. Two babies now is a lot more exhausting than when my other kids were little. That extra ten years makes a big difference."

Ten extra years. She looked to be about my age. See? I was already too old for a baby.

"Was that your daughter who opened the door?" Tyler asked.

Des nodded. "That's Paige. She's as good a hostess as Fontaine. And speaking of proper hosting, I have to admit this punch is awful. Tyler, want a beer? Come out on the deck with me and we can escape all this pink. I think Jasper is hiding there already."

"It's too warm outside for the baby," Sadie said, tipping her head at the mini-McKnight he was holding.

Des looked over at me, optimistically. "Would you like to hold her?"

Would I like to hold her? The baby? Would I like to hold the baby? That's what he said, but what I heard was *Would you like to jump from this plane with no parachute?*

"Um, sure."

I held out my arms as if he were passing me a porcupine. His motions were casual, comfortable. Clearly he trusted my ability, even if I didn't. But oh, good heavens. What if I dropped her? What if she cried? What if everyone could tell I hadn't touched one of these things since my internship rotation in pediatrics? That had been a mighty long time ago.

Still, a rush of warmth spread through me as I took her, repositioning her in my arms. She stared up at me, the picture of intense tranquility. As if she knew how untutored I was and was silently promising to make this easy.

And easy it was. So easy. Maternal feelings fluttered around my heart like springtime butterflies, tickling just a little. She was beautiful, and squeezable, and warm. She smelled like baby powder and pure heaven.

My uterus howled like a lonely coyote.

Damn it. I did want one of these. I really, really did.

My glance up at Tyler was involuntary.

He looked at the baby.

And then at me.

Then he looked at the baby again as if she were Pandora's box about to burst open. And maybe she was.

His cheeks flamed red.

Des thumped him on the back and gave an amused huff of laughter. "You need a beer." It wasn't a question, and Tyler turned and walked away without making eye contact with me again.

"That's Shelby you've got," Sadie said when the men had left us. "This one is Sydney. Do you have kids?"

The inevitable burn of cheek flush stole over my face as I began to stammer. "Me? No. Not yet. I mean, well, no. I think I may have missed my chance on that."

She expertly flipped the baby up to her shoulder and patted its back gently. "Why?"

"I'm thirty-five." I held up my left hand. "No husband. Kind of want one in the picture."

"Understandable. You've got time, though. I'm thirty-six, and it all went fine with these two."

"Yeah, I don't see it happening." I looked out toward the deck where the men were standing around a keg, laughing and talking with animated gestures. Tyler looked visibly more relaxed than he had when staring at me with the baby in my arms. I understood his reaction. He knew I wanted one of these. I hadn't made it a secret. And it wasn't my fault that holding her had set off a primordial chemical reaction in every maternal cell in my body, making me sway like a human metronome.

Sadie's gaze followed mine, and we were silent for a moment. When she turned back to me, her smile was sincere. "You know, there aren't many secrets in this town."

That made me laugh. "Yes, I've learned that."

"Yeah. Well, for what it's worth, everyone in this town thinks Tyler is a pretty good guy."

He was. There was no denying it. Tyler Connelly was a good guy.

"Yes, he is," I finally answered. "And very sweet. He's also eight years younger than me. What does this town say about that?"

Sadie's smile broadened. "They say you're probably having a really good time."

Chapter 26

THE SUN WAS SETTING OVER the lake, and a soft haze in the air gave our surroundings a muted, mystical quality. Or it could just be that I'd had two glasses of wine at dinner. Maybe it was my vision that was hazy. Either way, it was a warm, beautiful evening as Tyler and I strolled aimlessly along the docks of the Bell Harbor marina. He pointed out various boats, discussing aspects of each one as if they were old friends. He'd grown up at this place, and every captain we encountered as we walked had a smile and a wave for him.

"That's the *Mongoose*, a thirty-eight-foot Tiara Express," Tyler told me, pointing at a white boat with a navy-blue top. "Lots of extras on that one. And next to that is the *Fishing Fortress*. It's a Sea Ray Express. Most of these have dual big-block Chevy engines."

He said this as if it meant something significant. It didn't. Not to me. But I didn't have the heart to tell him all these boats looked pretty much identical, or that I didn't know a big-block engine from a big block of cheese. Mostly I was just enjoying his enthusiasm and silently wishing he could somehow manage to restart his father's charter business.

"Did you know it's bad luck to take bananas on a fishing boat?" he said as we got to the end of one dock and turned around to go back.

"No. Why?"

He shrugged. "Not sure exactly, but it has something to do with the old trading days. I guess tarantulas would hide in the banana crates, and once you had a couple of mating tarantulas on your boat, it was hard to get rid of them."

My whole body shuddered. "Oh, that's awful. I'd have to jump overboard if I was on a boat full of big, hairy, badass spiders."

Tyler laughed and wrapped an arm around my shoulders. "I had no idea you were afraid of spiders."

"I'm not, usually, but being surrounded by an extended family of scary tarantulas is different. Ugh!" I shuddered again but saw a perfect opening. "By the way, speaking of being surrounded by scary families, how would you feel about coming to my parents' wedding?"

Tyler laughed. "Nice segue. Are they venomous?"

"Tarantulas or my family?"

"Either or."

"No to both, but I do have a sneaking suspicion my mother's personality has been supplanted by an alien. Long story. But the good news is, my family isn't that big and they're all sick to death of coming to my dad's weddings, so it should be a pretty small crowd. It's next weekend."

"Next weekend?"

We stopped walking and stood face-to-face. I think I'd surprised him.

"Next Friday I'm working, but I can see about switching with someone, I guess."

"I'm sorry I didn't mention it sooner. I've blocked the whole thing from my mind, and now suddenly here it is. It's in Bloomfield Hills, so we'd have to spend the night on Saturday."

One eyebrow rose. "I assume I'd have my own room. I'm not the type to shack up with a woman at some cheesy motel."

"It will be a very nice hotel."

He smiled. I tingled.

"In that case, I will happily shack up with you."

"Excellent." I rose up on my toes and kissed him. Then we started walking again, our hands linked and swinging.

"So, there is something I've been meaning to talk to you about," Tyler said. "Something I've been thinking about for a while. I'm not sure what you'll think."

He suddenly seemed a little pensive, and so suddenly, so was I. Any conversation that started with *there's something I've been meaning to tell you* usually ended up with someone being very upset. Or someone being very surprised. Or someone being very broken up with.

"OK. Let's hear it." We stopped walking again and I braced for impact.

He gazed out over the water for a minute, his lips pressed into a line until he finally started talking. "I've been a basic EMT for almost three years now. I've advanced as far as I can without additional classroom training. So . . ." He took a big breath and blew out the last part, "So, I'm thinking about enrolling in an advanced paramedic training course."

"Paramedic training?" I'm sure I sounded surprised, not by what he'd said, but purely from relief over the absence of bad news. This was great news.

He nodded and started rapid-fire talking, as if he'd been saving up all these words for just the right moment and they were finally pushing their way out, like a seed breaking through the soil in time-lapse photography.

"Yeah, there's an excellent program in Grand Rapids that I could do and still keep my job at MedPro. I'd have to keep working, obviously. I need the money. But those shifts would count as part of my internship. It'll take a while, a year and a half in the classroom, plus

I'll have to take an anatomy and physiology course. But I think I can do it. Tuition is about nine grand, which I don't exactly have right now, but I'm working on that."

He ran out of breath and stared at me expectantly, watching for my reaction.

A paramedic?

"Tyler, I love that idea."

Relief flooded his features. "You do? You don't think it's too . . . you know, simplistic?"

"Simplistic?"

"Yes. Simplistic. Evelyn, you've made it all the way through medical school and residency. Being a paramedic doesn't really compare to that."

The fact that he would think that hurt my feelings, but I guess I could see his point. Still, I wish that thought had never occurred to him.

"It's not a contest, Tyler. Plus being a paramedic is an incredibly hard job. We both know that. I've been in the emergency department enough times when those guys show up to know there's nothing easy about what they do. Plus I think you'll be fantastic. You're a natural."

He smiled, and I could practically feel the tension easing out of him. We started walking again. "How do you figure that?" he asked.

"You just are. You take care of people constantly. Look how wonderful you were with me when I had the flu."

His laughter echoed over the water. "Buying you Popsicles because you puked is hardly proof I'll make a good paramedic. You're being overly generous."

"I'm not. And I don't understand why you didn't tell me this sooner."

"I don't know. I guess I wanted to look into it a little more before saying anything. I've been in such a holding pattern waiting for the legal stuff to get resolved. The delay with that is frustrating."

I felt his elation bottling back up. I leaned closer against him as we headed back toward the buildings of the marina.

"What does your lawyer say about the delay?" I was tempted to mention that his lawyer was my best friend's husband who may or may not be having an affair, but it didn't seem relevant. And either way, Steve might be an asshole, but I had no idea if he was a good attorney.

"My lawyer says be patient. Scotty turns twenty-one next week, so at least the assault charges will be sealed forever. That's a huge load off everyone's mind, and he's heading off to Fort Jackson at the end of the month."

I lowered my voice. "Does your lawyer know it was Scotty who stole the Jet Ski?"

Tyler's gaze darted around but no one was close enough to hear us. "He didn't steal it. He borrowed it. And no. There was no point in telling him that."

"I disagree. I think you should tell him everything. It might influence things in your favor." Like the amount of crap Steve believed about Tyler and his family. And the amount of crap Hilary believed too.

"This is all being handled, Evie. OK? I appreciate your concern, but you don't need to worry about it."

His phone chimed in his pocket and he pulled it out. His face went pale as his eyes moved over the text message. His voice rasped with frustration. "Here's something to worry about, though. God damn it. My mother's been caught by security at Mason's Jewelry Store. Shoplifting."

Chapter 27

"ARE YOU SURE YOU DON'T want me to take you home first?" Tyler asked as we jumped into his Jeep to head over to the jewelry store where his mother was waiting, presumably in handcuffs.

"No, it'll take you twenty extra minutes to drop me off. Just take me with you."

His jaw was set, muscles clenched. I couldn't blame him. This was hardly the best way for me to meet his mother. I could tell he was angry with her, and worried and embarrassed. My mother had a great many flaws, but at least shoplifting wasn't one of them. This was awkward.

The drive was silent but mercifully short, and within minutes we pulled up in front of the store.

Tyler started to say something, then just shook his head. "You may as well come with me."

Dark-haired Tilly Mason, owner of Mason's Jewelry Store, met us at the front door. The closed sign had been turned around and most of the lights were off.

"Come on in, Ty," she said as if this wasn't the first time she'd been through this scenario.

"Hi, Tilly. Thanks for not calling the police. I owe you one."

She shut the door behind us and locked it. "No, now we're even. Thanks for saving my dad's life when he had that heart attack. But Ty, she can't take stuff from here."

We walked to the back of the store as he answered, "I know. I'll talk to her. And the next time she comes in, you just shoo her right back on out."

Tilly opened another door leading to a small room, and there sat a pretty, petite woman who looked very much like her son, with blonde hair and bright blue eyes. She looked tired, though. Not just from fatigue or from the situation. Her forehead had the kind of creases that come from life nipping at you constantly. I could do something about those lines if she wanted me to, but it would be rude to mention it, under the circumstances.

She stood up from the chair and reached out to hug him. "Oh, Ty. Thanks for coming. I would've called Carl, but, well, it's his bowling night, so I called you instead."

She stepped back before reaching him and sniffled into a damp tissue. She'd seen me, and her eyes went round in surprise.

"Oh, goodness. My goodness. You must be Dr. Rhoades." She reached up to smooth her disheveled hair and blushed furiously. She straightened her blouse and threw a glare at Tyler, as if to say *how could you?*

"It's nice to meet you, Mrs. . . ." My voice trailed off as I realized I didn't know her last name. She'd had two more husbands since marrying Tyler's dad. Plus, all things considered, it wasn't really that nice to meet her. Not under these conditions. I gave her a clumsy little wave and retreated into the corner of the room.

Tyler stepped closer to her, his voice stern. "Mom, the next time you try to lift something from Mason's store, Tilly is going to press charges. You're lucky as hell she didn't call the cops on you this time. What were you thinking?"

His mother's lips trembled. "I wanted to get Scotty something nice for his birthday."

"By stealing it?"

"I wasn't stealing it. I was carrying it closer to the window because the light was better over there. If that heartless Tilly Mason didn't keep this place so dark, I wouldn't have had to do that. A mole couldn't shop in here, it's so dark."

She peered around Tyler toward the store owner, her pointed glance an empty accusation.

Tilly crossed her arms. "That watch was in your purse, Donna. I'm not an idiot. And I'm not heartless either. If I was, you'd be in jail. Maybe I should call the police now instead of letting Ty take you home with a warning."

He held up his hands between the two women. "OK, OK. Let's get this settled as amicably as possible." He turned to Tilly. "I really appreciate you being discreet about this, Tilly. I'll take my mom now and we'll get out of here. How does that sound?"

"That sounds good." She leaned around him and shook a finger at his mother. "But don't you come back in here, Donna."

Tyler's mother sniffed. "As if I would. And don't you shake a finger at me, young lady, or I'll tell your mother how you used to smoke outside St. Aloysius instead of going in to mass."

Tilly leaned forward, shaking her finger again. "You tell her that and I'll tell everyone you drank communion wine every Wednesday when you were supposed to be dusting the altar."

I pressed my lips tight. I shouldn't be laughing. Shoplifting was a criminal offense and clearly this wasn't the first occurrence, but the image of Tyler's mother with a feather duster in one hand and a gold chalice of cheap red wine was damn funny. And any minute now these two ladies were going to start a slap-fest.

"OK!" Tyler said again. He grasped his mother by the wrist. "Come on. Let's go."

"Where's my purse?" Donna asked as she trotted along behind him, and I followed.

"It's on the counter near the front door," Tilly said. "So you won't have a chance to stuff anything else in there."

"Thanks again, Tilly," Tyler said gruffly as we walked out the door.

I walked past her and gave up another awkward wave. "I'm Evelyn, by the way. Nice to meet you."

She smiled for the first time since we'd arrived. "Evelyn? You mean Bonfire Evelyn? Nice to meet you too."

─⋀⋀─ ─⋀⋀─

The ride from Mason's Jewelry Store to Tyler's mother's house was oppressively silent until Donna finally said, "Well, Dr. Rhoades, what you must think. But all I can say is I never in my life stole anything. That Tilly Mason drinks, you know."

"Mom. Stop talking," Tyler said. "Just. Stop. Talking. Please."

His mother's house was a beige-and-brown structure designed to look like a Swiss chalet set against a backdrop of huge white pine trees. An old, rusted, mint-green pickup truck sat next to the garage. It looked like it had been parked there for a decade and a half. Tall beach grass grew up all around it.

Gravel crunched under our feet as we got out and three black Labrador retrievers bounded into the yard, greeting us with effusive barking. Carl was on the front porch smoking a cigarette. His face was in shadows, but the blue terry cloth robe was a dead giveaway. I could just barely see it in the fading light.

"Donna, where've you been?" he called out. "I had Salisbury

steak and tater tots all heated up and ready to go for dinner. It was my night to cook." He stepped forward. "Oh, well, hiya, Doc."

He ground out his cigarette on the porch railing as we walked up the steps. My peripheral vision caught Tyler shaking his head.

"Carl, you remember Evelyn?"

I held out my hand. "Nice to see you, Carl."

He caught up my fingers and kissed the back of them, arching a white eyebrow. "A pleasure, Evelyn. Welcome to our home. May I interest you in a sloe gin fizz?"

"Carl, Mom has something to tell you," Tyler said, taking my hand from his stepfather's grasp and leading me inside. "It's eighty degrees out here. Aren't you a little bit hot in that bathrobe?"

Carl smoothed the lapel. "I love this robe. You mother gave me this robe. Didn't you, Donna?" He leaned over and kissed her cheek. "But where've you been?"

"Shopping," she said noncommittally.

We walked inside. The house was a mishmash of tacky collectibles; tarnished framed photos; old, tattered magazines; mismatched furniture; and dead animals. Fortunately, those animals were just heads mounted on the walls. A few deer, a fox, a rabbit, and what looked to be your average, garden-variety billy goat.

"What do you think of my hunting trophies, Red?" Carl asked, walking in behind us and lighting up another cigarette.

"Did I mention Carl's a taxidermist?" Tyler whispered in my ear. "These are all things he's shot himself."

A goat? Where was the sport in killing a goat?

We walked through the cluttered family room into a yellow kitchen with gold-flecked linoleum. A scarred-up pine table filled the center of the room. Everything here was frayed and well used.

"I'm sorry about the state of the house, Dr. Rhoades. We've been meaning to clean it," his mother said.

"Oh, it looks fine," I assured her. "Please call me Evie."

Her smile was strained, and she reached up to pat her hair again.

Carl stepped around us. "Move over, Donna. I was just about to make the doc here a sloe gin fizz. You want one, Ty?"

"No drinks for us, Carl. We just came to drop Mom off. She had a little episode at Mason's Jewelry Store."

Carl turned and looked at his wife, and then at Tyler. "What kind of episode?"

"She tried to steal a watch."

Donna stepped forward and put her arm on Carl's. "It was for Scotty. He's leaving soon and it's his birthday, so I wanted to get him something special."

Carl's eyebrows lifted, his lips pursed. "A watch, huh? You never stole me a watch."

"I think you're missing the point here, Carl," Tyler said, visibly deflating.

His stepfather shrugged. "No, no. I get it. She's not supposed to steal stuff. Donna, Donna, Donna. Shame on you. Do you want a sloe gin fizz?"

He turned back to the counter and started pulling bottles from the cupboard.

Tyler sighed and looked at me, his gaze vulnerable and raw. I smiled back, because what else could I do? I reached out and took his hand. I wanted to kiss him then and tell him this was all fine. Hilary might be right. His family was a fucking train wreck. But they were his family, and so that was that. It didn't change my opinion of him, and I wanted him to know.

"I'd like a sloe gin fizz," I said. "And then can you show me your dad's boat?"

About half an hour later, we made our way down a dirt path to an ancient barn. Tyler unlatched the door, and the hinges creaked as it swung open. It smelled like straw and old wood inside, and off to the left I could see what looked like a workbench covered in tools.

An old red pickup truck was right in the front, but what caught my eye was what was behind it.

"There it is. A thirty-eight-foot Bertram. Sturdy as hell. You could take that thing out into the ocean if you wanted to."

I walked over and touched the hull. "Why does it seem so much bigger than those boats we saw at the marina?"

Tyler's smile was indulgent. "Because it's not half underwater?"

"Oh. Yeah. For a smart girl, I guess I should have figured that out myself. So what would it take to get this in the water?"

He looked at me as if that question was just as silly as the first. "A trailer?"

My hands landed on my hips. "I mean money-wise, smartass. How much would it cost to start up your dad's charter company again?"

He looked down. "Oh, that. A lot. Probably forty or fifty grand by the time I made repairs to the boat and got it tricked out with fish-finding sonar and rods and such. Plus there's the monthly rent on the slip out at the marina, and the gas for this thing is diesel, so that's not cheap either. It all adds up pretty fast. At least keeping it here is free."

"It's such a shame to have it just sitting here."

He stepped closer and put his hands on my hips, right over my own hands. "Well," he said, "it is just sitting here. But it does have a comfy berth. Should we check it out?"

I looked around this dusty old barn and looped my arms around his shoulders. "Tempting. But I have a better idea. Let's go to my place and I'll float your boat over there."

Chapter 28

MOVING DAY! AT LAST IT was moving day. Tyler was there, helping me pack up the last of my few meager belongings.

"I've never seen so many scraps of paper," he said as he walked around with a trash bag.

"Careful what you throw away. Some of those little scraps are very important," I answered.

"Then maybe you should keep them in a file or something instead of all over the place," he teased.

"Why do you think I'm moving? So I have a house with file drawers."

He continued picking up my litter as I folded the last of my clothes and put them into a suitcase to drive across town. The moving men had arrived to put my few pieces of furniture into a truck. In just a few hours they had all the bits and pieces of my life loaded into the back of a U-Haul.

I looked around my apartment and felt a little bereft once everything was gone. I stared at the now-barren room. Tyler had grown quiet, standing beside me.

He'd been quiet for the last hour or so. A subtle change in mood and I wasn't sure why.

"Are you all right?" I asked, looping my elbow around his.

He paused. "I'm good. Just tired. And I have someplace I need to be for a couple of hours this afternoon. Remember?"

"I remember. Where are you going again?" He hadn't told me. In fact, he'd been downright evasive, and I didn't want to push him to tell me, except that I was pushing him to tell me. Because, yes, I did want to know.

"Just some stuff for my brother before he leaves town. I'll catch up with you later. You're all done here, it looks like." He nodded at the empty room.

"Yep," I said. "I guess this is good-bye. I had some good times here. *We* had some good times here." I squeezed his arm, but he kept looking forward.

"Yep." He turned and walked out the door. "We did. But it looks like it's time for good-bye."

-\/\/- -\/\/-

"All that crap goes straight down into the basement, girlfriend. No composite woods up here on the main floor," Fontaine said as I instructed the movers to take my bedroom dresser up to one of the guest rooms.

"This dresser needs to go in one of the extra bedrooms," I said.

Fontaine shook his head emphatically. "I've got it all under control. Trust me." He pointed to the basement steps, and the moving men obeyed. Fontaine might be little, but he was also scrappy and bossy.

"The last time you said *trust me*, I ended up with purple walls in my bedroom."

"It's Vineyard Passion and it looks fa-fa-fabulous. Wait until you see it with the bedding. You're going to love it. When does the boy toy get here? Isn't he supposed to be helping today?"

"He helped this morning, but he had someplace he needed to be. He'll show up later. We're having dinner tonight in my fancy shmancy new kitchen."

"Sounds delish," Fontaine answered, winking suggestively.

While the moving men unloaded my apparently unacceptable belongings, Fontaine took me on a tour of my own house. I had to give him credit. The place looked amazing, with funky new light fixtures; quirky, whimsical pieces of art; and freshly painted walls in bold but appealing hues. He was pretty good at this decorating thing.

Even my bedroom was gorgeous, with walls a deep, deep purple, so dark it was nearly brown. Apparently that's what Vineyard Passion looked like. The new furniture was rustic antiqued white, and all the accent pieces and bedding were in muted shades of charcoal and silver. The pillows on the bed were plumped up and happy, just waiting for a lusty couple to roll around on them.

Tyler was going to enjoy this room. I bet he'd enjoy my six-headed, sexy-time shower too.

This house was a dream. My dream. It represented the culmination of all my years of hard work. All those late nights on call and early morning rounds. All the cramming for medical school exams and long days of surgery. I'd earned this nice, big, beautiful house. It was my trophy. And I wanted to share it with Tyler.

I wanted to share dinner with him too. Gabby had dropped off all the fixings for a spaghetti bonanza, but it was nearly seven o'clock before I heard his Jeep in the driveway. Panzer walked around, trying to figure out where to stand for his barking frenzy.

I opened the front door before Tyler could knock. "Hey, it's about time. Where've you been?" Panzer licked his hand and got an ear scratching for his troubles.

Tyler hesitated on the porch, finally slipping off his shoes before I latched on to his hand and pulled him into the foyer. "Well, come on. Let me show you around."

"Sorry I'm so late. My stuff today took longer than I expected and, well, you know." He shrugged, and I moved in to hug him. The embrace was perfunctory. Whatever had started to bother him this morning was still riding on his shoulders. My joy dimmed.

"What's wrong?"

"Nothing. Just a long day." He wrapped his arms a little tighter around my middle.

"Want to tell me about it?" I asked.

He shook his head. "No, I want you to make me forget about it."

I smiled and squeezed. "I think I can do that. I made you dinner. I practically cooked."

"You did?" I should have been insulted by his level of surprise, but other than the soup I'd heated after having the flu, he'd never seen me so much as toast a bagel.

"Yes, I cooked. Sort of. I used two separate burners on the stove. I think that counts." I stepped back and led him toward the kitchen. "Do you want the tour first, or should we eat? I'll have to reheat everything anyway since I thought you'd be here half an hour ago."

"I told you I had stuff to do." The snap in his voice startled me.

"I know you did. It's not a problem. I just meant that the pasta cooled off."

"I'm sorry." A fauxpology. He sure didn't *sound* sorry. He was still grouchy, and I still had no idea why.

"Maybe we should eat first."

He looked around, turning slowly in a circle. "I think we should. Something tells me the tour might last awhile."

"Sit down then. Want some wine? Gabby brought over a wonderful cabernet." I was already on my second glass, celebrating the warming of my home.

"Do you have any just regular beer?" He said it as if wine was simply too pretentious.

"Sure." I opened the refrigerator, glad I'd thought to pick up a few necessities, like beer, coffee, and toilet paper. As long as we had those three things, we could be set for quite a while.

I handed him the bottle and he popped off the top.

Dinner was quieter than I'd hoped. He wasn't very chatty, but the food and drinks seemed to rub away some of the sharp points of his mood. He took my hand at the end of the meal.

"This was nice of you. Thanks."

"You're welcome. Thanks for all your help."

He shrugged. "I didn't do anything."

"Of course you did. You helped me pack, and helped load the truck, and you've helped me with the dog, and—"

"OK. OK." He nearly smiled.

I pulled his hand up to my lips and kissed it. "So, what's on your mind, Tyler? You're not yourself. Don't you like the house?"

"I do, Evie. Of course I do. Even what little I've seen is amazing."

"OK, then why so blue?"

The sun was dipping beneath the edge of the lake, turning gold shadows to gray, and I could hear the waves rolling in over the sand, just as I'd longed for. This moment should be sublime. It should be perfect, but it was all wrong. Tyler was in a funk, and it tarnished everything.

He pulled his hand from mine and stood up, picking up our plates and carrying them to the kitchen sink. "I went to see my lawyer today."

My very full stomach fell hard to the ground. "You did? Why didn't you tell me that's where you were going?"

He turned around and leaned against the counter, frowning again. "I don't know. I just didn't want to." That hurt my feelings. I knew he was embarrassed by all of this, but he shouldn't be. And he should certainly trust me enough by now that he could tell me. "So what happened?"

His sigh was big and came from deep within. He crossed his arms and looked down at the floor. "I have to pay for the dock, which I expected. But this guy is saying I also messed up his shoreline and he had to have a landscaper come out to fix it. It's bullshit, of course. I didn't mess up his shore. That's not the worst of it, though." He paused, and unease brushed over me, like a spider on my skin.

"I was hoping the Jet Ski could be repaired," Tyler continued. "I didn't think there was much damage, but according to the owner, it has to be replaced, not repaired. That means more out of my pocket."

"How much will a replacement cost?"

His jaw clenched for a second before he answered. "About five grand. So right now, with the dock and the yard and the legal fees, I'm looking at close to fourteen thousand and some change."

"Fourteen thousand dollars?"

"Yep. But if I try to fight it, if we go to court and I lose, I could end up with a misdemeanor on my record. And I didn't realize this before, but Evie, if I get a misdemeanor, I'd lose my job at MedPro."

My heart squeezed tight. "Oh, Tyler. That's terrible. I'm so sorry."

I stood up and walked over to him. He didn't look at me. He just stared down at the floor. My beautiful, site-finished mahogany floor that probably cost as much as this settlement.

"Does your brother know this?" I asked.

He shook his head, slow. Sad. He finally looked up at me. "No, and I'm not going to tell him. He doesn't have the money either, Evie. Plus he leaves for Fort Jackson in two days. It's done. I'll pay it. It just means I have to put off the paramedic training for a while. A long while."

"Why? Couldn't you finance that?" I reached out and touched his arm, but he moved away from the sink, and away from me. He walked into my professionally decorated living room with my real suede sofa that probably cost more than his Jeep.

"Why? Because I'm already making payments on my medical bills. And my mom needs some help with her mortgage. So even if I could set up a payment plan for tuition, I can't take on another bill. Not right now. I'll just have to keep working until I'm caught up."

My bright, shiny house suddenly felt ostentatious, and my joy over it insensitive. I was angry at Scotty for putting him in this predicament, and I was angry at Hilary's husband for not being a better lawyer. None of this was fair. Tyler was wrong to get on that Jet Ski after drinking. There was no question about that, but he'd been trying to help when all of this spiraled downward.

I walked over to where he stood. He practically crackled with tension, and I didn't know how to help. Ironic, really. Making people feel better about themselves was a big part of my job, but fixing how they looked on the outside was far easier than fixing how they felt on the inside. This situation was fraught with elements I had little control over, and neither did Tyler. All I knew was that I wanted very much to cheer him up. Or at least distract him for a while. I slid my hands down his arms and took hold of his hands. "I wish I could fix this for you."

"I know. It'll be fine. I'll figure it out."

He would. He always did.

"I have something upstairs that might make you feel better. Do you want to see it?"

He sighed, and a tiny, resistant curve curled the edges of his mouth. "What is it?"

"A shower. A six-headed steam shower. Maybe if we went in there I could wash all your cares away."

For a minute, I thought he was going to turn me down. My skin flushed with rejection, even if he did have a perfectly valid reason for it. But then he smiled. It didn't quite reach his eyes, but I hoped with a little effort I could make him happier.

"I have a lot of cares," he said finally. "They're sticking to me everywhere. You'll have to be very, very thorough with your washing."

"I will. I promise."

It wasn't much to offer. A short-term fix, but I was desperate to wipe that sad look away from his beautifully symmetrical face. I led him up the stairs and watched his wary reaction to the rest of the house, as if he was suspicious of it. But once inside the bathroom, he let out a little chuckle of resignation. I turned on the water.

"Time to steam things up," I said as I unbuttoned the first button of his shirt.

"Your bathroom is bigger than my apartment," he said.

"It's a little excessive. I realize that, but I just couldn't resist this party shower." I undid another button, and another as we talked. "Guess what I thought of when I first went through this house with my Realtor."

"How many surgeries you'd have to do to pay for it?"

I shook my head and pushed his shirt off his shoulders. "Nope." I kissed his neck, and he gave up a throaty little sound.

"How many gallons of water you'd use?"

I smiled. He knew me. "Yes, actually, but right after that, guess what I thought of." I ran my hands into his hair and tilted his head down so he'd look at me. "I thought about you being in there. In that shower."

"No you didn't." His lips curved a bit more. Some of the tension eased. His hands reached up to my waist, inching up under the hem of my shirt. "You're just saying that to make me feel good," he said.

"No I'm not." I raised up on my tiptoes.

His fingers traced a line around the waistband of my shorts, sending shivers into every cell of my body. Making him feel better was going to make me feel better too.

"You looked at this house months ago. You hardly even knew me then," he said, pulling my shirt up and off and dropping it to the floor.

"I know. That's why the idea of you in there was so . . . tantalizing."

"Tantalizing." Now he smiled. "That's a nice four-dollar word. I don't think I've ever been called that before." He deftly unclasped my bra, and I let it slide off my arms.

Bare skin to bare skin, I pressed against him. And I liked it.

"I bet you've been called that lots of times. Just never to your face. So, see? With me you get full disclosure. I'll always be honest with you."

I was teasing, trying to lighten his mood, seduce him. But something in his expression shifted again, and the humor drifted away. He looked down at me as if he wanted to say something more, but instead he kissed me, hard, stealing my breath, and suddenly I couldn't tell if it was the shower steaming the room or the heat between us. Our shorts went the way of our shirts, and then we were in the luxury shower, water streaming down, pulses speeding up. I'd wanted to take our time in there, enjoy the suds and novelty, but he was intense, insistent, focused. There was a tension there, still. A heaviness he'd carried since he'd walked in my door tonight. I wanted nothing more from this moment than to take that weight away. And so I let him set the pace. He knew my body by now, and I knew his. He knew what I liked, and I responded, giving as I received.

But when all was said and done, I couldn't shake the feeling that he was still so sad.

We fell into my bed sometime later, and Tyler pulled me close against his side, like a shield. I pressed my hand against his cheek and turned his head toward me.

"Hey. You know I'm crazy about you, right?" I said, following it up with a kiss on his shoulder. "No matter what."

He kissed my temple and sighed. "I know. I'm crazy about you too. No matter what."

Chapter 29

I DREAMT THERE WERE SEVEN dwarves working on my house. They each had their own pickax, and they were tap-tap-tapping against my bedroom door. Then I woke up and realized the tapping was real. Fontaine must have let himself in to hang pictures. It was nice to know how little my opinion about such things mattered to him.

Tyler was still sound asleep beside me, his face pressed into the pillow. I'd loved him once more, during the night. Slow and sweet and full of comfort.

In the shower, it had seemed as if he'd been trying to prove a point or deny the frustration that lingered from bad news, but when the moon was high and we could hear the waves rolling over the sand, we'd taken our time. Defenses down. In bed we were always equal.

I slipped into the bathroom and freshened up, pulling on a pair of shorts and a T-shirt. Then I went downstairs to tell Fontaine to find something else to do until Tyler woke up. I found him in my home office surrounded by thick black picture frames.

"Good morning, sunshine!" Fontaine sang out.

"Shhh!" I pressed a finger to my lips. "Tyler's sleeping."

Fontaine arched a dark brow. "Oh, is he now? Wore him out, you little minx? It's always the quiet redheads who are such vixens."

"That's me," I said. "Anyway, what are you hanging?"

"Your diplomas, girlfriend. You left a pile of them on your desk, and I couldn't resist. I had them matted and framed so they all match. Do you love it? Tell me you love it, because I'm about to hang them regardless."

He'd arranged them in a geometric pattern on the floor. All my years of hard work represented on card stock, now turned into lovely artwork. I'd moved those darned certificates from shitty apartment to shitty apartment, hardly having a place to stash them, much less a decent spot to hang them. Now that wall of frames would be a constant, lovely reminder of all I had accomplished. I blinked back a tiny little tear.

"I do love it, Fontaine. It's wonderful. Can I help you?"

"Can you hammer a nail?" He had the nerve to look speculative.

"I'm pretty good with my hands, Fontaine."

"All right. But be careful. I've marked the spots on the walls." He handed me the hammer and nail. "See the dot? Put it right there."

Tyler found us fifteen minutes later, just as I hung the very last diploma, and I realized in my excitement over this project I'd forgotten about trying to be quiet.

"Hey, good morning. I'm sorry if I woke you up." I leaned over to kiss his unshaven cheek. He didn't react, almost as if I hadn't touched him at all.

"What's this?" he asked.

"Those are all of your girlfriend's diplomas. Can you imagine?" Fontaine said. "This is one smart woman. She's practically a Rhodes scholar. Oh, hey! Get it? A Rhodes scholar? I am hilarious!" Fontaine snapped his fingers while I stared at Tyler staring at that wall.

And it didn't take a Rhodes scholar to see that all those framed certificates were making him see something he hadn't before. The breadth of my education.

"That's awesome, Evelyn," he said. "It looks great."

Evelyn? Since when did he call me Evelyn?

"Listen, I have to run, though. I have to take care of some stuff for Carl. And I work the next few nights. I'll give you a call."

His smile was so patently false he looked as if he'd had a bad injection of Botox.

"Tyler." I wasn't sure what I was going to follow that up with, but it didn't matter anyway, because he was already out the door.

"And then he just took off?" Gabby asked.

She and Hilary were at my new house for dinner. Now that I had a kitchen, I wanted to show everyone I knew how to use it. And so we ordered pizza.

"Yeah. He's taking this court thing hard." I stole a glance at Hilary.

She shrugged and set down her virtually uneaten slice of pizza. "Well, what do you want me to say? Steve's a shitty lawyer. He's a shitty lawyer and a shitty husband."

Gabby shook her head.

"Hilary, you have to talk to him about this. *Acho que você é fazendo tempestade em copo d'água.*"

"What?" Hilary snapped.

Gabby patted her hand. "I said you're making a mountain out of a molehill."

"You think him cheating on me is a molehill?" Hilary sat up straight, pushing her plate away.

"No, I think assuming your husband is cheating on you because he's had lunch with a coworker is the molehill. Talk to him. Get it out in the open. You've been festering over this for months, and it's time to deal with it."

Hilary slumped back down. "I know. I know. I will. This weekend. I will for sure. I guess, it's just . . . what if I'm right? What if he is cheating on me and I find out that all this time we've been living a lie? What if this whole relationship was a sham?"

I wrapped my arm around her shoulder. "Of course it's not a sham. That's crazy talk, Hilary. You guys have had a great marriage. And I think it's still great."

She sniffled and picked up a napkin to dab her nose. "It's just . . . I followed the rules and married the kind of guy we always talked about. I had a list too, remember, Evie? I wanted to marry a smart, professional guy, and so I did. But all he does is work, and talk about work. And work some more. And I see you all aglow with Tyler this and Tyler that. It makes me think I made the wrong choice. Maybe I should have fallen for some unconventional guy like you did. Then I'd be happy now."

Suddenly her recent behavior started to make some sense. Just as I'd felt betrayed by my mother when she fell back in love with my father, Hilary was feeling betrayed because I hadn't followed the rules we'd set up back in our residency days. And she had.

"Hilary, honey, your relationship with Steve has nothing to do with my relationship with Tyler. We are different kinds of women, and we have different taste in men. Plus you seem to be forgetting the wonderful eight years you've had with your husband. I know you're worried about things now, but I'm certain you're going to work this out. If my parents can get back together, you guys certainly can. You just need to have a little faith."

Have a little faith? Where had that come from? And since when did I start doling out marital advice? But deep down, I knew I was right.

"She's right." Gabby confirmed it. "Talk to him so we can all move on. And speaking of moving on, back to Tyler and the settlement. What do you think he'll do now?"

Hilary sniffled.

"Are you OK?" I asked her.

She nodded. "We can talk about Tyler now. Even I'm sick of talking about me and Steve."

I stared at her, just to make sure she meant it, but she seemed sincere. Then I turned back to Gabby. "I don't know what Tyler's going to do. Keep working and paying his bills, I guess. I just wish I could make it go away. It's so unfair. He didn't even—"

Hilary and Gabby both looked at me with interest. "He didn't even what?"

I stopped myself in the nick of time. I'd nearly said, *he didn't even steal the Jet Ski*. "He didn't even tell me he was seeing his lawyer that day," I said instead.

Gabby shook her head slowly. "That poor guy needs a do-over."

"A do-over?" I took a bite of pizza, but suddenly it had lost all flavor.

"Yes. You know. Like in a game. You have a bad shot or a bad play and you get to call do-over. He needs a chance to just wipe the slate clean and start over. If he could magically get all that stuff paid off and do the paramedic training, he'd be great. It would be a whole fresh new start for him. He needs to win the lottery or something."

A clean slate. A fresh start. A glimmer of excitement sparked low in my chest and grew with every passing beat of my heart. I was formulating an idea. A fabulous idea. I wanted to shout it out, but it was another secret for me to tuck away. I couldn't share it with anyone. Not even these two.

I looked down at my watch and yawned. "Yeah, he needs a clean slate for sure. And I need to get to bed. Sorry to kick you guys out, but we need to wrap this up. Gabby, do you know what time my first patient is in the morning?"

I stood up and collected their plates.

"Probably nine. Why?"

I put the plates into the dishwasher. "No reason. Just hoping I can sleep in."

But I didn't sleep in. I was in the office at eight in the morning with a box of doughnuts for the staff and a teensy little request for Delle. I pulled her into my office and shut the door.

She looked nervous, as if I was about to reprimand her. As if I could.

"Delle, can you keep a secret?"

Her eyes went round behind her tortoiseshell frames. "Of course, Dr. Rhoades. I am a bastion of secrecy when the occasion calls for it."

"OK. This occasion calls for it. I really, truly need you to keep this to yourself."

She made the sign of the cross. "I'm your girl, Dr. Rhoades."

"Excellent. You have access to patient billing, right?"

"Yes."

I took a big breath. This was just the first step in my plan, and I hoped it worked. "I want to pay off Tyler Connelly's medical bills. Not just the ones for our office, but all the bills from his emergency room visit too. Can you manage that?"

She stood, spine straight. For a moment I thought she might salute me. "I can certainly take care of that for this office. It might be a little trickier for the other bills, but I have a very reliable friend who works in the hospital billing department. She'd help us, and she can be trusted, especially if you took care of a little mole she has right here." Delle pointed to the side of one nostril.

"Done," I said.

She rubbed her hands together. "Oh my goodness, Dr. Rhoades. This is like a caper. I'm very excited."

It was a caper, and that had been the easy part. Dealing with the other bills was going to require a little more effort. As soon as Delle left my office, I made a phone call.

"Good morning. Pendleton, Whitney, Pullman and Frost, Attorneys At Law. How may I help you?"

—ᴧᴧ— —ᴧᴧ—

"What the hell are you thinking, Evie? Tyler's a nice kid and all, but come on. This is a lot of money you're talking about. Is he really that great in the sack?"

Steve Pullman sat across from me, a mammoth oak desk between us. He was clearly compensating for some sort of short-coming with a desk like that. He'd lost a lot of hair in the last year or so, and he was starting to show his age. Maybe this alleged affair was his midlife crisis.

"Yes, he is that great in the sack," I said defensively, "but that's not why I'm doing this. I'm doing it because he deserves a break. He didn't steal that Jet Ski. His idiot brother took it out for a joy ride and Tyler was bringing it back. I mean, really, did it never occur to anyone that a thief doesn't return stuff?"

"Of course it occurred to people. That's why the larceny charges were dropped, but he still crashed into the dock. He only has to pay for stuff he was actually responsible for." Steve loosened his tie, a tie that probably cost as much as Tyler made in a night serving at Jasper's.

I moved to the edge of my chair. "Do you really think that Jet Ski needs to be replaced? Or is this guy just taking advantage of an opportunity?"

Steve shrugged. "It doesn't matter. If your boyfriend doesn't want to fight the charges in court, then he has to pay the restitution. I don't care who took what or who brought what back. The owner wants to be compensated."

"Fine. Who do I make out the check to?"

Steve stood up and put his hands in the pockets of his navy blue pants. "Seriously? You really want to do this?"

"Absolutely."

"You won't get your money back. The kid's broke."

"I don't want the money back. It's a gift."

He paused, then leaned over and pushed a button on his phone. "Bertie, bring me the Connelly file, would you please?"

Steve's efficient secretary was there with it almost immediately. She handed it to him, perused me, and then left.

He sat back down and ran a hand over that thinning hairline. He looked up at me. "You must really be crazy about this guy."

I was. I couldn't explain it. I wasn't sure when it had happened, and I sure as hell didn't understand why, but one fact was clear. I was in love with Tyler Connelly. A man eight years younger with no immediate interest in marriage. A man who waited tables and drove a beat-up Jeep and an ambulance. A man whose highest ambition was to fish. And still I loved him, because in spite of all that, he was the sweetest, kindest, sexiest man I'd ever met. I loved the thrill of him. The caring and the loyalty. The raw edges and the vast potential. Like an undeveloped sculpture, Tyler was a work in progress, and I wanted to be there to see what emerged.

"I *am* crazy about him."

Steve stared at me with the expression I must have had on my face when my parents told me they were getting back together. Disbelief. Suspicion. Concern.

"It's just like how you used to feel about Hilary," I said.

Oh, God. Where had that come from? Stop talking, Evie. Stop talking.

Steve frowned at me. "Used to feel? What's that supposed to mean?"

Shut up. Shut up. Shut up. Don't say it.

"Hilary thinks you're cheating on her."

Oh, crap.

This town had turned me into one of them. Now I couldn't keep anything to myself either. I'd become a Bell Harbor blabbermouth.

Steve's face went pale for the space of a heartbeat, then turned a scalded red. "She thinks what? That's insane. I'm not cheating on her. I would never cheat on her."

This was so none of my business, but I'd kind of stuck my foot in the bear trap now. I owed it to Hilary to try to fix this.

"Then why have you been so secretive? And why are you working out at the gym all the time? And what's with the tax-coding whore?"

"The . . . the what? The tax-coding . . . what?" He stood up and started pacing. I probably should have wrapped up things for Tyler before diving into this quagmire, but I was in it now, all the way up to my chinny-chin-chin.

"She says you can't stop talking about this new lawyer who specializes in tax code. Let's start with that."

He scowled at me. "No, let's end with that. First of all, I've been going to the gym lately because my wife goes to the gym. All the time. Do you know what it's like trying to keep up with her? She looks just as beautiful as the day I married her, and I'm losing all my hair. Look!" He bent low and jabbed a finger at his scalp. He was right. It was shiny.

"I'm trying to get fit so she'll pay more attention to me. She's buying sex toys now, you know. Sex toys for herself. Where the hell does that leave me? Have you ever seen a Vagazzler? That thing can give her an orgasm and then make her a Frappuccino. I can't compete with that. I don't know how to make a Frappuccino."

Steve sounded pretty sincere. I think Hilary might have been wrong about this after all. She'd be so relieved, just as soon as she was done being furious with me for nosing into her business.

Steve was still pacing, sweat coming out of every pore. He loosened his tie a little more and then just yanked it off and threw it on his big oak desk.

"Seriously? She's talked to you about this? She thinks I'm cheating on her?"

"You changed your e-mail password."

"So? I had to. Somebody hacked me. I didn't change it so she couldn't read them. God, you think I don't know she reads my e-mails? She's always read my e-mails, and I don't care. Most of it's boring as hell." He crossed his arms and glared at me, trying to kill the messenger. "And which *whore* are we talking about, exactly?"

"The new hotshot lawyer who just joined the firm and works with tax codes."

Steve wiped the back of his hand across his gleaming upper lip. Man, that guy could sweat. He leaned over and pushed the button on his phone again. "Bertie, would you please see if Felicity could come in my office for a minute. I have a quick question for her."

The wait was awkward. Steve continued to pace, and I continued to wish I'd minded my own business and let Hilary take care of her own damn marriage. I was there to help Tyler out, not her.

A soft knock sounded on the door a minute later. It opened, and in walked Felicity. She was impeccably dressed, with fluffy blonde hair and big dark eyes. Like Hilary, she had mile-long legs. She also had an Adam's apple. No amount of hormone therapy was going to hide that thing.

"You had a question, Steve?" Felicity's voice was low and breathy, just this side of gender reassignment.

Steve gestured in my direction. "Felicity, this is Evelyn Rhoades. She's decided to pay off the legal fees for one of our clients, and I just wondered if, by any chance, that was tax deductible."

She smiled and shook her head, flipping that long hair over her shoulder with a manicured hand. "No, I'm sorry, it's not unless perhaps the fees were incurred by a charitable organization. If it's just for a private citizen, you're out of luck."

Steve crossed his arms again. "That's what I thought. But you're the tax-code expert, so I thought I'd check with you." He glared at me again.

"Thanks so much, Felicity," I said. "So sorry to interrupt your day."

"No problem. Is that it?" She looked at Steve.

"Yes, I think you've answered all of Evelyn's questions."

She left and Steve flung himself back into his chair. "Are we good now?"

I leaned forward and whispered, "How could you fail to mention to Hilary that Felicity used to be a man?"

"Why would I? I had no idea my wife thought I was cheating on her. I think that's the bigger secret here. And why the hell am I finding this out from you instead of Hilary?"

I sat back in my chair, suddenly feeling utterly drained. "That's a fair question, Steve, but I think from here on out, you two should talk to each other. I've stirred up enough as it is. Can we get back to Tyler now? Who do I make this check out to?"

Chapter 30

I HADN'T SEEN TYLER IN five days, not since he'd left my house after seeing the diplomas all over my wall. We'd talked on the phone a few times, but the conversations had been stilted since he was in the call room at MedPro with paper-thin walls and his coworkers coming and going. Yesterday I'd texted him a picture of Panzer's belly with a note that said, "We miss you." I'd gotten a smiley face back for that, but nothing more.

I was anxious as hell to tell him I'd paid off his debts, but that had to be done in person. Not because I wanted credit, but because I wanted him to stop worrying. This was such a good thing, and I was giddy at the prospect of seeing the relief on his face.

In fact, it had felt so good paying his bills, I'd even called the paramedic training center and put his name on the registration list. I'd very nearly paid for that too, since I was on a roll, but something held me back. It seemed presumptuous, so in the end, all I did was pay the one-hundred-dollar deposit to save him a spot so he could start in September. It would be perfect.

I heard his Jeep in the driveway just as I finished putting on my jewelry. We were heading to my parents' wedding, an event that was bound to be interesting, if not altogether enjoyable. I hoped my father had some defibrillators ready, because when my mother heard the details of Tyler's background, she was bound to have another cardiac incident.

I lugged my weekend bag from the bedroom down to the front hall and opened the door just as Tyler was lifting his hand to knock.

"Wow. Look at you in a suit." It was dark gray, and he wore a white shirt with a gray-and-blue patterned tie. Tyler Connelly might be broke, but he looked like a million bucks, if maybe a little bit tired.

He flushed and smiled. "Look at you in a fancy dress."

I twirled in my champagne-colored, quasi–maid of honor dress, and he laughed. The sound warmed me through. This weekend would get everything back on track for us. I wanted to grab him and kiss him and strip that nice suit right off his body. But we were already late. I settled for a fast hug and a tiny kiss.

"I'm so glad to see you, but we should get on the road," I said. "Grab your bag. We can take my car."

His gaze narrowed just a hint. "You don't want to show up in Bloomfield Hills in my rusty Jeep?"

"Your Jeep has a charm all its own, but for a drive this long, no offense, let's take my Mercedes. But you can drive." I pulled the door shut behind me and tossed him the keys.

He caught them like they were hot and finally held tight, but an odd expression fell over his face.

"Um, this is a little awkward, but I worked last night and I'm beat. I was kind of hoping to catch a little sleep in the car. Would you mind?"

Sleep? But we had so much stuff to talk about. I took the keys back reluctantly. "Of course you can sleep. Better during the ride than during the wedding, I guess."

He smiled and picked up my bag, hoisting it over his shoulder. "Where's the dog?"

"At Hilary's house. She owes me one for saving her marriage."

"You saved her marriage?" His brows rose in unison.

"Yes. Long story. It starts with a man trapped in a woman's body, but I'll tell you all about it later."

The drive took longer than I expected, and I found myself getting antsier and antsier as we approached Bloomfield Hills. Tyler snoozed away, and I was glad for him. And for me. He needed to be well rested for all the naughty things I had in mind. In the meantime, I pondered how to best introduce him to my parents. I wanted them to get to *know* him without actually hearing anything *about* him. I wanted them to be captivated by his charm, his easy smile, and his sense of humor before they discovered he was a dog-walking college dropout. Of course, I knew he was so much more than that, but I'd had time to learn about all his finer attributes.

Tyler and I arrived at the bed-and-breakfast where the wedding was being held, and I instantly understood why my parents loved it here. It was a romantic old Victorian house nestled in a cluster of huge old oak trees. The ceremony would be on the back patio overlooking a lush forest with a bubbly stream running through the back. It was so quaint I expected to see Snow White and Sleeping Beauty wandering though the glen.

"Evie, at last!" My mother walked up and hugged me as I came through the front door and into the lobby. Her hair and makeup were already done, but she was wearing a blue satin robe. It reminded me a little of Carl. I smiled over my shoulder at Tyler.

"Sorry we're late, Mom. We hit a little traffic. Nice robe."

"Thanks. Your father gave it to me as a wedding present. And that's the advantage of renting out the whole place. I can wander around wearing it. And who's this?" Her eyes gleamed at Tyler.

I took a big breath and exhaled silently. "Mom, this is Tyler."

He reached around me to extend his hand. "It's a pleasure to meet you, Dr. Rhoades. Congratulations on your marriage."

She tried to eye him surreptitiously, but I could see her taking inventory. She'd already figured out that his suit didn't cost much and that he was younger than me. But her smile was genuine.

"Tyler, thank you so much for being here. I hate to send you off on your own already, but I need my maid of honor. Do you suppose you could entertain yourself for a bit? I think the men are watching some sort of game or something in the library."

I looked up to gauge his reaction, but he seemed fine. Relaxed. Still a little sleepy.

"Sure thing," he said.

I squeezed his hand. "I'll see you in a little while."

He smiled and wandered down the hall as my mother took my wrist and tugged me across the lobby into another little sitting room with a couch and two chairs. Her wedding dress was hanging from a hook, and two floral bouquets were waiting in a bucket.

"He's gorgeous," she said as soon as the door was closed.

I expelled another big breath. Apparently I'd been holding that one. "I know."

"And young."

"Yes."

"Good for you. We don't have too much time, though. Can you help me with this dress?" She took it off the hanger and shook it out. Chiffon floated outward. "So, how old is he? Either he's very young or you've done some excellent work on him."

She was teasing, and I started to relax. My mother was in a good mood, which was an excellent thing since it was her wedding day.

"We don't have to talk about Tyler, Mom. We should talk about you. How are you feeling?"

"Me? I feel great. This will be a piece of cake. Your father is nervous as hell, though, which I think is hilarious. You'd think with all this practice, he'd be fine. But I want to hear about your guy." She handed me the dress and took off her robe. She had on lacy underwear. Totally appropriate for a blushing bride, but one look at that and I was the one blushing. It was awkward. I held open the neckline of her gown so she could step into it, and averted my eyes.

"OK, well, Tyler is younger than me. A little bit. He's a paramedic." That was stretching the truth but it was very nearly true. "And he grew up in Bell Harbor."

She pulled the dress up and turned her back to me so I could zip her up. "How did you meet him?"

"I gave him stitches after he had an accident with a Jet Ski."

My mother looked back at me. "A Jet Ski? That's not the guy who got arrested on your birthday, is it?"

Oh, shit. I'd completely forgotten I'd told them all about that at dinner. Damn it. Damn it. Damn it.

"That was all just a big misunderstanding. We should really be talking about you and Dad." I finished with her zipper and reached down to pick up her sandals from the floor. "Sit down and I'll help you get these on."

She perched on the little sofa, careful not to wrinkle her dress. I waited for the recriminations, the admonishments, the lecture. I knew what she'd say. He's too young. He's irresponsible. He's not a doctor.

"Evie, Evie, Evie," she finally said. "I assume the sex is good, though, right?"

My mouth dropped open and a little squawk of surprise came out. She patted the seat next to her and I sat down. Fell down, really. She took a sandal from my hand and started to buckle it.

"Well, is it?" she asked.

I caught my breath and answered. "The sex is phenomenal."

She took the other sandal. "Well then, that's all that matters. The rest of the stuff you can work out later. Relationships are all a crapshoot anyway. At least if the sex is good, then, well, then at least the sex is good."

I fell back against the cushion. God bless those aliens and whatever they'd done to my mother.

"He doesn't meet any of my requirements, though." I'm not sure why I was arguing with her. I think it was just out of habit.

She stopped buckling her sandal. "Your what?"

"My list of requirements. You know, all the qualities that would make him a perfect husband?"

She stared at me for a full ten seconds, and then she burst out laughing. "Perfect husband? Oh, honey, haven't you learned anything from me at all? There is no such thing as a perfect husband. Or a perfect wife. Or a perfect marriage. Sometimes love supersedes logic, and the best thing to do is just follow your heart."

"Follow your heart?"

Someone knocked on the door, and a few seconds later my aunt Sally stuck her head into the room. "Debra, are you about ready? Garrett says the game is over."

"That's so romantic," my mother answered. "Tell him I waited twenty-three years for him to wise up. He can wait ten more minutes for me."

She stood and picked up a necklace and handed it to me. "Would you hook this for me?"

I wrestled with the little clasp and finally got it secured. We turned together so she could see her reflection in the full-length mirror. She looked gorgeous. Radiant; ethereal even. My mother had always been attractive, but at that moment I realized it was love that made her beautiful.

She reached up and touched my hand where it rested on her shoulder. "Evie, darling, I won't presume to give you relationship advice. In fact, I've finally learned that one of my biggest flaws was thinking I knew everything. So all I'll say is that I'm taking a giant leap of faith by remarrying your father, and I've never been happier. I hope this Tyler person is as good as you deserve, because you deserve the best. If he makes you happy, then that's all that really matters."

My parents' wedding was lovely, intimate, and romantic. My father looked reverent in his black suit but joyful as he spoke his vows. He sounded as if he really meant them his time. I guessed I should take that leap of faith with my mother and give him the benefit of the doubt.

As maid of honor, I stood next to her for some of the brief ceremony, but when I sat down, Tyler was next to me. I reached over and held his hand. He was a damn good sport for coming to this shindig with me.

At dinner I was between him and my father. I tried to field questions between the two of them as best I could. It was like being line judge at Wimbledon. I was tense waiting for what *might* happen.

"What do you do for a living?" my father asked. That one was as inevitable as bad weather.

"A little bit of a lot of things," Tyler answered, "but mainly I'm an EMT."

"Tyler's planning to take the paramedics course soon," I added. He glanced at me from the corner of his eye.

"Eventually," he said.

My father took a sip of scotch. "Good for you. Tough job."

"Not as tough as yours," Tyler volleyed back. He was holding his own against my father. Of course, it helped that my father was mellow with matrimony. And malt whiskey.

"I'll take an anesthetized patient over one who's awake any day of the week." My father chuckled. "I prefer them heavily sedated whenever possible."

I couldn't tell by Tyler's reaction if he was intimidated, entertained, or indifferent to my father's response.

"Tyler grew up in Bell Harbor," I said, hoping to steer the conversation away from medicine in general. "It's really such an amazing town."

"Small, though," my father said.

I could say something inane, like *it's cozy*. Or something artificially pretentious like *it's a lovely microcosm of Americana*. But I didn't have time because Tyler answered for me.

"Yep. It's pretty small."

My father nodded, and I felt the skin prickle under my arms. I didn't know why I cared about this. What difference did it make if my father liked Tyler? *I* liked him, and that's all that mattered. And what difference did it make if Tyler *didn't* like my dad, because I didn't particularly like him either. I took a big swallow of my wine instead. These two were on their own.

"Lions fan?" my dad asked.

Tyler paused. "When they give me a reason to be."

And then they were off, talking sports like a couple of dudes, and suddenly my job here was done. They didn't need me anymore. I looked over at my mother. She was smiling and listening to my aunt Sally tell some story. She looked happy, glowing even. She'd taken that leap of faith and I was proud of her. And so far marriage agreed with her.

Chapter 31

"SO WHAT DO YOU THINK of all this?" I asked Tyler as we sat having a glass of wine on the back porch after dinner. The reception was already winding down, with most of the guests sitting in small, comfortable groups scattered throughout the first floor of the bed-and-breakfast. At the moment, it was only Tyler and me outside, and this was the first chance I'd had to get him alone. He'd been attentive all evening, but quiet.

He looked out over the grass. "What do I think? I think it's very nice. Nice ceremony. Nice place. Nice people."

He smiled at me, but I couldn't shake the feeling he was holding something back. It wasn't just the fatigue of having worked the night before. It was the same awkward guard he'd had up since the day I moved.

"And what a nice, neutral answer," I said. I guess I couldn't blame him. He knew marriage was a goal of mine. That being the case, it was bold for him to even be here, and so far he'd done a good job of avoiding that whole deer-in-headlights look I'd been expecting.

"It is nice, though," he added. "It's amazing that after so many years your parents got back together."

"I guess it is. For me it's very strange, but I'm trying to adapt."

He tugged on the cuff of his shirt. "Adapt. Yeah, speaking of that. You know how we've talked before about plans, and how sometimes they don't go like we expect?" He didn't look my way when he said this, and my stomach flipped like a pancake.

"Yes."

He paused, and the pancake flipped again. "Well, I guess it's no secret that this business with the boat dock has been a total clusterfuck—"

I'd wanted to wait until later. Later when we were in our room and had some real privacy before I told him, but the secret was burning inside and I had to blow it out. I had to make that sad, sad look on his face go away. Just like he'd done for Scotty, I was going to rescue him from this mess.

"I know it has been," I interrupted, "but I have something really good to tell you."

He looked at me. *There* it was. The deer-in-headlights.

I reached out and took hold of both his hands. "You have been so selfless and amazing taking care of your family that you inspired me."

He frowned. He should start looking happier any second now.

My nerves twanged, but I kept on talking. I needed to get this out. To make him feel *better*. "I know what an incredible person you are, and what an amazing paramedic you'll be. It's not fair that you should have to wait because of other people's mistakes, or even because of just fate, in general." I gestured to the area around us, where fate resided.

He leaned back. "Evelyn, what are you talking about?"

Breathe in, breathe out.

"I paid your bills."

His face blanked, but the pulse in his neck sped up. "Which bills?"

"Your medical and legal bills. Everything that had to do with the boat dock and Jet Ski is taken care of. You have a clean slate. I'm giving you a do-over."

He stared as if I'd spoken Portuguese. I hadn't, had I?

"You know," I said, talking a little louder as if that would make everything more clear. "Like in a game. A do-over. If anyone deserves one, it's you."

He stood up and walked toward the railing of the porch.

I waited, my heart pulsing like a strobe light. He finally turned back to me.

"Are you kidding me with this, Evelyn? You paid my bills?" His voice was quiet, and far too serious. Frown lines became caverns across his face. But I was expecting the dimples. I was expecting joy. Where was the jubilation? Where was the happy? He just looked . . . pissed. Thoroughly and utterly pissed.

But I smiled anyway, to prove my point that this was a *good* thing. Because it was. A good thing.

"No, I'm not kidding, and I'm so glad I did it. You deserve this break, Tyler. Now you're free and clear to take the paramedics course and not have to worry about the other stuff. Those debts are gone. Erased." I swished my hand to the side. Swish. Erased. "And they're saving a spot for you."

"Who is?"

"The people at the paramedic training center. I put you on the list. You don't have to do it, of course. If you decide not to for some reason. But I wanted you to have a place if you were . . . you know . . . ready."

Judging from the pulsing vein at his temple, that last part might have been overload.

He turned on his heel and walked away from me, his posture stiff, his hands fisted, and I realized I'd screwed this up. Either in the doing or the telling, I'd made a mistake. A second passed, and then another. When he turned back, his face was grim, even more grim than before.

"This is unbelievable. Do you see what you've done, Evelyn? Now I'll never catch up to you. God, do you realize how long it'll take me to even pay you back?"

I stood up and walked over, as fast as my dread would allow. "I don't want you to pay me back. It's not a loan. It's a gift. That's the whole point."

His expression grew darker, stormier with every breath.

"A gift I can never equal. No matter how hard I work, it'll never balance out. I'll never match your education. And I'll never be able to give you anything that compares to what you can afford to buy yourself. Like that house you're living in now."

"My house? What does my house have to do with anything?" What was he even talking about?

He stepped closer. "Financial equality. It was right there at the top of the list."

"What?" My stomach plummeted like a canoe over Niagara.

"The list, Evie. The husband requirement list. I saw it. Advanced degree. Economic equality. Intellectual compatibility. I read the whole fucking thing, and other than being a man, I didn't qualify for any of it."

"Oh my God, Tyler. That list was stupid. It was for the Bell Harbor Singles profile. Where did you even see it?"

"I found it when you moved. It was folded up on the floor under your couch. I only opened it because I thought it might be important." He scoffed and scowled. "I guess it was."

On the floor? My mind raced backward. Gabby had the list in her pocket when she came over to tell me about breaking up with Mike. I thought I'd thrown it away.

"That list is irrelevant. It means nothing."

The air around him seemed to pulse. "It means everything. It's what you want in a man. And the stupidest part is you tried to tell me. Over and over. Those first few times I hit on you, you kept trying to tell me I wasn't good enough for you. But I ignored you because, God, I wanted you so bad. From that very first minute I saw you."

He scrubbed his hand over his jaw, and I wanted to stop him from talking. I wanted him to stop before he said more and I felt even worse, but Tyler Connelly had more to say. He paced as he spoke.

"Here's the problem as I see it, Evelyn. No matter what you do, no matter how many bills you pay or classes you sign me up for, I'm never going to be the guy on that list. That's what you want, and I'll never measure up. I realized that when I saw your house, but you doing this just makes me certain that I'm right. And we're all wrong. This is never going to work out between us."

"No, we're not wrong. I don't want you to be one of those guys. I want you to be yourself. Tyler, I never said you weren't good enough. I said you weren't *old* enough. That's completely different. And this thing with the bills, I was just trying to help."

His pacing sped up, and I started to sweat. My heart was slamming so hard against my ribs I thought one might crack.

"I don't need help," he said, finally stopping, and glaring at me as if I'd done something unforgivable. "I'm not a kid, I'm not a victim. When my dad died, I stepped up. Me. My older brother took off, but I stuck it out. When my family needs me, I take care of them. I don't need someone else to bail me out. God, I can't believe—how did you even do that? Pay my bills. Who knows about this?" He started pacing again. "Jesus, the whole fucking town is going to know what you did, and they'll think I talked you into it. It's bad enough everyone believes I stole the Jet Ski, but at least that was my decision. Now they're going to think I seduced my way into your bank account." .

Everything inside me twisted, kicking the breath from my lungs. This was not how this was supposed to go. This was supposed to be a good thing. But all the air around me compressed, as if I were being sucked into a tornado while the trees around me stayed motionless.

"Hardly anyone knows," I said, blinking back a useless tear. "Delle in my office, but she's been sworn to secrecy, and I trust her. And your lawyer." And Delle's friend in the hospital billing department, but under the circumstances, I wasn't going to mention her.

"My lawyer. You talked to my lawyer?" His voice rasped.

"Here's the thing about that, Tyler. He's a friend of mine. Well, he's married to a friend of mine. So he'll keep this all on the down-low. No one has to know."

He stared at me, his expression so flat I knew it was only the calm before a storm. He stepped toward me, towering. His cheeks flushed, his voice burning in my ears as it rose. "Everyone will know. It's bad enough that Scotty can't find his ass with both hands, Carl wanders around in a bathrobe, and my mother steals jewelry from Tilly Mason, but now all of Bell Harbor is going to think I'm just as pathetic. God. I had a plan, Evelyn. I had a plan to get myself out of that legal jam, but you beat me to it, and now I'm more behind than ever."

How could he be seeing everything, *everything* so differently? No one was going to judge him. Bell Harbor loved him. They'd be happy he finally caught a break. How had I misjudged this so badly? How had I messed this up? Why was he so mad?

My aunt Sally's voice called out as she stepped onto the patio. "There you are, Evie. Your mother needs you. Can you come in?"

I looked at Tyler, but everything about him seemed unfamiliar. A stranger in a dark gray suit.

"We have to go in," I whispered.

"No, I don't have to go in. I need to take a walk. We're all done here, Evelyn. Do you understand what I'm saying? We're all done."

He turned, grinding his heel against the stone, and stalked away into the dark.

Chapter 32

"WHERE'S TYLER?" MY MOTHER ASKED when I came in from the patio.

"He's not feeling well, but he'll be inside in a minute." I gave her the biggest, brightest, happiest fake smile I could muster. Sure, my parents had ruined a few of my birthdays and most of my childhood, but I was not going to ruin their wedding reception because Tyler Connelly had just dumped me. At least I think he'd dumped me. God, it felt like he'd dumped me. It felt as if he'd ice-skated across my chest. My heart was broken in so many pieces even my parents couldn't stitch it back together.

"Oh, that's too bad. I hope his stomach's not upset from the lobster ravioli. Your father said it was too rich. We should have gone with the beef Wellington. I should have listened."

"Let that be a lesson to you, Dr. Rhoades," my father said, coming up beside us. "If you'd listened to me twenty-three years ago, we could've been together all this time."

"What? And give up that yearly gorilla-gram to celebrate our divorce?"

Both my parents chuckled, awash in the joy of their rediscovered love affair. And I burst into tears at the demolishment of mine.

"Evie, Evie, what's the matter?" My mother turned me by the shoulders to face her.

Please let someone invent teleporting right now. Please have them zap me to another space and time. I was not standing with my parents right now, crying like a sixteen-year-old girl over a thoughtless boy. I couldn't be.

And yet, I was.

"Where's the kid?" my father said, patting my back none too gently, as if he was trying to burp the tears out. I assumed by kid, he meant Tyler.

"He's taking a walk," I said, gulping in a mouthful of air and trying to compose myself.

"Come on. Let's go sit down." My mother led me to the tiny room she'd changed in before the wedding, and the three of us sat down on the tiny couch. My father's ice clinked in his glass.

"Evelyn, tell us what happened," my mother said. Her voice was no-nonsense, as if she were taking a patient history.

I shook my head and pressed my hands to my face. "I'm not really sure. Except I did something I thought was going to be a great thing, but it turns out it was a terrible thing." I still didn't understand how I'd ended up the bad guy in this scenario.

"But what was it?" she pressed on. "What did you do?"

"I paid his bills."

"His bills?" my father said.

I reached over and took his glass of Glenfiddich. This occasion called for a drink. "Yes, I paid off some of his debts so that he could afford to take a paramedic training course. Horrible of me, huh?" I took a sip. This scotch was officially mine.

"Well, I don't know, Evelyn. Did he ask you to?" My father brushed a lock of hair back over my shoulder. I tried to recall the last time he'd done something like that. I think my mother had finally succeeded in tenderizing him.

"No, of course he didn't ask me to. He'd never ask me to pay for anything, and now he's afraid everyone in town will think he's pathetic and needs my help."

"Ah, pride. That's a tough one. It takes a mighty strong man to show a little weakness. I think you might have insulted him." My father tried to take his scotch back but I held on tight.

"How is it insulting to help someone?" I asked.

"Because it implies weakness, Evie," my mother said, patting my hand. "I used to think every time your father tried to help me it was because he thought I couldn't do it for myself. And I'd get so mad, but he was just trying to be gallant. Isn't that right, darling?"

My father nodded. "I was so gallant she once cut all my ties in half."

"Shh. That was for something else. Don't ruin this moment." She patted my hand again.

I snuffled back another sob. "Tyler makes these grand gestures for his own family all the time, and I do this one thing and he can't see how it's the same? He kept his brother out of jail, he makes his mother's house payments, he brought me soup when I was sick. He does stuff for people all the time. It's what will make him a great paramedic."

"So where is he now?" my father asked.

"I don't know. We just had this fight on the patio and he took off."

I heard my mother scoff. "Oh, goodness. That doesn't sound so bad. Your father and I have had bigger fights over where to squeeze the toothpaste. I bet he comes back any minute."

My father nodded. "Yes, I'm sure your mother is right. She

usually is. And even if it takes him a while to come around, there are worse flaws than pride."

"Hey, I have some pride too, you know. It's not fair that he's mad because I tried to do something nice."

"Of course, darling," my mother said, smoothing out the chiffon of her wedding dress. "You have a right to be mad, but don't let it turn into a twenty-three-year argument. If he's important enough to you that you'd pay off his debts, I hope he's important enough for you to work through this."

My father put his arm around me. "Do you need us to sit here with you until he comes back? Because we will if you want."

My mother took my glass and sipped the scotch. "Of course we will. If you need us, we'll sit here all night."

Who were these two? These warm, compassionate, sensitive parents? Apparently the aliens had gotten to my father too. But I was grateful. Still, this was their wedding night. They shouldn't have to spend it babysitting me.

"I'm fine, you guys. Thanks. Go on upstairs. I'm sure Tyler will be along any minute."

"Are you sure?" my mother asked, handing back the glass. I felt adored by their attention. Maybe them getting back together was a good thing after all.

"Yes, I'm sure. Go on. Pleasant dreams."

They stood up, each squeezing one of my shoulders, then walked out of the room hand in hand, like a couple of high school sweethearts. *Adorável.*

I sat in that little room until I'd finished my father's drink and finally wandered into the lobby to wait for Tyler. Because surely he'd be back any minute.

Only he wasn't.

Eleven o'clock came and went. I talked to every person still downstairs, until it was just me and my drunk uncle Marv.

Midnight turned today into tomorrow, and still no Tyler. I couldn't decide if I was tragically wounded by his absence or ragingly furious. It was about forty-nine to fifty-one right now, except that I had to throw worried into that mix. I had no idea where he was. He could still be walking, I supposed. Maybe he'd planned to stalk all the way back to Bell Harbor. If that was the case, he'd be soaking wet now, because it had been raining for the last half hour. Or maybe he'd been eaten by a bear. If that was the case, I was kind of rooting for the bear right about now. Or maybe Tyler had wandered into a nearby tavern and was drowning his sorrows in a bottle of whiskey.

Or maybe he was up in our room.

Why hadn't I thought of that sooner? Maybe he'd been up there this whole time watching pay-per-view porn. That had to be where he was. I said good night to drunk Uncle Marv and headed upstairs. I got to our frilly, romantically decorated room.

No Tyler.

And no luggage either. I realized then we'd arrived so late that we'd never brought it in from the car.

This night was a bust. A horrible, awful, ass-kicking bust. All I wanted to do was climb in that bed and dream this day had never happened. But I wanted my toothbrush. And my fuzzy slipper socks. I couldn't sufficiently wallow in my self-pity without my slipper socks. I was going to have to go to the car. I found my keys, went back down to the lobby, and headed out into the drizzling rain.

I got halfway to the car when he said my name, and I nearly jumped out of my skin, spinning around and pointing my keys outward to jab my assailant. But of course, it was Tyler.

"Evie?"

"Holy shit! Geez, Tyler, you scared me half to death. What are you doing out here in the rain?"

He looked terrible. Aside from being drenched, his suit was torn and there were smudges of dirt all over that nice white shirt.

"That's kind of a funny story," he said quietly. "If you let me back inside the hotel, I'll tell you."

I wanted to say no. I wanted to stay mad. He'd hurt my feelings. He'd made me cry in front of my parents. And he'd broken my heart.

But he was Tyler. And so I said, "Fine. I just came out to get the luggage."

I opened the car door, and he reached in to get both bags. The walk back in was silent. I wanted to kick him in the shins for scaring me, hurting me, worrying me. And most of all, for making me think we had a great thing going and then tossing it away just because I'd nicked his pride.

We got back to the room, and he changed into a pair of dry jeans and a T-shirt in the bathroom. I wanted to change too. This maid of honor dress was miserable, and it felt like I'd had it on for about nine days. But all I had were my clothes for the drive home tomorrow and a slutty nightgown that I had hoped would have been ripped off me by now.

I sat in the middle of the bed, and Tyler came to sit beside me. I took that as a positive sign, but I still had no idea of the state of our affair.

"So where the hell have you been?" I asked.

He ran a hand over his hair. "Well, you know that beautiful creek that runs through the property? The one we could see during the ceremony?" He adjusted the pillows and leaned back.

"Yeah."

"Well, the banks of that are pretty damn steep. And slippery. And impossible to see once it gets dark."

"Are you telling me you fell into the creek?" I felt a spark of vindication. I wasn't proud of that, but there it was.

"Pretty much. I spent about two hours down there, trying to find a spot to get back into the yard. Pulling on tree branches that I could reach. Slipping back into the water. I took on a couple of muskrats. That was pretty scary. Mean little bastards." He moved another pillow and patted it for me. I ignored that.

He kept talking. "Then I finally scrambled my way up and out and back to the patio. I watched you talk to that old guy in the lobby for a while. I should've come in then, but I just felt too . . . absurd."

I nearly wanted to laugh. At him. With him. But I was still too upset. I couldn't help being a little bit glad that he'd been suffering. I was my parents' daughter, after all.

"Well, it serves you right. Why did you go stomping away like that? I don't understand why you're so mad at me."

He sighed, big and heavy. "I know. I know you don't, Evie, but I had a plan, and you messed it up."

He sounded like his brother. Whatever plan he had, this was not my fault. "What plan?"

"I sold my boat."

I turned toward him so fast my spine cracked.

"You what? Why would you do that? You love that boat."

His gaze at me was earnest, raw. "Yeah, I do. But I love you more."

Joy, confusion, frustration, hope—they hit me from every angle and with such varied intensity I nearly fell off the bed.

"I don't understand, Tyler."

He reached out and took my hand. "I saw that list of what you thought was the perfect husband, and it made angry. Not at you, at me." He looked down and toyed with the bracelet on my wrist. "I wanted to be that guy. And I could have been. I could've gone back to school, Evie, but it was easier to quit. Easier to blame my mom's situation or Scotty or my knee or whatever. But the fact is, I could've figured it out. I just felt sorry for myself. It was hard when my dad died. But shit happens, you know. You dust yourself off and try again."

"But that's what you already do. You *do* dust yourself off and try again. More than anybody I've ever known." How could he not see that?

"Yeah, maybe." His voice was frustration cloaked in resilience. "At any rate, I sold the boat so I could pay off those debts and give myself a clean slate. It's time to give up a dream that is never going to provide financial security. I need something more concrete. More reliable and lucrative. You see, the thing is, Evie, I don't worry too often about impressing people. I am who I am. People know me. But since meeting you, for the first time in my life, I'm wishing I was more. More because I want to be . . . enough for you."

My heart squeezed tight at his vulnerability. "I don't need you to be more. I just need you to be you. You are enough for me."

"You say that, but I'm not sure it's true. You want marriage and kids and financial security. I don't want to spend my life wondering if you have regrets about any of that."

"Tyler, the marriage and the kids can wait. And the financial security I already have. The only thing I don't have is somebody to share my time with. That's the thing I want the most. That matters more than degrees or income."

"Not according to your list."

"Forget the list. It was stupid and ignorant. And if I made one now it would have completely different things on it." I moved a little closer.

"Oh, yeah? Like what?" The tiniest of smiles tilted his lips.

"Like sense of humor, and honesty, and generosity."

He frowned a little. I scooted closer and lay down on my stomach so I was looking up at him as he leaned back against the headboard.

"Perfect facial symmetry."

And the smile was back. Finally, some dimples. "What?"

"Your face has perfect balance. It's one of the first things I noticed about you. But you know what I've learned about you since then?"

"What?" His voice dropped lower, huskier. I might get to wear that racy nightie after all.

"I've learned that you'll look after me when I'm sick, that you love dogs, that you'll do anything and everything necessary to take care of the people you love. That's the stuff that really matters, Tyler. That's the stuff that made me fall in love with you." I moved up as he slid down so we were lying side by side.

"You do?"

I nodded. "Very much. I love the way you laugh, and make me laugh. I love how you worry about me. And honestly, I love that you want to restart your dad's charter company. I'm incredibly sad that you sold that boat."

His smile dimmed. "I'm sad that I sold it not knowing you'd already paid those bills. But nothing has been signed yet."

"You think you could cancel the sale?"

"There's no money in fishing, Evie. I'll never be rich."

"I don't need you to be rich. I just need you to be you." I kissed him then, because I simply couldn't wait any longer. The last few hours had been awful, thinking he was gone from my life. Because I loved Tyler Connelly, whether he was a paramedic or a fisherman or a dog walker. None of that mattered. The only thing that mattered was that he was mine.

And mine I made him. We kissed, and we tussled, and we soared. My maid of honor dress was thoroughly dishonored by the time we were through, but Tyler and I were satisfied and happy. We were in love. It just took a little leap of faith.

Cuddled up on the covers a while later, I traced my finger along his tattoo. "So what's the first thing you noticed about me?"

Tyler chuckled. "Honestly?"

"Of course."

He smiled, big and bright. "The glitter in your hair. I was kind of drunk, you know. I thought you might be an angel. Turns out I was right."

Acknowledgments

No book is written alone, and I am truly grateful for the support and friendship I've received as this one grew from the tiny glimmer of an idea to a full-fledged love story.

Thanks to my dedicated and tireless team at Montlake Publishing. I appreciate you more than you will ever know.

Thanks to my agent, Nalini Akolekar. Your guidance, support, and sense of humor keep me sane and grounded. You are Wonder Woman, but in a more tasteful outfit.

Thanks to Elizabeth Otto for sharing, at a moment's notice, her invaluable insight into being an EMT. Thanks to Anna Pakiela for sharing her knowledge and patiently explaining to me various aspects of the legal system, especially since my own corrections officer was unavailable for comment. Thanks to Dave Pierangeli for providing additional legal guidance on this book. Any errors in those areas are entirely mine. (Now might be a good time to also thank Dave for moving furniture for me upon occasion.)

Thanks to the beautiful Madeline Martin. She knows why, but I'll let her explain that herself.

Thanks to Robin Allen for suggesting M&M's scatter when they hit the floor. That was just the metaphor I needed!

Thanks to Cherry Adair for her support, enthusiasm, and her Post-it plotting madness.

Thanks to the handy little translator inside my computer that magically adapted English phrases to Portuguese. I sincerely apologize for any mangling I may have done to that beautiful language.

Thanks to Kelsey Shipton for her wonderful help with *Hold on My Heart*, and for not being mad that I failed to thank her sooner!

Thanks to Samhita for always making me belly laugh, and for pointing out there is no sport in shooting a goat. Thanks to Jane, Sheila, and Kim for packing up my house so I could move three days after this book was finished. Thanks to Gabby, Hillery, and Meredith for being the eternal sunshine in my life. And for never revealing where I've hidden the bodies.

Thanks to Alyssa Alexander, Kimberly Kincaid, and Jennifer McQuiston. For so many reasons. They are countless but I hope you know them all. Thanks to Kieran, Liz, Catherine, Darcy, Ash, Tammy, and Kim. Your friendship keeps this job fun, even during those moments when it's . . . well . . . less fun.

Thanks to Adam Levine and Phillip Phillips for unknowingly providing the soundtrack to this story.

Thanks to Paul Walker for unknowingly providing inspiration to many a romance writer. A light has gone out. You will be missed.

And last, but never least, thank you to my husband, kids, sisters, and wonderful family members who have given me more support than any one person deserves. I am blessed. Without you guys, none of the rest matters.

About the Author

Allie Gadziemski, 2012

Past or present, Tracy Brogan loves romance. She read her first swashbuckling adventure at age sixteen and knew right then she was destined to become a novelist. She now writes fun and breezy contemporary stories about ordinary people finding extraordinary love, and lush historical romance full of royal intrigue, damsels causing distress, and the occasional man in a kilt.

Tracy is a Romance Writers of America® RITA finalist for Best First Book, and a two-time Golden Heart finalist. She's the bestselling author of *Crazy Little Thing*, *Highland Surrender*, and *Hold on My Heart*. She resides in Michigan with her husband, their children, and their overly indulged dogs.

Tracy loves to hear from readers, so please contact her at tracybrogan@att.net, or visit her website at TracyBrogan.com.